THE OTHER PILOT

ED BALDWIN

ACKNOWLEGEMENTS

My friend Steve Moesky created the cover. Steve is a commercial artist and designer in Austin, Texas, and he's an old aircraft enthusiast like I am. The cover is so good I expect Steve to find a whole new line of work designing book covers. And I expect a lot of readers to be attracted to the story by that picture.

Kimberly Hitchens of Booknook.biz was able to take my corrupted manuscript file, which had gone from Word Perfect, to Microsoft Word 97, 2007, then onto a Mac in rich text and make it beautiful.

Virginia Gilbert proofed the manuscript like the newspaper editor she is, and offered sound plot advice.

Mike Bertz owns and flies a restored P-51 Mustang. Together we researched the flight characteristics of the Messerschmitt and choreographed the dogfight Steve Moesky painted for the front cover. Mike was in my guard unit in Colorado and his expertise and enthusiasm for vintage warbirds drew me into the world of piston engine fighters.

Thanks to Nicola Nelson for enhancing my technical understanding of space systems and satellites.

So now read my story as it twists and turns through military culture and technology, pilot lore and old airplanes, action, romance, and politics; and don't turn to the last page until you've read the rest.

CHAPTER ONE

The general hated flying. Any other pilot would have been thrilled to have a brand new block 50 F-16 to tool around the country instead of using the airlines. Even with his aide there to file the flight plan for him, General Trusten Polk hated it. He hated the G-suit, and the helmet, and the boots.

"Trust One to Buckley tower. Permission for takeoff," he said, annoyed at the delay. They had his flight plan, there were no other aircraft leaving for hours. Why not just say, "Permission granted," and let him get airborne and out of here?

"Trust One, permission granted for takeoff. Have a pleasant day, sir."

General Polk keyed the microphone button on the stick to acknowledge the transmission, but said nothing. His left hand moved the throttle impatiently. The Falcon lurched forward.

The night before, an old friend had called in another favor, the latest in a long series of requests, tips, accommodations, lies, and fraudulent deeds. Like the round heeled whore he was, Polk had delivered with a smile.

The acceleration pressed Polk back into the seat as the aircraft rocketed down the runway. Polk had no sense of being in control, even though he wielded the stick and the throttle. He even considered closing his eyes, trusting that sheer inertia and the width of the runway would keep them on it until they reached takeoff speed.

"One sixty," Kevin Barnes said, calling out the takeoff speed from the back seat.

In two days Polk had to be in Washington to testify before the Senate Armed Services Committee. Tonight when he got back to Virginia, the FAX machine beside his bed would print out the questions, and the answers. No one cared what Trusten Polk thought about the issue, the four stars would speak. All he had to do Monday was read off the answers. Disgust choked him, like vomit in his oxygen mask. The Falcon's nose lifted gracefully.

He'd been a man once. A man who had occupied space, with a personality, a soul. He'd had dreams, friends, a past, and a future. Now Trusten Polk was virtual reality. Turn off the forces that controlled him, and there would be nothing.

Polk lurched forward as the engine, emitting a loud clang, exploded. He looked down into the cockpit, mind in transition from his self pity to the checklist for engine failure on takeoff. The right wing rotated quickly downward.

"Hey!" Polk yelled, as if Kevin Barnes in the back seat could do something if he were alerted. Instinctively he put lateral and backward pressure on the stick to correct the roll and bring the nose up, but before the Falcon could respond the right wing tip hit the ground and the aircraft cartwheeled forward at 250 knots. The nose hit a moment later and 12,000 pounds of jet fuel became an aerosol. The burning rear of the aircraft rotated into this cloud of fuel and ignited it with a muffled roar and a bright red fireball.

The firemen sitting on the crash truck east of the runway were already in their crash suits, so they had only to put on their boots and start the truck. They were rolling before the stunned air traffic controllers could notify them of the crash. In less than a minute they were at the site, pouring foam on the debris and looking for survivors. The black smoke was already 1,000 feet in the air.

The pilots had been admiring Mount Evans, sixty miles to the west and 14,264 feet above sea level. Had anyone been on the top that morning they could have seen the small plume of smoke on the eastern fringe of the Denver metropolitan area that marked the end of an illustrious, if unusual, military career.

CHAPTER TWO

The long thin blade crossed and recrossed the stone. In spite of a puddle of 30 weight motor oil, it made a high pitched grating sound that fascinated the dog. A black Labrador retriever lay with his face on his front paws and his eyes fixed on the knife as if he were to receive some precious insight from the event.

Boyd Chailland (SHYland) sat on the back steps of his rented farm house just east of the Denver International Airport. His gaze shifted from Mount Evans, to Longs Peak to the north, and back to the filet knife he was sharpening. From his vantage point in the prairie east of Denver he could see the whole city and the mountains beyond. He could look down the line of airliners descending from the east, and with the usual departure route to the north, he could marvel at how those huge loaded crafts could rise so quickly in this thin mountain air.

"You ready to chase some trout, Eight Ball?" he said to the dog as he wiped the motor oil on his jeans and stood up, admiring the blade.

The telephone rang. Boyd had only been in Denver a month and could think of nothing good that could come from a telephone call.

"Captain Chailland?" the voice asked.

"Yes."

"This is Colonel Bertz. We've had an accident this morning." There was a quiver in his voice. "General Trusten Polk crashed on takeoff at 0700. He and his aide were both killed. I'll be the chairman of the accident investigation board and I've assigned you to be the pilot member."

"Yes, sir. Should I come over now?" Boyd saw the image of Polk speaking just the day before. Earnest, decisive, and energetic, he had been wired with a collar mike and paced the stage.

"There are those in Congress..." Polk had said several times, straying perilously close to a political statement, forbidden to military officers. He had only touched on the anniversary celebration of Buckley being upgraded to an Air Force Base from an Air National Guard base, his reason for coming to Denver. The thrust of his talk had been toward preservation of U.S. military superiority in an uncertain world, and a caution to watch for, "those who would leave us open to a stab in the back from bitter enemies who covet this beautiful land."

That last statement had been the 20 second sound bite delivered as the lead story on the evening news the night before. With it had gone a complimentary piece about how the Colorado Guard unit was part of the backbone of America's might, with its state-of-the-art F-16s ready to deploy worldwide on a moment's notice. Boyd had felt pride for the first time since taking an active duty assignment as a pilot with a guard unit instead of another active duty fighter wing. His choice had been between a non-flying job or flying with the reserves.

"What happened?" Boyd asked the obvious question without waiting for an answer to his first one.

"Engine exploded on takeoff. Never even cleared the end of the runway," Bertz said woodenly, like he'd already told the story more than he wanted to, then added, "Yes, come over now. Wear ABUs and bring an extra change of clothes."

Boyd relived a take off; damn little of it before the end of the runway. Then he saw the general again, striding off the stage to applause, waving.

"Come to flight operations and we'll assemble before going down to the site. We usually bring in somebody from another base for the board, but you're new here, and you're an instructor pilot with combat experience in the F-16. Headquarters said to put you on the board. How soon can you be here?"

"Half an hour, sir," was Boyd's crisp military response. It masked his considerable aversion to the task and the disappointment in having his weekend plans changed so abruptly.

A change of clothes? Boyd thought as he stood in his kitchen looking south out the window. A smudge of smoke was visible high in the southern sky toward Buckley.

"Change of plans, big guy," he said as he filled Eight Ball's water dish and tossed him a couple dog biscuits. He strode back down the steps into the worn back yard and kneeled to rub the dog's ears and head. The dog looked up expectantly from his dog biscuit, brushing his heavy tail against the dust.

Boyd stood and returned to the house. He quickly threw a spare flight suit and boots along with a change of underwear and socks into a leather athletic bag.

The smell of the leather briefly took him back to the care-free leave he'd enjoyed in Italy while flying combat air patrol over Afghanistan. He'd felt invincible then, before the drawdown eliminated half the pilot billets and sent shit-hot fighter jocks to the airlines, parcel services, and graduate schools. Fighter wings were different now. Performance was not for pride as before, but to stay in the upper half of the top gun standings and avoid the next cut.

He turned off the lights, unplugged the coffeepot, donned the black baseball cap of the cougar squadron of the Colorado Air National Guard and walked out to his muddy and battered Chevy pickup. No need to lock the door.

CHAPTER THREE

Boyd stood stunned by the transformation of the aircraft he had flown almost daily for six years. It had changed from a graceful light grey ballerina of the clouds to a broken black beast, surrounded by a 150 foot circle of burned grass, and pieces. "Pieces of what?" Boyd murmured to himself with a wave of nausea.

The perimeter of the site was marked by day-glow orange ribbon and patrolled by guards toting M-16s. Boyd and Moses Eubanks, the crew chief on his aircraft, stepped out of a van only a few feet from the smoldering wreckage. The air reeked with the smell of burned and unburned kerosene, and burned grass, paint, plastic, and human flesh. The ground was singed inside the barrier. Firemen milled around, still carrying hoses and spraying water and foam on a few smoldering hot spots. Fire trucks, police cars, ambulances, and command vehicles, each chattered on their own radio frequency. All the doors were open. All the engines were running.

"Over here, gentlemen." A voice emerged from the chaos, and the accident board walked numbly toward it, their eyes still fixed on the wreckage. "I'm Major Graham. I'll be in charge of crash site security. Now that you're here we can enter the area. We'll stay together at first and take a quick walk around, then we can spread out and look for objects to chart. The pilot member of the board needs to be the first one to examine the flight controls and instruments so nobody touch the cockpit area until he's been there. The remains will stay in place until the flight surgeon has all the pictures and diagrams he needs. Don't pick up anything yet. When we begin charting parts, call for a technician to come over and measure how far something is from the center of the site and what compass reading it is. One of the actual board members will confirm and initial all notations." As he said this, the guards moved the ribbon and they walked onto burned grass.

The carcass of the F-16 lay on its side without the wings. The jet engine, really just a pipe with a fan in the middle, was blackened by the fire and its outer wall had a fist-sized hole on the right side. The fuselage that had surrounded it was gone. From the rear cockpit forward the outer skin of the aircraft was intact in a few places, missing in others. The canopy was broken, and only a few pieces of it were scattered about on the ground below the fuselage. Both pilots were still in the aircraft, their fireproof helmets, visors, and flight suits still in recognizable condition.

When the fuselage had collapsed on impact, the shape and size of the cockpit contracted and expanded drastically in a moment. This had fragmented the pilots' bodies and caused their fluids to form an aerosol like the jet fuel that had caused such a spectacular fireball. The explosion and fire after impact had been anticlimactic for them.

Moses Eubanks vomited immediately upon looking into the cockpit. Boyd a moment later. Most of the others followed within a minute or two. The security guards and firemen politely turned their attention to details in another direction from the vomiting accident board.

A gentle breeze was blowing from the north and by stepping into it one could get respite from the smell. Boyd turned and looked at the mountains, stood straight and breathed deeply and remembered the first and last lines from a poem all pilots know.

"I have slipped the surly bonds of Earth…

…and touched the face of God."

Others were looking at the mountains too, each making his own adaptation to cope. One by one each returned his attention to the subject at hand and began talking in low murmurs about various aspects of the crash.

Boyd returned reluctantly to the cockpit. The flaps were down, as they should be this close to take-off. The stick was in a neutral position, typical for the F-16, as the controls are actuated by pressure on the stick rather than movement. The airspeed indicator was stuck at 200 knots. The attitude indicator was correctly indicating 30 degrees of bank, which was about the position of the fuselage at this moment. The throttle was in afterburner, all the way forward; a desperate last ditch effort to stay in the air. The landing gear were in the locked down position. Things were just how they should be according to the pre-flight checklist. He stood back while the photographer recorded all findings.

"Wingtip hit here." Moses Eubanks called, standing fifty yards behind the fuselage. The others walked over to see the surprisingly narrow gash in the ground that was only a couple feet deep. A young man, not more than twenty years old, and wearing an orange jumpsuit, rushed over with a brand new construction tape measure and began documenting its exact location. He was ashen faced and seemed eager to get that far away from the aircraft.

"Look at this stuff all over the ground." Boyd said, standing beside Moses as the others walked around the site. The ground was littered with tiny bits of things.

"That's the plane," Moses said solemnly, stooping to pick up a piece of composite no bigger than a toothpick, and just as sharp. It looked like fiberglass. "You take the engine and avionics out of one of these things; four men can pick it up."

"No shit?" Boyd said, thinking about the 18,500 lbs it weighed empty and the 7,000 lbs of fuel it carried internally, and the 15,000 lbs of bombs or rockets it could easily carry. "I guess that's all it is, really. Engine, instruments, gas, bombs, and men." Boyd had to look at the mountains again after that. Pilots prefer to approach plane crashes in the abstract.

The different parts of the plane were discovered, talked about, catalogued and photographed. Before they knew it, it was noon. Lunch was delivered and they were all called over to eat.

Just before leaving the perimeter Boyd stopped and picked up something totally unexpected; they looked like a pair of vice-grip pliers, blackened from the fire and bent. Moses and Major Graham stopped to examine them and the airman quickly began the measurements.

"Vice-grips?" Boyd said to Moses as they washed their hands and opened a can of Pepsi. "I've never seen a Vice-grip on an aircraft before."

"They aren't vice-grips. They're dikes. We use them to cut the wire that tightens the bolts on the inside of the combustion chamber. The bolts have a safety wire attached to them that is twisted to be sure the bolt doesn't come loose and fly about. Sometimes dikes do get left in the aircraft. It doesn't usually cause a problem." Moses looked worried.

"Looks like they might have gotten into the engine and then it spit them out the side, rupturing the fuel tanks," Boyd said, still whispering.

"Maybe." Moses said slowly as he wrinkled his face, removed his hat and ran his hand over the top of his bald head as if he were smoothing down the hair that no longer was there. The head looked like a mahogany colored bowling ball.

They ate lunch in silence, without pleasure. Bologna sandwiches on white bread with one slice of American cheese and doused with mustard will stop any thought of additional food for a good six hours, and what is a meal for if not that?

By mid-afternoon the sun was high and warm and they were all working in their ABU pants and t-shirts. The firemen had packed up and left, and the security police were occupied with a small band of reporters who had been allowed to approach the site and report back to the army of journalists at the main hanger. Finally there was nothing else to do. Mortuary Affairs began to remove the remains. A final walk around, within, and a large circle outside, the perimeter failed to turn up anything new. They boarded the crew bus and were driven back to the briefing room.

Tired, thirsty, and smelling of fiery death, Boyd hopped out of the crew step-van at base operations and followed Moses Eubanks inside. The accident board walked silently down the hall, the pilots and admin people standing aside, out of respect and revulsion at the smell. Some were already stripping down in anticipation of the showers at the end of the hall.

"Chailland! Got a call," the Supervisor of Flying stopped Boyd in the hall. "Some guy says he has something for the pilot member of the board and won't talk to anyone else."

Boyd took the yellow phone message form from the major serving as SOF for the day and walked a few paces before looking at it. The call was long distance. Boyd stopped, angry, grumpy, and in the mood to argue.

"I need a class A line, this is long distance," he said, hoping someone would say he couldn't use the phone and he could crumple the note up and go shower with the rest of the guys.

Amiably, the major pointed to the phone on the SOF desk and left the room. Wearily Boyd sat down and dialed.

"Lamar Implement Company!"

"This is Captain Boyd Chailland, Colorado Air National Guard, here at Buckley. You left a message for me to call back."

"Oh yes, that was Mr. Switzler, hold just a moment please?"

"Hello, John Switzler. Thanks for calling back. I understand there's a board investigating that plane crash this morning. It's all over the news."

"Yes, I'm Captain Boyd Chailland, the pilot member of the accident board." Boyd said, crisp and formal. He wouldn't be at all sad to have this be short.

"Look, Captain, I'm not any happier to be having this talk than you are. I just want to be sure I'm talking to the right guy. I don't want to create any problems, and maybe I'm mistaken about this. So, if I have some information that's relevant to this case, can I just report it to you?"

"Sure, we may need to check back with you in person if it's something important."

"That's no problem." There was a pause, as if John were struggling to find a starting point. "Look, Trusten Polk and I were friends; college roommates; fraternity brothers at Oklahoma. We kept in touch for awhile, then I didn't hear anything until today. The last time I saw Trus was after the Viet Nam war. He was going to Libya to fly fighters there. I was living in Tulsa then and he came by the house. We had some beers, caught up on the good times. Right after that I heard he'd been in a plane crash."

"I'm writing this down. I haven't been over his personnel file yet, so I can't say if we need anything that far back," Boyd said, confident now he could bring this to a close.

"I'm not calling about any of that. The fellow on the television last night, the guy that made the speech; the one on the news this morning. That's not Trusten Polk."

"What do you mean it's not Trusten Polk?"

"Not the guy I knew."

"Maybe you knew a different Polk."

"On the news it said he went to OU, won a silver star in Viet Nam. I went to the Air Force web site and read his bio. It all fits; but it's not him."

"How could it not be him?"

"I was thinking maybe the news got the wrong picture."

"Yeah, that's probably it. We'll have his personnel file in the morning; with the official picture, finger prints, DNA; everything."

"It's probably just a mixup of pictures, or something. I'll just hang back, not talk to anyone."

"Good idea. Look, I'll get back as soon as I see the file; probably tomorrow afternoon. Keep it quiet till then."

"Deal."

Leaving the base Boyd felt dirty. In spite of a long shower the smells of the crash were still on him. He didn't want to take that back to the sanctity of his rented farm house and

Eight Ball. His spirit was wounded. He needed a beer, and Dozer's Bar was just the place. Way east of Denver International, Dozer's had opened when the initial grade work was being done. For more than two years heavy earth moving equipment churned the prairie to get the grade and elevation right for the runways, and Dozer's was the watering hole for the drivers.

Boyd had been to Dozer's a couple times since moving in a few miles down the road. The walls were lined with pictures of bulldozers, graders, dump trucks, survey crews, and mountains of dirt as it documented the construction phases of the new airport. Boyd entered and sat at the bar, ordering a long neck and swiveling around to look at the Saturday happy hour crowd.

A man stood in the door, his eyes adjusting to the darker interior. Tall, heavy, dressed in western style pants with a bolo tie and Wellington boots. He spotted Boyd and walked over, taking the adjacent stool.

Retired colonel, Boyd thought to himself. Sees my flight suit and wings from over there; wants to talk about the crash. Can't tell him anything. Don't even need to acknowledge I'm on the accident board.

"Captain Chailland?"

"Yes," Boyd said. How'd he know, was what he thought.

"May I buy you a drink?"

"Sure." This is just what Boyd had hoped to avoid.

"Let's sit over here, it's quieter." He nodded to the bartender to send over two more and walked toward a table in the corner. Boyd followed, taking a seat and watching passively as the older man sat, leaned his cane against the table and pushed another long neck across the table to Boyd.

Boyd took a long pull of his beer and felt the cold slice down into his middle. He waited for the questions to start.

"Trusten Polk was my best friend," the man said solemnly.

Boyd looked the man in the eyes for the first time, not hiding the surprise in his own. The man was intense, watching him.

"I have friends at Buckley. They called me after the crash. Too late then, of course, to do anything."

"Do anything?"

"About what he told me at dinner." The gaze was direct, piercing.

"Wait, who are you?"

"Barney Freeman, just an old retired colonel. Trus and I go way back."

"There's a form for the accident board; I have to document the previous 24 hours. I need to know what he ate, with whom, where, how much he had to drink. That sort of thing," Boyd said, trying to remember what else he needed to find out.

"Ate with me, at the Brown Palace, steak, one cocktail. That's not what's important for you to know. Listen, Trus was in big trouble. It was eating him up. He's gotten into something in Washington. Something illegal. Something big. Something that may have led to that crash."

"Wait, I gotta write this down," Boyd said, looking over at the bar for a legal pad, some paper.

"No. Just listen." A big hand pinned Boyd's arm to the table. "He was a member of the Delano Society. Mention that to your board chairman. Ask him to run that by the SecDef. You'll see some fireworks." Freeman stood, dropped a twenty on the table and walked out, he didn't use the cane.

CHAPTER FOUR

She was early, but waited in the car until the staff cars with the stars and eagles on the front unloaded in front of the chapel. The wives wore their church dresses and the guys their class A's. There was to be a burial at Arlington in two days, this was the memorial service for the Air Combat Command staff and those who might have known General Polk here at Langley in Virginia. Some big guys from the Pentagon and other bases had shown up here, to show support and respect.

Nobody knew Trusten Polk. Carmella De Beauvoir was sure of that. She entered the chapel with the bulk of the crowd, those who came in from their workplace in the uniform of the day, lining up to sign the guest registry. The lump in her throat became the first tear as she signed it herself. She'd been to a hundred of these, every active duty death on every base her husband had been posted to in a thirty year career. Bud De Beauvoir had led flights, squadrons, wings, and held staff jobs at every level. She would pull herself away from kids, or golf, or bridge, put on her best dress and meet him at the chapel or rush out to the car when he honked in front of the house. Most of the time she hadn't known the deceased, some young airman in a car crash, a pilot in a training accident, cancer, heart attacks, a boating accident. This was different.

"Will Colonel De Beauvoir be coming?" a young Airman from the ACC staff asked. He wore Honor Guard shoulder braid.

"No, he's TDY. I'll just sit in the back."

"The other staff colonels are in the second row. Could I escort you up there?"

She looked up to the second row, the place her husband's job entitled her to sit. Phyllis and Ned, Carol and Raphael, and Maxine without Tommy were all together. They were her neighbors, pretty good friends, and part of Polk's bridge club.

"OK. Put me on the far end of the row, next to Colonel Franks," she whispered. Maybe sitting next to Maxine would help her maintain composure. If she lost it, she'd be so far toward the end of the row it might not be noticed.

"Where's Bud?" Maxine Franks asked.

"He had to go to Randolph for a promotion board. He'll be back tomorrow. We're going up to the burial at Arlington," she said as she slipped in next to Maxine. Carmella dabbed her eyes as tears flowed. Who would take the guest registry when the funeral was over?

Bud had had the Wild Weasel squadron at Spangdahlem, ten years before. The dark, damp German winters took their toll and he'd had to spend a lot of nights shoring up morale at the club and at various gasthouses around the Eifel region of southern Germany. The Weasels were the squadron that went into a target first to take out the anti-aircraft radar. They went TDY to every hot spot and exercise in the hemisphere. Carmella played bridge. Brigadier General Trusten Polk, the wing commander, was her regular partner.

In the chapel at Langley, the music started, and Carmella De Beauvoir remembered Trusten Polk.

"Five, No Trump," he had bid, with authority, and a twinkle in his eye for Carmella. Their opponents folded and Polk proceeded to work through the cards, skillfully switching suits to trap their face cards and win the hand, and the tournament. Afterward, helping him clean up in the kitchen of the wing commander's quarters, she'd felt an attraction, brushed against him, flirted, and finally, they'd embraced.

Carmella was not a stranger to being felt up in the kitchen. Fighter pilots back from a long TDY or passing a big Operational Readiness Inspection celebrate, and some celebrations are marathon affairs going from house to house gaining momentum. A butt pinch or a tittie squeeze in the midst of general merriment is not a foul. This, however, was a long wet kiss with Polk's hands thoroughly exploring her plump butt and ample, matronly bust.

"Oh, God!" he'd said at the break, the blushing anguish on his face and the bulge in the front of his trousers told Carmella two things: Trusten Polk was not queer, as some had suggested because he was a lifelong bachelor, and secondly, he was a needy, lonely man.

Bud De Beauvoir, call sign "Debo", barged through life at full tilt, the little boy with the big dick, with one eye on the mirror and the other on his buddies; indestructible, fearless, restless. Sex with him was entertainment. He wanted lights and mirrors and always something new.

Trusten Polk, call sign "Trus", tall, broad shouldered and handsome like Bud, was very different. Carmella knew, even before their session in the kitchen at Spang, it was all an act. He could swagger and joke and talk about flying, gathering the young pilots like children around him to hear his stories and share his insights on the world situation, but he didn't feel it. He took her naked, full length, slowly in a darkened room, savoring every inch of her with his hands and face. He spent his seed in such a great rush of emotion, it seemed like pain, and she was drawn to him because of it. She wanted to see behind that mask, to know what he felt. Afterwards he was shaken, guilt ridden for committing the unforgivable sin of fucking a subordinate's wife.

Polk went to the Pentagon after Spang. Bud got National War College, then the Pentagon on Polk's staff, later his own wing. Bud was sure he'd get a star, and when he didn't it took something out of him. One day he was that boy who never grew up, mischievous and wild, the next day he was old, counting the days to retirement and an oblivious life of fishing. He lived two hundred yards from the ocean, and didn't yet own a fishing pole.

Langley was best for Carmella. Kids grown and at nearby colleges, Bud reaping the benefits of a successful career in a soft staff job with no flying and enough travel to make him feel part of the action, and Polk needy and guilt ridden as ever, giving up more and more pieces of himself. She was fascinated.

"Our Heavenly Father, we are gathered here today to remember one of our own." The Command Chaplain opened the service. Polk's own preacher, selected by him for the chance to become the only general officer chaplain in the Air Force, had three pages of notes. He played bridge too.

Trusten Polk was into something illegal, dangerous, and tied up with politics. It was affecting their sex life. He was like all boys – draining off some of that sperm seems to clear their mind, lets them see the world better. Anxiety about his problems was turning their trysts into confessions, complete with tears and entreaties of, "never leave me, I have no one!"

She'd calm him down, promise whatever, get his pants down, and get on him. Afterwards, he'd talk about a friend from Texas. She'd seen the friend a couple times at Polk's house, a stoop shouldered man with a cane. Things always seemed worse after he'd been around.

Polk would send Bud TDY about twice a month, usually for a day or two, and always with rental cars and full protocol honors, as befitting a senior staff officer of Air Combat Command rolling into town to kick ass and take names. Carmella would plan something for the early evening with friends, then on returning home turn out the lights except for her bedroom, and slip out for a walk. The security detail that watched Polk's street changed at 2300 hours, and she'd slip into Polk's back door. Boys are always telling sex stories, re-affirming among themselves that they're all getting it regularly. Carmella, middle aged and heavier than she would have liked, enjoyed knowing that she was keeping the brains of two of America's fighting men clear of that dreaded semen build up.

He needed to talk. "If the country only knew," was one of his favorite phrases. He'd check himself, then resume the endless discussion he always seemed to be wrestling with himself over – constitutional rights. He'd talk about how the media didn't understand why law abiding citizens would need to carry guns. Carmella didn't either, but Polk, apparently, did. Once she saw a film clip of him on the news from out west. He was standing in front of the F-16 he flew when he traveled, making a speech about the constitutional right to own property and control its use. She found it odd that an Air Force general would be speaking on such a thing and mentioned it to him. He paled, and asked her what channel and at what time. Had anyone else seen it?

The FAX machine in Polk's bedroom would begin to spew out paper at midnight. Carmella had learned that if the night's sex were not over by then, then it would be, because Polk got mad as soon as the thing kicked on to warm up. Unlike all the other documents Bud brought home and Polk had all over the house, these were not on letterhead, and the FAX cover sheet had no identifying information on it. It was pages of text, instructions, verbatim speeches, even testimony before Congress. From where? From whom? He wouldn't say.

CHAPTER FIVE

"I was standing right there, by the truck," the fireman said, dressed in his civilian khaki work shirt and standing in the open firehouse door. "I knew it was the general and wanted to see how he handled the Falcon. We had the tower frequency on the radio." He nodded at the open door of the fire truck, indicating a multichannel radio. "Just as his nose gear left the runway there was this little burst of fire out the other side in the back."

"Wait, don't get ahead," Boyd said, writing furiously on a yellow legal pad. He was at the firehouse halfway down the runway across from the tower. From the main door he had a panoramic view of the runway, and was close enough to hear the wind whistle across the control surfaces of a landing Falcon. "Start with what you saw while he was taxiing, and what you heard."

"I didn't see much before he got to the end of the runway, the taxiway there dips and you can't see from here. I didn't walk out until I heard them give him clearance to take off. He was in afterburner right from the start, and wasn't to the 5,000 foot marker there when he lifted off."

Boyd looked at the marker that was midway down the runway and not 100 yards from where he stood. It was a beautiful, sunny, June morning. He hadn't slept since the accident. He'd seen Trusten Polk's face all night; watched the speech as if played out in a silent movie; awoke in a start with both hands pulling the ejection handle between his legs; felt the impact; smelled the death.

"Right after that jet of fire came out there was a, a…" the fireman was struggling for just the right word. "Whump. Yeah, that's it. A whump." He said it again, louder. "Whump. Then pieces flew off of both sides of the rear of the aircraft and it was engulfed in fire. Right away. Then the afterburner noise stopped and it just drifted down to the ground. Well, it didn't drift exactly, but it did fall. The engine just quit."

"How about the wings?"

The fireman thought for a moment, then said, "They began to rotate this way," he said, indicating a counterclockwise roll.

"Left wing down?"

"Yes. No. It was the other way, because it was the right wing that hit the ground. Then it cartwheeled twice and just blew to pieces in a big fireball. We study all the time about how much of a fireball you get with 8,000 pounds of jet fuel, but you don't appreciate it until you see it. That fireball looked a hundred yards wide and two hundred feet in the air. I could feel the heat from here."

"How high did the plane get before it fell?" Boyd asked, turning the third page on the legal pad.

"Not more than thirty feet. It just barely had room to rotate that one wing underneath."

"That'd be a pretty quick roll, then."

"Yeah, I guess. It all seemed to be in slow motion. I watch Falcons take off all day when I'm working. Never get tired of it. Never thought I'd see this," he said sadly, looking down, turning away.

Returning to the hanger Boyd stopped by the pilot's lounge where a pot of coffee was always on and one could have some of the popcorn they made there. Into their standard popcorn popper, salvaged from a defunct movie theater, they put one scoop of oil, one scoop of popcorn, and one scoop of canned Jalapeno peppers. Not a treat for the weak of stomach.

"Hey Doc." Boyd said as he entered the room. Webb Collins, the flight surgeon, was just filling a bag with the popcorn. The smell of peppers was strong in the air. "How's your day going?"

Webb wrinkled his nose and shook his head. He filled his mouth with popcorn by drinking it out of the bag. He walked over to the bar and picked up a Dr. Pepper sitting there and flopped down on a leather couch, stretching his boots across a low table covered with magazines.

"We did the autopsies this morning."

"And you can still eat popcorn?" Boyd asked as he filled a bag and got some coffee. Webb seemed to brighten the day a bit. Even now Webb was optimistic and smiling.

"I didn't actually do it. They sent out a pathologist from the Armed Forces Institute of Pathology. I just watched. He did it down at the medical school."

"Find out anything?" Boyd asked, sitting down in a facing couch and stretching his boots across the same table.

"Not really. Just two dead guys. They'll do some toxicology; drug screens. Just in case. That will take a couple weeks."

"You ever do one of those yourself?" Boyd asked, wondering what it must be like to cut somebody up."

"Yeah. One. In medical school. It took me nine hours. This guy this morning did both in an hour and fifteen minutes. Of course, all the parts weren't there."

Webb finished the popcorn, and was looking at the pictures and awards that lined the walls of the lounge. The plaques and awards for feats of flying and bomb dropping went back twenty years. There were also some home-made awards commending certain after hours accomplishments not covered in the usual awards ceremonies. Webb pointed out a few of these as the two men walked around the room reading about events neither of them had been a part of.

"Who was flying it?" Webb asked.

"General Polk did the talking with the tower."

"The one with the stars on his flight suit was in the front. We'll have to wait for dental records and DNA to be sure it was really him. We got good footprints too."

"How'd you end up here, in the Guard?" Boyd asked after a minute, feet stretching out on the table again.

"Same as you, probably. My next assignment on active duty was a non-flying job in a general medical clinic, so I got out and joined the Guard. I do a couple shifts in an emergency room in the Denver area every week and hang out here the rest of the time trying to slime a flight or a TDY someplace. I'm a guard bum."

Just at that moment Colonel Bertz breezed around the corner with his coffee cup in his hand.

"Good. You're both here," he said, stopping suddenly. "I want you to take the D model and go to Langley to interview friends and family. Try to get the two weeks' activities laid out as best you can in two or three days and then come back here."

"Yes!" Webb Collins said as he jumped up stabbing his fist in the air in a triumphant gesture. Then added, "Sir."

"I'll have your orders cut today and you can leave first thing in the morning."

CHAPTER SIX

Boyd bought a seven-day dog food dispenser and left an outside faucet dripping into Eight Ball's water dish. Moses Eubanks agreed to check in every two or three days while Boyd was gone. At 0530 hrs the next morning Boyd and Webb met in the parking lot and walked into the hanger to check with the crew chief that the two seat D model was ready. They got a weather briefing, recalculated their fuel and flight altitude requirements based on the latest forecast and selected alternate stops in case there was a change. They checked notes from Langley for any local changes in operation.

Over coffee, Boyd went over standard emergency procedures and agreed to let Webb fly the plane once they were out of the Denver traffic pattern.

At 0630 hrs they donned their G-suits and carried their helmet bags out to the waiting aircraft. After the walk around, pre-flight, strap in and start-up they taxied toward the end of the runway at 6:56. At 7:00 the runway was opened for the first time since the crash and they were given permission for take-off. At 7:10 they reached 45,000 feet with Denver barely visible in their rear. Webb joyously controlled the stick and

Boyd reviewed the flight plan and spoke with the air traffic controllers.

"How do you want to do the interviews?" Boyd asked through the intercom. They were watching the dry prairies of eastern Colorado give way to the greener pastures and wheat fields of western Kansas.

"Doesn't make sense for both of us to interview everybody. Let's each do a pilot and pool our info."

"Who gets the general?"

"You want him?"

"No."

"Neither do I."

"You take United, I'll take American. The next one that checks into Kansas City Center gets the general and the other guy buys lunch."

"It's a deal," Webb answered. Within ten seconds a United 767 from Newark to Denver checked in, giving Boyd responsibility for documenting General Trusten Polk's whereabouts for the last two weeks.

"I want a steak for lunch," Boyd said, acknowledging defeat.

Webb bought Boyd a steak sandwich from the flight line cafeteria at Scott Air Force Base in Illinois, where they stopped for gas.

"Here are their personnel records and medical records. I have arranged for you each to have a car and driver to get around base or in town as needed. Lt. Colonel Barnes' family lives in Hampton and General Polk lived on base. He had no family." Boyd caught a momentary frown from Webb as this last bit of information was conveyed by the Langley base commander. "We're in somewhat of a quandary about General Polk's effects. I'm going to have Major Herrera, his other admin officer meet you at the general's quarters this morning."

Sitting down with Webb and the records, Boyd went right to the personnel file. Electronic now, there remained a paper file kept locally; the same with the medical file. He flipped to the back and saw that Polk had entered active duty from ROTC at the University of Oklahoma in 1970, just like John Switzler had said. There was a continuous line of performance reports, formats changing as the systems were updated every few years. Nothing fishy at first glance. He traded with Webb, who had finished scanning the medical records. Polk was 73 inches tall and had gone from 174 pounds in his initial flying physical to 199 at the most recent. The medical record documented a lengthy hospitalization in 1975 after a plane crash in Libya. He'd been evacuated to the burn unit at Brook Army Medical Center in San Antonio, Texas. Fingerprints and footprints were all there, ready to be compared by experts with whatever had been collected at the crash site.

Boyd arrived first at the general's quarters. He parked the staff car in front and walked into the yard of a very large two-story red brick residence on a tree-lined boulevard. All the houses were large, but General Polk's was the largest. It backed up to a bay which Boyd assumed connected to the

Atlantic Ocean only a mile or two away. The back yard was secured with a tastefully landscaped chain link fence, further setting the residence apart from its neighbors. The grass was cut and the flowers were cultivated. Azaleas were in fading bloom, and a magnolia was well on its way to producing those huge fragrant white flowers Boyd so remembered from his youth in southeastern Missouri.

"Captain Chailland?" His reverie snapped, Boyd turned to see a major dressed in class A blue uniform with the shoulder braid of a general's aide and shoes spit shined to a gloss that exceeded even that achieved by the plastic Corfam that some officers prefer. Boyd's salute was quickly returned and a handshake offered. "Sorry to have to meet under such an unfortunate circumstance. Did you ever meet the general?"

"No, sir."

"It's Wayne," the aide said as they stood in the yard admiring the efforts of the base grounds crew. "He was good for Air Combat Command. Quite the politician. Very good speaker. Had the Congressmen and news people in the palm of his hand. Good organizer; had Kevin and me hopping all the time mending fences, remembering favors, looking for talent. He left the tactical planning to staff. Let's go inside. I really don't know what we're going to do with his stuff. I don't want to rifle through his things, but someone's going to have to. We can take an overview now if you like." Wayne, with a Hispanic name and Nordic features, pulled out a set of keys and began trying them in the front door.

Not a closet smoker, Boyd thought as they walked into the foyer of the home. Once virtually universal among pilots, smoking is now forbidden in all flight line areas – frowned upon as unhealthy and because of its adverse effects on night vision. Still, one discovers closet smokers when the telltale odor is detected in their cars and quarters. The air was tainted only by the faint hint of air freshener. As they walked from room to room Boyd felt like a buyer being shown through a house by a real estate agent. Opening a kitchen cabinet he found clean, well worn pans and pots and various cooking appliances stacked neatly. In an adjoining cabinet were dishes and behind them a Family Services loan item receipt listing virtually everything in the kitchen.

"How long has he been in the Air Force?" Boyd asked.

"Thirty eight years."

"Thirty eight years, and doesn't own a frying pan." Boyd said, opening the refrigerator. "And, I didn't think there was a fighter pilot on the planet without beer in his refrigerator."

"The general was not a big drinker," Wayne said, almost in apology.

"Did he entertain? Here?"

"Sometimes. Catered by the club."

In the living room a bookcase revealed the complete history of World War II by Churchill, General Staff and War College texts, "Red Storm Rising" by Tom Clancy, a news magazine and an alumni magazine from the University of Texas. The silverplate in the dining room was complete with a receipt from Family Services. Upstairs everything was in order. The uniforms were hung neatly and the bed was made. There was a surprisingly small number of civilian clothes. Boyd opened the medicine cabinet.

"Stomach trouble?" he asked, taking out a bottle of Tums, another of Maalox and Pepto-Bismol. There was a large bottle of Metamucil, a packet of Senokot and a prescription bottle of Ambien.

"He was careful what he ate," Wayne said, still apologetic.

There were three kinds of toothpaste and two kinds of dental floss in the cabinet also. Below the sink were two bottles of mouthwash, a bottle of peroxide, Lysol, Mr. Clean, Tub and Tile cleaner and some wonder detergent sold by door to door salesmen.

"Can I take this?" Boyd asked, indicating the prescription bottle.

Wayne nodded and Boyd loaded up the contents of the cabinet into a shoeshine mitt he found on the back of the toilet. Probably shined his shoes while he's sitting on the crapper, Boyd thought.

Beside the general's bed was a fax machine, and on shelves beneath were three boxes of copy paper.

Boyd knelt and opened the top box; just paper. The other two were filled with faxes.

"Is this stuff official? Anything classified?"

"It's not marked classified. Anything classified is supposed to be marked and this house is not cleared for anything above

Secret. He never brought classified stuff home that I know of."

"It's just faxes, no letterhead, no official markings of any kind."

"Look at the fax, does it have a property ID on it?"

Boyd picked up the fax and turned it over, pulled the cord and examined that and the power cable it was attached to; no federal ID.

"I think this was personal stuff," Boyd said, looking up at the major.

"I guess so. Can you guys just take stuff like that? Don't you need permission or something?"

"We'll bring it back, we just want to look through it, to see if he had any special stresses nobody knew about."

"OK."

"Not much here," Boyd commented as they returned to the kitchen and looked out into the backyard. The bay was a mile or so wide and the city could be seen across it. The general had a private dock, as did most of the other residences that bordered the bay. There was no boat there.

"Was he much of a boater?"

"No. He had some friends who would come by occasionally. I don't know who they were."

Boyd walked out into the yard. The fence went down to the water's edge. The grass was sparse because of the shade of the several tall pines. They walked out onto the dock. It was a standard affair, attached to the shore with cables and floating on pontoons. It could accommodate several small boats. Walking back to the house Boyd looked down into the freshly cultivated flower bed just at the patio and saw a quarter sized depression in the earth. He slowed his pace just a bit and scanned the other side of the walk and the surrounding areas for others. There was another in the grass just under his feet. A cane? He thought to himself, yes.

"When did it rain last?" Boyd asked, matter of factly.

"Rains a lot here; couple times a week this time of year. We came in from Andrews last Wednesday in a C-21. It rained the whole time. The general and Kevin left the next morning for Denver."

"What time did he get back here Wednesday night?"

"It was after nine. I dropped him off."

"Still raining?"

"Yes."

"I guess you don't have to irrigate." Boyd said, handling the leaves of a camellia bush just at the back door, its leaves thick and green.

"Irrigate? Lord no!" Wayne said with a disbelieving laugh as he opened the door for Boyd.

"What kind of security does he have?" Boyd asked as they walked back through the kitchen. He had noticed a digital panel by the back door and warning stickers on the windows.

"There's a guard here at night. Usually in a car. Sometimes he walks around. When the General is out of town we just rely on the burglar alarm."

"Is there any security on the dock?"

"Just the guard, when the General's here."

"So there wasn't anybody actually here the last five nights?"

"No." Wayne was getting irritated because he couldn't see the point in this questioning.

"Does anyone keep a log of his visitors?"

"Only at the office."

"Did you ever meet any of his boating friends?" Boyd asked, realizing he was straining the cooperation of the aide and had better either fill him in or drop the subject.

"No" was the frosty reply.

"I get the feeling someone's tidied up here. I was just wondering if anyone has been here since the crash."

"Not that I know of. It is awfully clean. I hope no one ever has to go into my place like this. It would be an entirely different experience," Wayne said, less chilly now that he thought he knew what Boyd was trying to find out.

"Mine too," Boyd said, opening the front door. "I don't think there's anything to see here. Let's go back to the office and reconstruct the last two weeks using his appointment schedule."

A woman in a bright flower print dress waited by the car.

"Mrs. De Beauvoir! Good morning," Herrera said as they approached.

"Good morning, Major. Has any family surfaced, to take the general's things? I heard that a new ACC Commander is to be announced this week, he'll want to move in as soon as possible."

"Nothing yet."

Boyd thought her eyes might have moistened a bit, she was looking up at the house.

"The general and I were bridge partners," she said, turning to Boyd.

"I'm sorry, Ma'am, this is Captain Chailland, from Denver." Then, turning toward Boyd, "Mrs. De Beauvoir's husband is, or was, General Polk's chief of staff." Herrera was embarrassed by his gaff at not introducing them, and then further by the awkwardness of the tenses.

"Not a very interesting guy," Boyd commented after they had returned to the general's office and reviewed his flight record and appointments.

"The four stars create quite a wake. Sometimes they obscure the man wearing them," was Wayne's reply. "He sure put in the time. I can verify he was here till six or later every night. On the road he worked even harder," he added, in case the last statement seemed to detract from the late general's reputation. "And he had quite a combat record." This added just in case someone might think he had been disloyal.

"Captain Chailland, you have a call."

Boyd turned toward the secretary, brows furrowed.

"A personal call," she said, motioning toward an empty office across the hall.

"Coffee?" Herrera asked, getting up to refill his own and offering to fill Boyd's, and allowing some space for Boyd to take his call.

"Captain Chailland, this is Carmella De Beauvoir."

"Hello," Boyd said, confused for a moment, then flashing back to their brief meeting that morning at Polk's house.

"Are you an investigator?" she asked boldly.

"Well, no. I'm a pilot. I'm on the accident board."

"Could I meet with you, today?"

Boyd agreed and the conversation ended quickly. He felt unsettled walking back to Herrera's empty office. Carmella De Beauvoir was used to getting her way with men; an entrance, minimal pleasantries, a near tear, the introduction, then a call. Fighter pilots usually got the best looking women, the ones that aged well. He remembered her smile again as she turned to cross the street in front of Polk's house. She had a grace as she stepped off the curve, agile for a fortyish woman, and shapely, breasts bouncing as she skipped to cross the street ahead of a slowly approaching car. What would the wife of Polk's chief of staff have for him that the colonel himself couldn't provide?

Herrera returned with the coffee. But Boyd's mind was on Carmella; the dress, the smile. There was a secret there.

"I'll tell my husband you called," she said, setting the rules as she graciously showed him into the well furnished living room of their large red brick duplex, across the boulevard and down a shady side street from Polk's more palatial quarters.

"Yes, Ma'am," Boyd said, taking the proffered seat in an overstuffed chair next to a small fireplace with a dried flower arrangement in it. This was her show and he would let her set whatever rules she needed.

"Trusten Polk and I have been very good friends for a long time," she said, looking out the window rather than at Boyd. "Very good friends," she repeated, now looking at him. "His bridge clubs are legendary in the Air Force. Fighter pilots have taken up bridge, not a fighter pilot pastime," she smiled knowingly at Boyd, "just to get an invite to one of his tournaments."

She was right about bridge not being a popular sport with any jocks he knew, Boyd thought.

"I've been his partner for ten years." She looked at him, letting him draw whatever conclusion he might.

Boyd nodded. It wouldn't be the first time a man's career was enhanced by his wife boffing the boss, rare in the military, though. Close community, frequent moves, very strict code of conduct; adultery in the chain of command is the ultimate social taboo.

"I'm telling you this because," tears were coming now and she dabbed at her eyes with a handkerchief, "because he deserved better than to just," she fought back a sob, then sobbed, "disappear. Someone new will move into his house, his job, all of us will get orders, and there'll be nothing left of Trusten but a picture over in the headquarters building." She cried openly now, like a child, her shoulders heaving as she dabbed at her eyes and then blew her nose. "There isn't any family, there never was. He told me a hundred times there wasn't."

Boyd nodded, wondering how many women there were who thought they knew everything about a man, only to find out there was another wife, children he hadn't mentioned, a prison record. Men had pasts they didn't reveal, adulterous women could fool husbands into believing they had a true, loving mate. Perfidy is a finely honed human trait.

"Trusten was involved in something illegal, something so scary, he cried like a little boy at night," she said, head now bent almost to her knees as she sobbed, eyes covered with the handkerchief. "The last year, he wouldn't eat in public because he was afraid he would vomit."

"I saw him on television the night before the crash. He looked fine."

"Trusten was an actor, and every social event or meeting a stage. It's what attracted me to him ten years ago, I wondered what he really felt. He has the fighter pilot swagger down pat, of course, all you guys do. He can do anger, grief, gratitude, and sincerity. He's always on guard, always watching for the effect he's having on other people."

"Did he share any details about his personal life?"

"He didn't have a personal life; just me and bridge. Oh, and a tall guy with a cane."

Before Boyd left the ACC Commander's office he called the Langley Base Commander again. Though Polk and his four stars ran the command, the base commander owns the base and all the facilities. Being as nonchalant as possible, Boyd asked him to secure the general's emails.

At dinner that night Webb had two beers before, two during, and two after their meal while they pooled their information. Kevin Barnes had been a family man and the whole family was assembled for Webb's visit. He'd gotten way more information about the man and his activities than he wanted. It had been an emotionally draining afternoon. Boyd told him about the general's spic and span house but not about the cane print or any details about Carmella De Beauvoir.

CHAPTER SEVEN

Congressman Roscoe Kelly recognized Trusten Polk's picture in the Washington Post, the article about the crash appearing on the second page. As a fellow Delano, Kelly was supposed to attend the funeral, or at least make some appropriate gesture. The old lions of Delano were dying off now, forcing him to attend more funerals than he wanted.

He'd first met Polk more than a decade before, when he was first offered Delano. As junior members he and Polk had carried messages for senior members; no paper in Delano. Right after his Delano contacts positioned him to be Chairman of the House Financial Services Committee Polk showed up at one of his hearings. Odd to see an Air Force general officer sitting quietly in the back of a dull financial hearing, but there he was, accompanied by a tall stoop-shouldered man. After the hearing Polk had introduced them and then excused himself. The other man, Kelly struggled to remember the name but could not, had walked back to Kelly's office with him. An introduction by a fellow Delano was mainline access to the heart of power in Washington and was not requested, nor granted, lightly. This man had just asked a few polite questions. The next night they'd had dinner at "Seven K," the hot new restaurant frequented by K Street lobbyists. Two lawyers from Payton Baggs, the hugely influential Washington law firm joined them. They'd had a wonderful night and the lawyers seemed to enjoy Roscoe's take on the current political situation and hear his plans for the banking industry. He'd assumed they were there to gather information and insight.

Pondering this chain of events, Kelly stood, sipping his coffee, and looked out on Independence Avenue. Carl and Ralph, the two lawyers he met that night, had become good friends and remained so today. They shared his love of fishing. Carl was on the board of the Washington Yacht Club and had arranged a special Congressional Membership for him, enabling Kelly to keep his boat at the foot of 7th Street, less than a mile from the Capital. He didn't think of Ralph and Carl as lobbyists, he struggled to recall if they had mentioned being registered as such. A twinge of anxiety emerged as he recalled all the nights they'd spent dining on fish they'd caught in the Chesapeake that very day prepared to perfection by the talented chef at the yacht club. Drinking, laughing, telling tales, mostly about fishing, Carl and Ralph were his main diversion from the stress of being chairman of one of the most powerful committees in Washington. A guy can have friends!

"Ginny, find out if Carl Taylor and Ralph Vincent are registered lobbyists," Kelly said, opening the door to the front office to make sure they were alone before speaking to his secretary.

CHAPTER EIGHT

From 42,000 feet the Blue Ridge Mountains look like wooded hills. The small roads don't show up so it appears to be a vast, unspoiled wilderness. Boyd's and Webb's route was more to the south as they'd filed a flight plan to Little Rock AFB for gas and lunch.

"When we get to Little Rock, I'll get you the best barbecue sandwich you ever tasted," Boyd said over the intercom, his mouth tasting it already. Webb was wielding the stick again. Talk was sparse as they traversed Tennessee, enjoying the scenery, thinking about the unfolding mystery.

"Redeye One. Descend and maintain flight level two five zero," Memphis Center interrupted Boyd's thoughts.

"Redeye One, descending to flight level two five zero," Boyd touched the hot mike button by the throttle. Then let up on it and said over the intercom, "We're there. I have the aircraft." He wagged the wings back and forth to demonstrate that he was in control. The Mississippi river was just below them, a shining ribbon of brown with the trees of the bottom land providing an accent.

As they passed through 25,000 feet Boyd said, "Memphis Center, this is Redeye One, cancel IFR."

"Redeye One. Squawk one two zero. Confirm, cancel IFR."

Rather than change his transponder frequency to the VFR frequency, Boyd turned it off. He pushed the throttle forward and said over the open intercom to Webb, "My home town is just off the end of the runway at the old Eaker AFB, about 50 miles up the Mississippi. We're going to drop out of sight here for just a moment and do a flyby."

The Viper, as fighter jocks prefer to call the F-16, accelerated in a slow descending turn to the north.

"It's there at your eleven o'clock. We'll kick it up to point nine mach and go inverted at eighteen hundred feet down the main drag, then just at that intersection west of town we'll go back upright, hit the burner and go vertical to ten thousand feet, do a vertical recovery then dive back for another pass."

"Shit hot!" Webb said, ready for it.

At close to seven hundred miles per hour the five stoplights flashed by quickly. Boyd heard Webb grunt into the G maneuver as he whipped the aircraft upright just before going vertical.

"You still back there?" Boyd asked after the second pass and right turn.

"Oh yeah!"

"I'll show you the house I grew up in. It's a mile east of that cemetery up there," Boyd said, slowing down drastically with the speed brakes.

"Shit! It's gone," he said a moment later, rolling inverted and looking back over his shoulder. He made a tight left turn and came back, flying over the cemetery. "Damn," he said, his voice descending. "Bulldozed it and planted cotton."

"Are you sure?" asked Webb, sensing the sudden change in the mood of their adventure.

"It was right by that big oak tree."

"Redeye One. Squawk one two zero." Memphis Center was apparently sensing they were through with their little detour.

"This is Redeye One. Understand you are not receiving squawk." Memphis gave them another transponder frequency and Boyd turned the transponder back on. Should anyone complain there would be no actual record of their deviation, although it wouldn't take much to figure it out. Certainly everyone in Kennett, Missouri knew Boyd Chailland was passing through.

"I'm the only one left and we didn't own the land. Wasn't much of a house." He remained silent except for communications with Little Rock Approach Control, now only minutes away. After landing they removed their G-suits and helmets and stowed them in the travel pod. A crew van took them to flight operations where they requested a loaner car to take into town for lunch. Arkansas is in the middle of the barbecue belt, and Boyd knew a place that served pulled pork sandwiches almost as good as Horton's in Kennett.

The little house and the old man on the porch filled Boyd's thoughts as they waited for the car. Webb remained silent. The old man's passing three years before had been difficult. For Boyd he lived on in memory in that little house, surrounded by his big dogs and waiting for Boyd to come home and share his new adventures. Now the house was gone and Boyd's loss was complete.

"You might as well tell me about it," Webb said, after a long silence.

Boyd nodded in the affirmative but didn't say anything. The car pulled up and he got in the driver's side. The base wasn't as familiar as the town a couple miles down the road. He drove through the gate and turned toward it.

"It was the water that kept us there. Dad was a farmer. When I was six he turned over a tractor and fractured his pelvis. He could walk only with a crutch. My mother was already gone. We lived on Social Security Disability. Dad wouldn't move to town. It was a share cropper's house and had a hand pump in the kitchen. The water table is so high here you can dig a well just by driving a pipe into the ground a few feet. This well must have hit some kind of super aquifer because the water came out cold and clear and sweet. You never got tired of it. The landowner put in an electric pump on another well in the back yard so we could have a toilet and shower, but the water wasn't as good. He let us stay there without rent all those years. I guess I can't blame him for wanting another half acre of cotton. Wonder if the quail are still there."

In his mind Boyd heard a bobwhite and he was back at the little house sitting on the front porch, feet dragging in the dirt of the front yard. Two dogs lounged under the porch and one on the step. The old man in faded coveralls sat in his rocker and they each had a tall glass of that water. In his hand was the acceptance letter from the Air Force Academy. A quail in the fence row behind the house was calling to his chums across the road. It was the happiest day of Boyd's life.

"This is a great sandwich!" Webb interrupted his thoughts.

A beer would have hit the spot, but they had 900 miles yet to fly.

CHAPTER NINE

"Room! Ten Hut!" Surprised, the accident board turned to see who was coming in before starting to stand. They were half up when the "At Ease!" was called out by the major general who entered. Young for the two stars he wore, he strode to the front of the room like he was used to control. He wore aviators wings and below them a parachute insignia. Among his many ribbons were an Operation Iraqi Freedom campaign ribbon and a Distinguished Flying Cross.

"Sorry to interrupt, gentlemen. I was supposed to be here yesterday but the regular embassy run from The Hague was weathered in by a spring storm over the North Sea. I'm Bob Ferguson, Air Force Adjutant to the Commander U.S. Forces, NATO. The new ACC Commander has asked me to help out with this investigation. Please, continue with your discussion. Col. Bertz can brief me later on what you've covered already this morning."

The surprise was so complete and the uneasiness of having such an unexpected authority this early in the day so unnerving, the board members had to ask the recording secretary who had been talking when the general entered to even continue the meeting. Webb had just finished the autopsy preliminary report. Boyd was next, reporting on the flight plan and his interview with the tower. He began the summary of the two weeks prior to the accident.

"Let's hold that for later in the investigation, Captain," the general broke in. "If we get too bogged down in detail now we won't be able to see what we have accomplished investigation wise and what remains to be done. Let's just give overviews now so we all know where we are."

That made sense to everybody and the meeting continued until the maintenance group began to speak. The general was very interested in what parts of the aircraft had been found and what, if anything, had not been found. This took the rest of the morning.

Lunch was brought in, and during their break, General Ferguson got around to meet each member individually. He was soon discussing the post Gulf War strategy as it affected NATO, and how the new Africa Command was going to be focused on taming the vast Dark Continent. It was after two before the board re-convened with the maintenance progress report. The afternoon was filled with discussion about the engine and whether it had been the GE or the Pratt and Whitney and how much did it weigh and how much should it have weighed before the crash. Plans were made to get in an industrial scale to be exact.

Bored beyond distraction, Boyd began to leaf through the personnel file on General Polk. The flight records indicated he flew the F-16 only rarely, preferring his C-21 with its comfortable executive's interior. There were an incredible 38 years of officer performance reports there. The ones on top were completed on a word processor and signed by the Air Force Chief of Staff himself. According to the glowing praises in the narrative section, General Polk was responsible for everything good that had happened to ACC and the Air Force during his tenure as commander, some three years. These immaculately prepared documents were almost as dull to read as the litany of found and missing engine parts that had droned on in the board room that morning, or the discussion about how much the engine weighed in the afternoon. The room was growing stuffy in the late afternoon. Boyd scanned the reports going back through this glorious career; Vice-Commander of ACC, NATO Headquarters, European Command, Air Group Command, Wing Commander, Squadron Commander, War College, a graduate degree. Intermingled with the glowing performance reports were letters of commendation from senior leaders. Several times Boyd stopped reading, intending to pay more attention to the board proceedings, but each time he couldn't maintain interest and went back to the personnel file.

Beneath all this fine paper and carefully crafted verbiage and just above the undergraduate pilot training record was a performance report written on a manual typewriter, in green ink, with a coffee stain in the center of it. A coffee stain? Someone had set a cup of coffee on the performance report of a four star general? It was dated November, 1972 and Polk had been just a second lieutenant, stationed at Phan Rang, Viet Nam, flying the F-100. The report was signed by Ben Culpepper, Maj., 488-48-9922.

"During Operation Giant Anvil, Lt. Polk flew twelve combat missions in three days, bringing back two heavily damaged aircraft. He volunteered to fly the missions of other pilots, as well as his own. His bombing and strafing over the city of Hue was instrumental in turning the tide there. His leadership is responsible for the high level of morale in this unit. In the mud and rain and confusion that is war in Viet Nam, Lt. Polk stands out as the shining example of what a pilot; a man, should be."

Boyd wanted to meet the man who wrote those words, and hear about the man he wrote about. He wanted to feel what it was like to praise a man as if he were the stuff of myth, and then set a coffee cup on the report. There was some odd stuff going on with Polk, was this real or had someone planted it in the file? He copied down the name and service number. No one noticed.

"I haven't seen him in over twenty years," was the flat reply from the telephone the next day. It had been a simple matter with name and social security number to find retired Lieutenant Colonel Ben Culpepper through the Air Reserve Personnel Center, conveniently located at the old Lowry Air Force Base in Denver.

"Did you know he'd been killed in that plane crash last week?"

"Yeah. I heard."

"I'm just trying to find out what kind of guy he was, to see if personality or whatever had anything to do with the crash." Boyd hadn't expected it to be so hard just to get Culpepper to agree to see him. He lived only 70 miles from Denver.

Silence.

"Was there some problem? From the performance report it sounded like you had a high opinion of him."

"Best pilot I ever met," Culpepper said, grudgingly.

"I could come up this afternoon."

Following the directions given him by Culpepper, Boyd drove north almost to Greeley and turned off on a county road to the east at LaSalle. A hundred years ago someone found that the simple addition of water channelled down from the melting snows on the Rocky Mountains some sixty miles to the west turned the marginal prairie grasslands into some of the most productive farmland on the planet. Onions, pinto beans, sugar beets, and corn make Weld County an agricultural powerhouse. Just across the South Platte River Boyd saw the hanger with Culpepper Aviation written on the side and top.

The new steel building had a neat gravel parking lot with one old pickup truck in it. The hanger doors were closed. Boyd tried the office door and found it open. There was no one there behind either of the two desks. The door between the office and the hanger was open and through it Boyd could hear tapping on metal. He stepped into the hanger and his heart thudded in his chest. Along with the smell of aviation gasoline and lubrication fluids was the smell of agricultural chemicals, familiar to a farm boy from cotton country. It was the airplane that caused the excitement. A large biplane with an enclosed cab, huge radial engine and a three-blade metal prop was being tended by a portly middle aged man, standing on a ladder leaning into the cockpit. He wore a nomex flight suit, stained badly by various oil-based substances. The patches and rank were removed, but the name tag still said, Ben Culpepper, LTC, USAF. He frowned when he saw Boyd.

"Did you go to Hayti to pick this up?" Boyd said with a confident smile as he walked over and rested a hand on the prop.

The frown vanished and the droopy face turned a quarter turn to the side and showed a faint smile, as if to say, "You know this plane?"

"King Cat. A standard Ag Cat upgraded with a twelve hundred horsepower Wright radial engine. Mid-Continent Aviation, Hayti, Missouri. Practically my home town."

"If you're gonna haul anything at this altitude in the summer, you got to have some balls."

"This, is balls," Boyd said, walking around the prop and looking at the engine.

"Not many people know this plane. They recognize it as an Ag Cat but are stumped when they see the engine," Ben said, wiping his hands and then the canopy as he closed it and descended the ladder.

"I grew up in southeast Missouri. They do a lot of spraying. They were putting 450 hp Pratt and Whitneys on a Stearman back in the sixties at Mid-Continent. I remember being fascinated during spraying season whenever they would come over in one of those things. We used to drive over to Hayti just to look at the planes they had parked around the lot at Mid-Continent. Sometimes when I make a bombing run down on the range I wonder what it would be like to do it in one of these."

"You get a better look at the scenery," Ben said, holding out his hand. "Ben Culpepper. Sorry I gave you such a bad time. I have very mixed feelings about Trus Polk."

"I would appreciate hearing about it." Boyd said, trying to keep it simple.

The smile disappeared and the frown returned. Ben was going to tell his story but he wasn't going to like it. It was apparently so unpleasant he was having trouble finding a place to start. "He was my best friend. The best friend I ever had. He ruined my military career and broke my heart." With these last words Ben's face turned hard and he looked Boyd in the eyes as if to add, "Yes, a man can have that good a friend!"

Boyd didn't say anything. The moment passed. Ben turned and walked into the office. On top of the Coke machine was a ring of keys which he used to open the machine. He took out two beers and tossed one to Boyd.

"We met in Viet Nam. I was on my second tour, Trus was just out of pilot training. We flew F-100s out of Phan Rang, a crappy little base on the coast. The Hun was a great airplane. The F-105 guys were always swaggering around talking about their speed, but shit, once they were over the target they were worthless. The Hun really gets down to the target. You see the enemy up close and personal," Ben said with a wicked grin.

"Trus was the best stick I ever saw. Once we briefed him on how we flew our missions he did it right the first time. By his tenth mission we were learning from him. Oh, we did some shit!" Ben was not reluctant now, the story was flowing better. "Flying as low as we did, anti-aircraft fire was a real problem, especially if you were the second or third ship onto the target. He'd come over first, white hot and firing his guns at nothing in particular, drawing all the attention in the valley. One of the rest of us would be right behind, low and slow and get the eggs down before they saw us. Another trick was to coordinate two ships coming in from two directions and cross the target at the same time. You have to be precise or the one who is a second late flies into the bomb blast of the first." Reliving this was bringing the twinkle back to Ben's eyes. He was sitting on one of the desks, drinking the beer.

"Napalm was his specialty. Marvelous weapon. Down in the south the VC would set up an anti-aircraft battery in a rice paddy. They would dig down and sort of fill up the sides a bit. Not so much that you could see it well or anything. Then throw camouflage netting over it. They had that Russian 23 millimeter gun that is especially good against helicopters. They'd just sit there out in the open and yet invisible and wait for a flight of Hueys to come along. Sometimes there wouldn't be anybody left to even tell what had happened. A whole flight, gone. If we found out where they were and came in with steel bombs they had a pretty good chance to get us on the way in. If we missed by, say a hundred feet, not that bad really, the bomb sinks down into the mud five or six feet before it goes off. All that shock is vectored up by the huge crater it leaves. The dinks just duck, then bust your ass on the way out. Trus would come in low and lay the napalm on the paddy, like a water skier, and fly right into the gun emplacement. He'd push the pickle and pull the stick. He never missed."

"Laid it on the water?" Boyd said, incredulously. "Didn't it go off when he pushed the pickle button?"

"Oh yeah! But, you're going three hundred and fifty knots and you just fly out of the fireball. Scorches the tail a little. You can't miss, and they can't get the gun to point down at you as you are coming in so you don't even get shot at. Well, not every time anyway. When the rest of us learned to do that we put the little cocksuckers out of business. Either the Russians quit sending them the guns or they found some other way to use them. Trus used to come in with some of the damnedest things sticking out of or stuck to his aircraft; trees, posts, clothes."

"Clothes?"

"Came in one time with a nav light out on the right wing-tip. His crew chief found a piece of somebody's black shirt flapping out of the hole, caught on the broken glass."

"If he couldn't shoot 'em or blow 'em up he'd run over 'em," Boyd said, emphasizing the other man's story. Ben nodded in agreement as he finished the beer and headed toward the Coke machine.

"As the little bastards began to thin us out, Trus took it personal. If somebody went down, he'd keep flying by there, hoping to see something. If nobody saw the crash he'd detour into the probable area whenever he had the gas, always looking. If someone didn't feel good, Trus took their mission. If someone took a round through the wing or something and brought the plane back, Trus wanted to go right out and even up the score; to get back at the enemy for hurting one of his friends. That was when he saved my skin. I took one of those 23 millimeter rounds right through the fuselage. It took out the whole instrument panel. Coming off the target we flew into a goddamned monsoon. Thunderstorm 50,000 feet high and rain so thick you couldn't see thirty feet. Without instruments I was history. Somehow he found me and flew fingertip all the way back home. Sometimes his wing overlapped mine to stay in sight."

"I read your OPR on him. I don't understand where the coffee stain came from."

"Oh that was Trus all the way. We didn't give a shit about paperwork. That's why I wrote it in green ink. Just to piss off the fat asses back at headquarters. Yet, I knew he might want a promotion or a medal or something in case we didn't get killed, which we all assumed we would. Hell, if you thought you might actually live through it you'd probably start trying to drop the bombs from above the trees and really be a target for the gunners."

There was no reluctance now, the story had begun to positively flow.

"It wasn't all flying. Sometimes we'd be rained in for a week at a time. We'd go to town, not much there. No women. We'd drink, play cards. Trus went monkey hunting one time. Another time we all went fishing down on the river that was nearby. Caught some fish too. And he was always talking about the goddamn Sooners. You never met a more boneheaded football fan. He'd do anything to see a film of an OU game. He'd gone through ROTC there and I guess those Okies are a loyal bunch."

"Football loyalties run deep."

"We'd go to Saigon for weekends when we could. He was a hell raiser! They'd send a chopper to take us into town and the whole way in there he'd rag me about what we were going to do. 'What's it going to be, Pepper?' He'd ask. 'The usual, booze and broads.' I'd say. 'Yeah, but which kind of booze?' 'Scotch,' I'd say. 'No. Beer. San Miguel. Ice cold.' He'd say. 'OK,' I'd say. Then he'd say, 'No. Scotch. Black Label.' Then I'd say, 'OK. With soda.' Then he'd say, 'No out of the bottle.' Just to rag me. Just to make me think about it and want it.

Likely as not we'd end up drinking gin and tonic or champagne."

"Then we'd go through the same thing about the girls. How many did I think we were going to need? He was always wanting to start with six for the first go 'round. That was a rodeo term he used for the time it took us to drink up our initial supply of booze and each one fuck all the women. Usually it was about a day, but sometimes we'd get distracted and not get finished in the whole weekend. I felt six was too much like a crowd. I preferred four. Two was too intimate. Like a love affair or something."

Boyd leaned back on the desk and laughed loud and deep. The image of these two pilots shouting back and forth in the helicopter planning their weekend and then the crowd in the hotel with all those bar girls was just too much. The paroxysms increased when he thought about it again and saw the happiness on the face of the grease stained crop duster as he relived the most intense time of his life. Boyd took a sip of beer and choked on it as he thought of the black shirt on the F-100 wingtip. His broad shoulders heaved and he had to stand up and cough to stop the choking on the beer and get his breathing started again. Tears came to his eyes from the laughing and choking.

Seeing the effect the story was having on Boyd, Ben was eager to continue. "Sometime during the weekend we would have to go eat. Usually this was at the end of the first go 'round. The whole bunch would load up in a taxi and we'd go to a real Vietnamese restaurant. Not one of those fancy French places, but one where they ate the sauce made with the rotten fish and it all laced with chili peppers. We were quite the sight with the girls all giggling and laughing and Trus and I passing out five dollar bills to everyone waiting on us and the manager scurrying around trying to find enough ice to cool down the San Miguel right at the table so we wouldn't have to keep sending for it. We'd usually order 'One of everything.'

"Sometimes when things would be slow for a few days he would cook up some of his 'Slope Stew.' He called our hosts 'Slopes', I don't know why. The stew was a large can of tomato juice, a bottle of Tabasco, a can of Spam, and nuoc mam, that fish stuff. I can still see him bartering with some of the locals trying to trade Kool-Aid or peanut butter for the nuoc mam. He'd throw in some vegetables and potatoes and cook it all day."

"Sounds terrible."

"It was. Took a real man to eat it. We'd fill a bowl with crackers and pour it over the top. Gave us something to do. Usually had three or four of the locals standing in line for some at the end of the day. Sometimes they'd bring some monkey meat to throw in or a dog or something. It added variety."

"You ate dog?" Boyd asked, thinking of Eight Ball and curling his upper lip.

"Probably. Who could tell in that." Ben laughed. Boyd thought he was probably kidding about the dog.

"Our hootch was the gathering place for the locals as well as some of the pilots. Trus's exploits didn't sit well with everyone in our unit. The locals would hang around to trade stuff with us and we got some info on what the VC were up to. We'd spread some bullshit that way too. Told 'em once we were going to try a new gas weapon that would make their dicks drop off and their balls swell up to the size of bowling balls. Then we'd kill 'em easier cause they couldn't run when the planes came over. You should have seen the look on their faces with that one. I'm sure it got back to the VC. Trus drug out the story to nearly an hour, adding all sorts of bogus scientific details. Hell, by the time he finished I had my balls tucked in a little tighter too!"

"Sounds idyllic."

"We lost a lot of guys. The weather was unpredictable and the terrain was weird. You were always dropping bombs in a valley. Never on top, always in the bottom. Getting in and getting out was more hazardous than the antiaircraft fire. Then sometimes a guy just disappeared. We figured a Mig would slip down under the CAP and pick someone off every now and then."

"You had a falling out?"

"The tour ended and the squadron was rotated back to the States. Before they could make us IPs or give us a desk to fly I talked Trus into putting in for a tour at Wheelas. No one wanted to go there so it was easy. We went right away."

"Wheelas? Never heard of it."

"Libya. We used to be right cozy with the ragheads. It was before Khaddafy kicked us out. You could travel almost anywhere in the Mediterranean in a three day weekend. It was great. That was where Trus crashed. He was out on a routine patrol with another F-100 and flew into a sandstorm. We don't know if they got disoriented and ran into each other or what. They both crashed. We looked for three days. Couldn't find a trace. We hadn't given up, but it didn't look good. On the fourth day some guys came in from headquarters with some lighter, slower aircraft and found him."

"Did you see him?"

"Just a glimpse. All bandaged up. Nearly dead, they said."

"Talk to him at all?"

Ben shook his head. Lips tight, he said, "Never saw him or talked to him again."

"Why not?"

"They flew him out right away and he was in the hospital at Weisbaden for a week or so, then back to the burn unit in San Antonio. I took leave and went by there to see him but they said he'd just had another operation and was in isolation. He sent me a brief note after that, thanking me for the thought. Three months later I got a longer letter telling me he was going to go to a staff job and then Air Command and Staff College and he'd gotten religion and didn't plan on ever seeing me again." Ben stopped talking and looked at the floor, then out the window.

"Just like that? Like you were a bad influence or some-thing?"

Ben just shrugged his shoulders.

"So what did you do?"

"It just wasn't fun anymore. I still flew out my tour in Libya, but I didn't enjoy it. They tried me as an instructor for awhile, but I was cranky and hard to get along with. Finally they made me the deputy maintenance officer of an obscure and obsolete weapons system with the Logistics Command in Georgia, a desk job. That filled in my twenty and I got out."

"So, now you're in the ag business. Got a wife or family?" Boyd asked, sensing the good stories had come to an end.

"No. Wouldn't wish that on somebody I liked. Had a wife once. Treated her terrible. Still feel bad about that."

"What did Polk look like, size, shape?" Boyd asked, think-ing of the tall, handsome man on the stage at Buckley.

"He was a small, wiry guy. I have some pictures at home. Snapshots. He was five nine, weighed about one fifty."

"Any tattoos, marks, scars?"

"I don't remember any, but I'm sure he has some now. They said he was really burned bad."

Boyd called John Switzler in Lamar on his cell phone driving back from La Salle. He apologized for taking so long getting back to Polk's old college roommate, and said the official picture was not in yet. He asked if Switzler could send any pictures he had of Polk. Switzler readily agreed.

Boyd detoured east on the way back to Denver to lengthen the trip and try to sort out his new insight. The man who had paced the stage in Denver Friday, holding an audience captive with his patriotism, and then ridden the F-16 into the ground on Saturday was not the same man who laid napalm on the rice paddies and cooked up dog and monkey with the natives in Viet Nam. The recent flight physicals mentioned nothing of any disfiguring burn scars, and he was over six feet tall.

The performance report and the war record were the base upon which someone built a hell of a military career. Did someone meld a politician with a glorious war record and create a general officer? Were there other manufactured general officers out there? Was it the Air Force or the federal government or just a small group of officers looking for the promotion fast track? Was the real Trusten Polk a forgotten skeleton in the Sahara Desert? How many friends or relatives of Trusten Polk were treated to a letter ending their relationships? Who was Barney Freeman? What is the Delano Society?

Whoever broke Ben Culpepper's life so casually could have also grown tired of the re-created Trusten Polk and had a pair of dikes left in his engine intake. Three pilots down and counting.

CHAPTER TEN

The retired colonel, Barney Freeman, waited in a van with tinted windows parked at the small strip shopping center two miles down the road from Boyd's house. He had called Boyd's cell phone just as Boyd was leaving Buckley and asked to meet him on the way home. It was Friday evening.

"Sorry to be so mysterious. I just wanted to talk for a minute. I have some documents you'll want to see. Maybe I can add something to what you already know."

I'm sure you can, Boyd thought. This was not legal, but if it cleared up any questions he had about this manufactured general it was an acceptable detour.

"Did you know General Polk in Viet Nam?"

"No." Freeman seemed content to be interviewed. "We met after that, at War College."

"Did you go to his house at Langley after he died and take things that were there?" Boyd asked, cutting through all the hours of talk that could circle around this thing and lead nowhere.

The eyebrows went up and the colonel leaned back in the captain's chair he sat in.

"I just got back from there, and someone had tidied up his house."

Freeman didn't answer immediately, looking directly into Boyd's eyes; surprised, thinking, trying to decide whether to answer and if he should tell the truth. Then he shook his head, but said nothing.

"You were here in Denver the day of the crash, that was just last week. You went to Langley, docked your boat at his dock the day after he died and went into the commander's house, didn't you?"

"Nope."

"Do you have the code to the general's security system?"

"No."

Boyd felt Freeman was lying, but the eyes remained steady, searching him out. He was interrogating, but he felt he was being searched. Odd.

"What's this Delano Society you mentioned?"

"You haven't told your board chairman about it yet, or you'd know."

"I don't want to spout off with something half-baked and look like a fool. I'm new to all this," Boyd said, realizing he was on the defensive now.

'Shit will hit the fan when you tell them, trust me on that. As to what it is, exactly, I'm not in it. I just heard Trus talk about it."

"Do you live in Denver?"

"No, I came for a meeting that Trus was supposed to speak at tonight. I'm headed out there now. As you're in official status investigating the crash it would be appropriate for you to be in uniform. Do you want to come along?"

"There are some constitutional issues here, Boyd, that you should be aware of. Trus and I have been concerned about the drift in this country for years. Our government has lost sight of some of the foundations that have made America what it is today," Freeman spoke earnestly, leaning back in the captain's chair in the back of the van. Boyd occupied the passenger seat, swiveled around to hear. Jerry, the driver, was Freeman's administrative assistant, and bodyguard.

They drove east on Interstate 70 for awhile, then exited onto a state road.

"Criminality has been hiding behind the face of tolerance. Organizations claiming lofty goals are really trying to destroy our country. You know them as espousing a New World Order. They're the people who want to reorient all humans on the planet into one big happy family. Well, it won't work."

"Sounds like a pretty innocuous idea," Boyd said blandly. He was here finding facts and investigating a plane crash. If this guy had some weird political base, best find it now.

Boyd turned as they bounced over a cattle guard at a fence line. Large signs on either side of the road warned of dire consequences should any, "unauthorized persons" dare trespass.

A burst of automatic weapons fire just over the hill ahead of them was joined by more. The background random single shots told Boyd it was a firing range and not a revolution before they crested the rise to see the pole barn and mobile home.

A half dozen men wearing combinations of camouflage, work clothes, and hunting garb were firing a steady stream of lead into the backstop at the base of a low hill. Forty miles to the west, Denver was visible beneath its blanket of brown haze, and the still-snow-covered Rockies shimmered in the summer heat beyond that.

The dust cloud behind them caught up when they stopped, and the middle aged man, dressed in a khaki work shirt with camouflage pants, striding out to meet them was momentarily obscured. The door to the van opened and Freeman stepped out into the dust.

"Colonel Freeman. Sir, welcome to the Unorganized Colorado Militia."

Boyd was introduced and warmly received by the dozen or so militiamen setting up rented chairs in the pole barn, his presence in uniform lending an official air to the proceedings that Boyd sensed was wrong. Military officers don't do politics, but apparently Trusten Polk did, as this had been scheduled featuring him. When Boyd offered no information about Polk's crash, or anything else, attention focused on Freeman, who talked confidently about other militia groups around the country.

At last out of the spotlight, Boyd strolled toward the firing range. Blazers, Range Rovers, farm trucks, a BMW, and an assortment of family sedans were parked along the fence. The gramma, or buffalo grass, underfoot indicated this area had very recently been range land. The mobile home was not new, but the lack of grass or weeds growing around it indicated it was new here.

A stocky man in a work shirt, jeans, red suspenders and wearing a black baseball hat with "Range Officer" on the front, strode up and down the line, advising, encouraging, instructing, and warning. He held the butt of a cigar clenched between his teeth as he laughed and joked with the men, mostly in their thirties or early forties, blazing away with pistols and one AK-47. Periodically someone would buy some ammunition from a foot locker he had opened on a metal desk. After an hour, he closed off the firing, checked the guns to be sure they were unloaded before they were taken back to the cars, and closed down the range. The shooters drifted toward the barn.

"Firepower demo," he said in answer to Boyd's unasked question as he returned from a worn pickup with an arm load of paint cans. "Grab a load."

Boyd carried two loads of old paint cans, filled with something, out to the backstop.

"John Rigdon," the range officer said, offering his hand after the second load. He had arranged the cans in two stacks, head high.

"Boyd Chailland."

"You active duty or guard?" He reached up to take the cigar out of his mouth. He was missing the distal third of his right index finger.

"Both, actually. I'm active duty Air Force serving with the Colorado Air Guard. The billet is called Active Duty Reserve."

"Well, you're certainly welcome here. You gonna speak tonight?"

"No, I'm just along to watch."

"Well, being active duty probably keeps you from joining up, but anytime you want to come out and use the range, come on. Hell, you can't go full auto just anyplace." He pointed the stub of his amputated finger at Boyd when he made his point.

"Well, that's a fact," Boyd said, trying to match John's earnest candor.

The cattle guard rattled as a new arrival crossed the fence line and both men turned to see. A worn white Volvo coasted into the parking area and found an empty space along the fence line. The single occupant was a young woman.

"Oh. Colleen's back. See you later," John said, abruptly turning away from Boyd to meet the Volvo. The red suspenders made his body seem wider, and his gait was wide too as he approached the car, talking already, arms waving in gesture.

"Hey Colleen! Ready for another shooting lesson? We're gonna demo some of the big stuff in awhile. You ought to stay for that." He held the door as she stepped out, smiling warmly. Shoulder length mahogany colored hair, tight jeans, and a ready smile had John wrapped around her merest whim.

Leaning into the fence, Boyd chuckled to himself as he watched them walk over to the range. Soon she was firing at a man-sized target with a small automatic, John hovering, correcting her grip, stance, and sighting.

"If they come to get your guns, what will you do?" Freeman said earnestly, standing awkwardly in front of the hundred rented seats that had slowly over the past two hours become half-filled. "Will you shoot your sheriff, police chief, your neighbors deputized for the task, or the National Guard?"

The room was silent. They had come here to strut their bravado, to brag about how effectively they could defend their homes, and to see a full fledged Air Force four star general. Instead, they were getting a retired colonel they'd never heard of and a captain that didn't say anything. Still, they were a rapt audience.

"Will it come to that awful moment when you will have to decide?" His voice was thin, but adequate to be heard if all remained quiet, which they did.

The afternoon had ended with a burst of automatic weapons aimed at the paint cans filled with water dyed red. A hundred rounds, fired from four assault rifles within the space of five seconds had blown water and paint cans all over the target area. The show had gotten the crowd into a festive mood. Then there had been hamburgers and hot dogs around the charcoal pit, the official opening of the militia meeting, during which the men sat with their squads in front and the handful of women and children in the back, a prayer, the pledge of allegiance, a rambling introduction and finally, the man himself.

"It won't happen that way," Freeman said, turning to walk along the front row. "The Jews went quietly to the gas chambers because they came from a long line of non-violent, peaceful people, and because they had been disarmed. No, our crisis will be different. We have affirmed and exercised our right to bear arms, and everyone knows that some of us will fight."

Heads nodded as people turned to their neighbors.

"Did you know that this land, right here," He stooped and grabbed a handfull of sod and held it up to the crowd, "has been designated as part of a critical prairie 'Bioregion,' and as such, comes under the protection of the UN Biodiversity Treaty?"

The room was silent.

"Who owns this land?" Freeman looked around the room, still holding the clump of sod.

"I do," John Rigdon held up his hand.

"For how long, if I may ask?" Freeman inquired.

"My great grandfather homesteaded it, in 1872."

"Is it mortgaged?"

"No."

"Did you pay your taxes last year?"

"Yes. I always pay my taxes," Rigdon said, beginning to seem irritated.

"Were you invited to attend the meeting last month in Denver where stakeholders were elected to make policy decisions about how this land should be used?"

"Didn't hear about any meeting," John replied, brow furrowed.

"Our President signed a treaty with the UN agreeing to the formation of Bioregional Councils, composed of stakeholders to make decisions about this land. You are considered an agricultural professional and are one of the many types of people eligible to be on such a council."

"But, I own the land!"

"The word 'own' doesn't appear in the treaty," Freeman said, voice softer now. People from the back of the room were, one by one, moving to the front. "The real power brokers in these councils are the nongovernment agencies, which is another word for activists, some sponsored by grants from our own government. You've heard it, and it's true. The pen is mightier than the sword."

Every head in the room was craned forward to hear.

Freeman shuffled to the center of the room, one hand on his cane he leaned into the front row, his voice now a croaking whisper. "They won't come to get your guns. They'll take your land."

"Are you a militiaman?"

Boyd turned, startled, to look into arresting green eyes framed by mahogany hair. Her gaze was direct, her hand extended.

"I'm Colleen Chamorro.

"Boyd Chailland," he said, still off balance from the talk about UN treaties and land. He'd expected a Second Amendment speech about the right to bear arms, instead he'd seen a room full of farmers and ranchers turned into a cohesive political unit in less than half an hour, by a man whose lack of public speaking skills worked as an asset.

"Are you a militiaman?" She repeated.

"No."

"A firearms expert?"

"Not really." Words were failing Boyd here. She was taller than she'd looked earlier, and the flannel shirt stretched across just enough cleavage to take the edge off of one's concentration.

"I'm an English teacher," she said simply.

"I'm a fighter pilot."

"Does the militia have an air force?"

"No. I'm in the United States Air Force. I'm attached to the Air National Guard in Denver. I was talking with Col Freeman and he invited me to come to hear him speak."

"Did he say, 'Come, see the strong right arm of patriotism'?"

"Something like that. How about you? You don't seem the type to want to spend a Friday night watching machine gun demonstrations."

"I was in a gun shop and asked who might teach me to shoot. They recommended the National Rifle Association, and John Rigdon was the instructor. He invited me to use the range here. He's been very kind."

"Keeps me awake," Boyd said, as they approached the refreshment table with a coffee pot perking away.

"That's a shame. Only a conscience should keep one awake," Colleen said brightly, taking a cup of coffee.

"I suppose the machine guns are a dull alternative to dropping actual bombs. Do you get to do that here in Colorado?"

"We drop practice bombs every day. Live ones a couple times a year, just to be up on how it feels when a ton of weight comes off your aircraft all at one time," Boyd answered, eyes flicking around the barn as the crowd stayed tight at the front. No one interested in being the first one out of the parking lot tonight.

"That must get the old adrenalin rushing. Two thousand pounds of steel and death, controlled by your very own hands." The words were harsh, but the eyes remained pleasant.

"So, what do you teach?" Boyd asked, taking a homemade cookie and leading her away from the crowd, lining up to join the militia movement by giving names and addresses to Jerry, who tapped them into a laptop. Jerry was also taking donations by swiping credit cards and scanning checks on a portable check scanner. John glared from within the group, close by Freeman.

"I teach women's literature at the University of Colorado," she said, then looked up from blowing on her coffee to see his reaction. There was challenge in her eyes.

"What's that?" He asked with pure innocence.

"Touché, you beautiful man. I won't tease you any more. Come, tell me about the life of a fighter pilot." They walked out into the night.

"Was all that true? All that about the United Nations taking people's land. That seems a bit far fetched," Boyd asked, bouncing back across the cattle guard, nearly the last car out of the area.

Freeman had stayed to talk politics and strategy. He had told them of his political action group that had worked for conservative causes and now was becoming the Patriot Party. Trusten Polk was to have been their candidate for Congress from a congressional district in Oklahoma.

"Yes, Boyd. It's all true. I didn't have to exaggerate. The language of the treaty and the press releases of the UN and the Nature Conservancy are my only sources of data. The stuff is all on the Internet, the addresses are on the back of that pamphlet you have there. Of course, there is opposition in Congress, but that could change." Freeman spoke earnestly, and softly. His voice was gone already. "Land is important to these people we met tonight. We have other issues, and I'll share them with you later."

"So you and General Polk have been working together?"

"Yes. For twenty years I've worked to build an alternative to the criminals who are running our country today. I have an infrastructure now. People who agree and are willing to help." Freeman was leaning into the center of the van and speaking softly. Boyd leaned in also, to hear.

"Trusten Polk was to have been the mouthpiece of our organization. His stage presence and military background would have given him credibility when he stood in a public forum and exposed the Delano Society as a corrupt oligarchy illegally running our country for the past sixty years. It's so wrong that, suddenly, he's not here." Freeman seemed on the verge of tears, then recovered. "Boyd, this country is about to change forever," Freeman put a hand on Boyd's arm, eyes piercing, focused, intense. "We're not going to stand by and let them muzzle us."

Boyd drew his arm back, uncomfortable with the other man's proximity.

"America is on the verge of discovering the granddaddy of all scandals. Congress drove a spigot into the federal treasury by guaranteeing mortgages, and it wasn't long before crooks got it running wide open. There's so much money sloshing around Washington now they can't spend it all, and the folks who will have to pay it back are going to find who did it and how. Both political parties are in it up to their necks. The backlash is coiled and ready to strike, and when it does, and the public finds out all those lofty ideals were just talk and that it's been about power and self-dealing all along, well, the Delanos will just be in the first wave at the guillotine, with more, many more to follow." He spoke with a sadness, as if he were relating an inevitable calamity.

"I've been reading about the mortgage loan thing," Boyd said defensively.

"That's just the distant rumble. Wait till the storm gets here," Freeman said, shaking his head. He leaned back in his chair, took a sip of water from a bottle and looked out the window as a full moon lit the prairie night. He sighed as if it were all out of his hands. After a moment he turned back. "Join us Boyd. We need your help." The intensity of Freeman's stare told Boyd this was the punch line.

"I can't speak out for a political party," Boyd said, annoyed that this kept coming up.

"Trus was both a part of the existing power structure and active in trying to find an alternative. That's why I must know how he died."

"I can't tell you anything," Boyd said.

"Unofficially, like you might tell a trusted friend," Freeman said, with an eager look, as if Boyd had just said yes instead of no.

"What is so critical about General Polk's accident?" Boyd leaned back, putting more distance between himself and Freeman.

"Some people in government are beginning to be afraid for their necks. I need to know if they killed Trusten to stop him from exposing them, or was it just an accident?" Freeman sounded worried. "Boyd, America is an oligarchy. There are only a few dozen people in charge. Polk was one of them, but he was a man of the people, and he took notes."

"Notes?"

"Notes. Proof…. Proof of treason. He knew every member of Delano."

"Treason? A strong word."

"Yes a strong word. Allegations of corruption and misuse of power require proof, and we're up against a pretty crafty lot; mostly lawyers, so they know how to operate without leaving tracks. Polk could stand up and point a finger; now it'll be harder to do. We've been building a base, an infrastructure to counterbalance what's been going on. The Patriot Party was to be the public expression of outrage, but there's more. We're much bigger than anyone knows."

"How big?"

"Knowledge and position are power. A few people in a large organization, well placed and powerful, like Polk, can be very effective when called upon to perform some small function in the name of the highest ideals. Thousands have heard of the Patriot Party and pledged to help. Since last week I have been able to find out that you have no living relative; finished in the lowest third of your class at the academy; got a speeding ticket driving a borrowed convertible belonging to the wife of the mayor of your home town the last time you were there, and have a real knack for close air combat. I'll let you think about how I got all that information while you're sitting on your porch tonight with Eight Ball."

Freeman's confidence gave Boyd an insecure feeling, thinking of Eight Ball sitting under the porch, trusting, waiting.

"OK. I don't know much, and I hope I don't have to hear any of this on the radio," Boyd said, trying to look intimidated. "There were some vice-grip type devices in the wreckage. If someone had left them in the air intake and they were sucked into the engine on take off, they could have caused an engine failure at just a critical moment. On the third day of the investigation a major general from NATO showed up to help with the board. When we got to the part about what General Polk had been doing the two weeks prior to the accident he shut me up and said we should come back to that later. Bob Ferguson was his name," Boyd said, spilling the details to seem candid, to learn more.

Freeman nodded with this apparent complete capitulation and accepted it without so much as a smile.

"Someone's not sure what happened, so they sent Ferguson to slow it down until they know. That was really stupid. I've been on accident boards, and the regulation doesn't permit the addition of a general officer, so they've left a trail. Good. As far as the vice-grips, those are probably dikes; they're wire cutters and laying around jet engines everywhere. It's an interesting theory to use them to bump off a general; pretty hit or miss for my money. We'll see. Now, I have something for you." Freeman opened his calf skin briefcase and took out a manila envelope.

Boyd held it in his hand without moving to open it.

"Trusten Polk's medical record. A rising young pilot died in a plane crash in Libya, and some high ranking Air Force officers were able to switch another guy into that identity. Someone threw this into the C-130 they sent to fly the medical team back to Germany. Polk saved it as proof. I've had it for a dozen years, just in case."

"His identity was switched?" Boyd tried to fake incredulity.

"Delano Society. Ask about it."

"I don't understand."

"Sure you do. Someone in power was making a future congressman or senator, only Trus wasn't good enough, or they weren't as smart as they thought, so he just made four stars."

"This could just as easily be faked as anything else…" Boyd began, mind racing at how the paper could have been artificially aged, the ink…

"Of course. But, there are names in there. Doctors, medical technicians, nurses. After the switch, the Air Force created a new record for him, altered all the official documents. This will lead you to contacts they didn't know about, and so couldn't alter."

"So, who was the other pilot, the guy who became Trusten Polk?"

"He never told me," Freeman said earnestly.

CHAPTER ELEVEN

Polk was a fool, always had been, Col. Freeman fumed in the cab on the way to Centennial Airport and his waiting Lear 35. Jerry would be along separately, after he'd wiped fingerprints and returned the rental car and thrown off any tail they might have picked up. His name wasn't Freeman, and he wasn't a retired colonel.

He'd been incredulous during his visit to Polk's quarters at Langley to discover that Polk had kept souvenirs of their activities, framed photographs of himself and some of the bigger fish they'd landed with their rallies, even snapshots in an album. What was Polk thinking? The FBI would've been all over them in a week, if they'd suspected anything. Apparently they didn't.

It didn't matter now, it was all but over. Polk's masters in Washington were old and sloppy. All these years they hadn't seemed to care what Polk might be up to. Had they found something? Had Polk's aversion to playing both sides in the political game led him to do something stupid; stupider than usual? Was he, Freeman on the verge of arrest, or was he still the black hole he had fastidiously tried to maintain for 20 years?

It was a risk, but he'd come back to Denver and filled the scheduled speaking date with the Colorado Unorganized Militia to get a look at John Rigdon's ranch and to have a reason to talk to that young captain on the accident board to leak the Delano story and find out how much trouble he was in. Now he knew. The Delano boys were smelling a rat, that's why they had their general attached to the accident board. Not at all kosher to just add a two-star to an accident board. Accident boards are supposed to be independent, but it had happened. That was proof of meddling from on high. So, did they bump off Polk to stop him from blowing the whistle? Did they even know about the scam he and Polk had been running right under their noses for twenty years? Probably not, he thought, but not certain yet.

Leaking information has always been a two-way street; you tell me something and I'll tell you something. The game is about who gets the most out of what they've told. It's a dangerous game. The loser can light his funeral pyre with the spark from his leak. With Polk gone, this was the end game, and the longer the Delano boys in Washington thought they were the hunters the louder the noise would be when the trap slammed shut. His knee began to hurt just thinking about all he had to do to get ready.

So comfortable they were, congressmen and senators, and chiefs of this and that. So sure their contacts and their secret back room machinations would protect them, regardless of elections – superficial elections from the standpoint of those with their hands on the levers of power. Silly Democrats, silly Republicans, expending all that energy on campaigns and candidates when it didn't make any difference. The same people were going to be calling the shots. That was all going to come to a big end in about six weeks. Payback is a bitch.

He paid the driver and entered the general aviation terminal at Centennial Airport, a civil aviation airport on the other side of Denver from Denver International, meeting his copilot in the pilot's lounge. They got a weather brief, and the colonel reviewed the flight plan before the copilot filed it with the FAA. Jerry arrived and the three men went out to pre-flight the aircraft. In half an hour they were at 30,000 feet crossing the Sangre De Cristo Mountains.

CHAPTER TWELVE

Except for the fist-sized hole in the right side, the engine appeared intact. Boyd and Moses Eubanks were in the hanger, still ripe with the smell of burned kerosene three weeks after the crash.

"The third stage fan assembly, the one that spins the fastest, disintegrated and sent pieces through the engine housing. See that hole there?" Moses pointed out the hole in the side of the engine. The burned carcass of the engine had been opened and showed chaos in the aft one third of the titanium fan assembly.

"The engine is surrounded by fuel tanks in this area and that piece went right through one, spraying fuel out the side as it headed who knows where. Right behind the piece was a jet of pure fire and it set off the fuel. Kawhump!" Moses said as they walked around the engine.

"Why did the third stage fan assembly fail? Was it because a pair of dikes were sucked into the air intake?" Boyd asked without taking his eyes off of the gaping hole in the aluminum engine housing.

Moses fidgeted and turned away. "I don't know. We're going to have to take down the first two assemblies and look at the parts real close to see if there are any marks a foreign body might have made as it came through there. Then we'll have to look at the broken ends of the fan blades in the third stage to see if one of them was defective or fatigued or if something hit one and broke it off. We might be doing this for six months." Moses was apologetic.

"What did the technicians from Langley say when they took this apart?" Boyd asked, wondering what they sent back in the way of opinion.

"Nothing. Pretty clear what happened. Why is the big question. This happens about once a year. Sometimes it's signed off as a defective turbine blade, one that had a tiny defect in the metal. Sometimes it's signed off as 'unknown', whatever that means. Sometimes it's foreign object damage, FOD. The F-16 is bad to FOD itself. You ever see one on a wet day? You can see it sucking up the water off the ground when they rev up the engine."

Boyd remembered seeing F-16s on rainy days with wet runways. The water would vaporize into a cloud on take off, showing the vortex of high wind velocity around the wingtips. On the ground when taxiing you could see a similar vortex swirling up from the ground into the air intake under the nose. Did the general's plane pick up a pair of dikes from the ramp where it was parked? Did someone leave them in the air intake or back in the engine somewhere? How much air would it take to suck them from the intake into the engine? Would they just sit there until the afterburner kicked in and then fly into the fan assembly?

Boyd sketched jet engine fan assemblies through the afternoon as another interminable meeting droned on. This one dealt with the witnesses' accounts of the flight and how testimony taken the week after the crash conflicted on several points, not important points in Boyd's estimation. That night he pored over his F-16 flight manual, trying to figure how a pair of dikes could have been left in the engine in such a way as to sit harmlessly until the afterburner was ignited. "How" burned his mind until after midnight when he put away his manual and went to bed. "Why" was beginning to take shape, and that left him awake until the birds began chirping in the pre-dawn darkness. It was interesting that the person who seemed to know the most about dikes and accident boards was Freeman. Who was that guy?

CHAPTER THIRTEEN

Dawn found Boyd seated on the back steps of the farmhouse watching the mountains catch the reflected glow from the clouds in the east ten minutes before the sun rose. Eight Ball was seated on the step enjoying Boyd's hand on his neck, his tail quiet for the moment. As the sun appeared above the horizon and the first clean ray of light shot across Colorado, the snow on the Rockies changed from a soft rose color to crisp white as quickly as if someone had flipped a switch. That seemed to settle things for Boyd and he snapped out of his reverie, course decided and mind clear.

Trusten Polk appeared to have been a fake, manufactured to accomplish some political purpose Boyd couldn't understand. He had had an extracurricular relationship with Colonel Freeman, drumming up opposition to the party that put him in power. Why? Someone may have killed him. Which side? Why?

Then there was the militia movement, was it a sinister threat to civil order, or the last chance to preserve America as it was founded? Or was it both?

He had decided he trusted Ben Culpepper. It would have taken an elaborate ruse to set him up, and they couldn't have known about Boyd's appreciation of old crop dusters and Mid-Continent Aviation. That big King Cat in the hanger, and Ben's obvious experience with it, was just too much to have been arranged. And where was the payoff in fooling Boyd anyway? All they could hope to get would be some information about the board. There would be easier ways to get that.

The uncertainties of who to trust and what to do next were cut through by the obvious course of action. It's always correct procedure to go to your immediate superior when in doubt. In this case that made more sense than ever. If Colonel Bertz had been a part of any of this, there would have been no need to contact Boyd.

"Could we take a walk over to the hanger," Boyd said quietly, close to Col. Bertz's ear, later that morning as the colonel poured some coffee in the pilots lounge.

The colonel turned with a look of impatience on his face. "I have some work to do here, maybe after lunch."

"This is the most important thing you or I ever did. General Polk was an impostor," Boyd said and turned to walk casually out of the lounge and down the hall, the colonel catching up.

"The man in that airplane was the ACC Commander, but he wasn't Trusten Polk. Trusten Polk was killed in Libya in 1975. Someone in the Air Force was able to substitute another officer into a war hero's identity, then guide his career through assignments and promotions all the way to four stars. Air Force general officers were enabled in this fraud by their membership in something called the Delano Society; a group of Washington insiders."

"What? That's impossible," Bertz said, struggling to keep up with Boyd's longer strides as they exited the wing operations building onto the flight line.

"There's more. General Polk was a busy guy. He was getting orders from the people in Washington who made him and at the same time fomenting revolution with right wing paramilitary organizations on the side as he traveled around the country."

"What? That's treason! You jump to that wild conclusion with what proof?"

"Three unrelated people have told me General Polk was not the same guy as Lieutenant Polk, two gave me pictures and one gave me the first guy's medical record."

"Why didn't you say something?"

"General Ferguson stopped me, remember?

"He was just trying to get oriented, to catch up."

"Or slow it down. There's more. One of the guys who came forward said he had dinner with Polk the night before the crash. I needed that for the 24 hour time line required by the accident board, so I met with him. He said Polk was all tied in knots about something he'd gotten into in Washington, something illegal. He told me the Air Force switched identities and gave me the proof, and he told me about this

Delano group. He said if we mention that to the SecDef the shit will hit the fan."

"You're not mentioning anything to the SecDef, and neither am I."

Unfazed, Boyd continued walking, Bertz's face still inches from his. "Polk had a girlfriend at Langley. She said he was tied in with something illegal, but she didn't know what. Massive stress, she said."

"A girlfriend? There's always a girlfriend."

"Corroboration, the stories all fit."

"Who was the girlfriend?"

"I think I need to maintain her privacy for now; there are other people's lives involved here."

"Oh, right."

"You read the Air Force Instruction on accident boards?"

"Certainly, several times. I passed out a copy to you and all the board members on the first day."

"Anything in there about a MAJCOM sending a general officer to oversee the process; to help out?"

"No," Bertz said defensively. "But this is a high profile case."

"All the more reason not to meddle. But they did. Why?"

"Look, you've got to stop this. If this gets out..., well, it just can't!"

Bertz was cracking already, Boyd thought, and he didn't even know half the story yet.

"Look, we've got to tell someone about this, and it should be in the chain of command."

"Right, I'll call the wing commander."

"No. Call the new ACC Commander. He's more likely to be free of all this."

"I can't do that!"

"Sure you can. You're the board chairman. Those big guys love it when some subordinate gives them the hot skinny on something. It might torque the wing commander here that you jumped the chain of command about ten levels, but you'll have some serious top cover."

"You said you had proof; pictures, a medical record. Where is it?"

"Right here," Boyd held up a thick manila envelope.

"All evidence is supposed to be entered officially into the board proceedings, and witnessed by two board members."

"The board's been out of session for a couple days, and I just got this. Two board members; me and you." Boyd handed the envelope to Bertz, who handed it back.

"Where are we going?" Bertz seemed to suddenly realize they were in transit.

"There's more evidence for you to see. We catalogued some dikes at the crash site, on the day of the crash. Master Sergeant Eubanks and his crew have re-assembled the aircraft. You need to see how neatly they fit into the hole in the side of the engine."

"Dikes?"

"They're like vice grips; pliers."

"How'd they get there?"

"How, indeed?"

"Oh, God! I should have put my papers in. Donna's been after me to punch out. Why didn't I listen?" Bertz stopped in his tracks and clenched his fists like a stubborn child refusing to enter the daycare center.

"Sir, we didn't do anything but look. The evidence is there and we found it. Let's don't make it worse. Make the call."

They showed their ID's to the guard at the hanger door and signed into the secured area as members of the Accident Investigation Board. Moses Eubanks was there tinkering on getting a piece of a wing flap to fit on the re-assembled F-16. Together Boyd and Moses walked Bertz through the possible scenario of dikes being left in the air intake and being sucked into the engine.

"Possible, but also could be a coincidence," Betz said, more confident now that he was on familiar ground.

"Did you actually meet these guys?" Bertz was going over the pictures and medical record.

"I talked to Switzler on the phone and he FedExed the pictures to me. Culpepper I met. We can get back to them pretty easy. Freeman, who gave me the medical record is kind of mysterious. He just shows up."

"We'll need to get some iron clad ID, make sure someone's not scamming us."

"You think it's wise to wait until we do. It could be days, and if someone talks it'll be all over the news."

"Oh, God! Why didn't I retire?" Bertz covered his eyes with his hands and slumped down on his elbows, hiding, it seemed.

"Let's just make the call. You want me to stay?"

"Yes, I'm not taking this bullet alone!" Activated now, Bertz jumped up. "Come on, we'll use the secure line in the Command Post."

The new commander of Air Combat Command, General Charles Kreitz had been on the job only a day and it had been dicey to even get him on the phone. Bertz had refused to talk to anyone junior and thoroughly annoyed the entire ACC command staff. Finally he got the big man on the phone and gave him one brief sentence about finding something fishy about General Polk and Kreitz had stopped him and insisted on a teleconference to include his lawyer. Half an hour passed while they set up the top secret conference room. The cameras were adjusted and each pair could see the other, the official backgrounds in the conference rooms providing a kind of verification of identity.

"Ok, Colonel Bertz, and Capt. Chailland, this is Brigadier General Upchurch, ACC JAG. I've asked him to sit in. Tell me what you have, and be brief."

Two sentences into the story he stopped them again. "Wait. I'm the appeal authority for your board, bringing this to me now jumps the appeal authority to the Chief of Staff of the Air Force. Is this so important it can't be handled at a lower level?"

Bertz was shaking, literally unable to continue. Boyd took over.

"Sir, three people have told me General Polk was an impostor. While meeting with one of those I discovered evidence General Polk had been involved with a group of right wing para-military organizations, even while in uniform and attending official Air Force functions."

"Stop." Kreitz muted his mike and talked to the lawyer for half a minute. "OK. Stay where you are. Don't leave the conference room. I'm going to have my security officer come in here and keep you guys company. Don't make any calls and don't leave, even to go to the bathroom. I'll be back." He left the room and a colonel entered and sat down and made small talk. The lawyer left.

An hour passed, Bertz begged to go the bathroom but the colonel refused, telling Bertz to find a styrofoam cup in the cabinet and use that. Bertz fidgeted for another ten minutes then found a cup and, huddling in the corner, pee'd in a cup.

Upchurch returned and relieved the colonel. He asked for their full names, social security numbers, dates of birth, and dates of rank, then left and the colonel returned. In ten minutes he was back and relieved the colonel again and sat, making more small talk. Kreitz returned.

"Boy, you guys stepped in it big. I don't know what this is, and I'm out of it, so don't tell me anything. Both of you, stay on base tonight. Get billeting and stay there. Don't talk to anyone. General Upchurch and my vice, Lieutenant General Gomes will be there tomorrow morning. When you reconvene the board, carry on as you see fit. The issue of some irregularity in General Polk's background is not, at this point germane to the board's inquiry, so don't take it up. Captain Chailland, be ready in the morning to take General Gomes' C-20 to Washington. You'll meet with some people in the Sec-Def's office. Bring your documentation. Speak to no person about this until then. Is that clear?"

"Yes, sir." They said in unison.

"Dismissed."

CHAPTER FOURTEEN

"Impressive view," Dan Ames said after Boyd had been announced, brought into the Office of the General Counsel to the Secretary of Defense, seated in a single seat located squarely in front of the big man's desk, and given a fresh cup of coffee. Boyd was transfixed, looking over the man's head at the United States Capital across the Potomac River from the Pentagon.

"Yes, sir." Boyd sat rigid, the pictures and medical record in a courier's briefcase still chained to his arm.

"How was your trip?" Ames was a fit-appearing middle-aged man in an expensive tailored dark suit. If the SecDef were to have a lawyer, this is the guy one would expect to see.

"Fine, sir."

"Good. Back to the view. It isn't an accident, you know. That the Secretary spends his days looking across the river. This job is a political appointment; he serves at the pleasure of the President, who lives over there, behind the Washington Monument." He pointed out the White House, up the river a bit from the Capital. Boyd stood to see. "His resources come from the Capital, and they can and do summon him to testify, sometimes under oath, about the goings on of the department. This may look like an important job, and it is, but we have our masters. The Secretary of Defense doesn't usually become involved with matters such as this. Allegations of impropriety need to be researched, worked through. That's my job."

"Yes sir." Boyd was beginning to feel the skids being greased.

"You're here because you did an extraordinary thing, and managed to keep your wits about you to bring it here before it got out. You've given us, and them," nodding across the river, " some time. Thank you."

"Yes sir."

"Now, let's hear it." He leaned back in his seat, eyes searching Boyd's. Ames must have been a prosecutor at some point in his career, because Boyd felt like an insect pinned down and examined under a dissecting microscope.

Boyd related John Switzler's call, his encounter with the enigmatic Colonel Freeman in Dozer's Bar, finding Ben Culpepper's Officer Performance Report in Polk's record and his subsequent reminiscences of Polk's Viet Nam adventures, the cane print at Polk's quarters, the FAX machine with four years of FAXes neatly boxed, Carmella De Beauvoir's friendship and observations, and finally John Rigdon and the Colorado Unorganized Militia. He ended the half hour monologue with, "And I have what documentation I've found so far right here," and produced the key to open the cuff around his wrist.

"That won't be necessary, Captain. It's all true, at least the part about Polk not being Polk. I already knew that."

Boyd drew in a breath as the gravity of that sank in.

"Tell me more about that militia group. Were there any Nazi flags, any pamphlets advocating the overthrow of government, any firebrand speeches other than Freeman?"

'No. Just a bunch of guys who like to shoot off guns and grouse about government impinging on their rights."

"Humm. Did you see any illegal firearms; machine guns, hand grenades, rocket launchers?"

"Some AR-15s in full auto. I don't know if that's legal or not."

"Nothing heavy?"

"No."

"After General Kreitz called yesterday I talked to some friends over at Justice. They already knew Polk was a fake, but there didn't seem to be any way to connect that with anything they could prosecute. But, you've raised another issue. We didn't know Polk was meeting with militia groups, and that he's been working for some kind of right wing political party. That is prosecutable. They want more information. To help you get that information I'm going to tell you an incredible story. The Delano Society exists. I'm going to tell you as much as I know because you've been told part of it, to create a disturbance, a smoke screen to hide something else. Colonel Freeman is up to something and he is apparently using what he knows about Delano for a diversion. He was right about one thing, your finding out Polk was in Delano got our attention.

" I'm not a member, but the Delano Society is a poorly kept secret in Washington; most people who've been here for awhile know about it. Who is in it is a popular cocktail party conversation – the Delanos don't announce it when they take someone in. Delano had an innocent beginning, expedient at the time, perhaps even necessary. It evolved over the years, and mistakes were made. One mistake, the biggest one now in retrospect, was meddling with personnel matters in the Air Force. Some general officers in Delano created Polk, thinking he would be useful. He wasn't, but they had him and had, after all, erased his prior identity so they couldn't just dump him. He was due to retire in a few months. He seemed like such a cypher, we had no idea he was into anything subversive." Ames seemed to be making excuses to Boyd for the shortcomings of the Delano Society.

Ames stood and walked to the side cabinet and poured himself another cup of coffee, then continued. "In 1944 Franklin Roosevelt had a stroke. He'd had high blood pressure for years and he blew a gasket or something, in the spring. He was partially paralyzed on one side, the right I think, and he couldn't talk at all."

He paced behind Boyd and spun the world globe in a decorative stand in the corner as he spoke. "He was running for re-election against Tom Dewey, and the invasion of Normandy was only a few weeks away. Henry Wallace was Vice-

President. Wallace hated both Roosevelt and Dewey, and Churchill thought Wallace was a communist. Stalin didn't trust Churchill and no one trusted Stalin. The whole alliance against Germany might have come apart if something happened to Roosevelt. The night it happened, Harry Hopkins, Roosevelt's chief of staff, summoned Wallace, George Marshall, Edward Stettinius, Harry Truman, Harlan Fiske Stone, and Sam Rayburn to the White House. They decided to settle their collective differences and govern the country by a committee of themselves and prominent Republicans to be brought in the next day, as if Roosevelt were still competent. It worked, and Roosevelt rallied and was able to actually give a few speeches and, miraculously, beat Dewey in November, with Truman as his running mate. The following Spring, 1945, Roosevelt died, and Harry Truman continued to consult with that small group of men. They called themselves the Delano Society, after Roosevelt's middle name." Turning to Boyd he asked a rhetorical question, "So, are they legal?"

Ames took a breath and looked out the window a moment, collecting his thoughts. "Maybe. In the collective sense, since 1944, no. Cooperation across party lines is not treason, but these guys are rumored to have been making major policy decisions behind closed doors, arranging committee chairmanships outside of majority party process, writing legislation with the help of lobbyists and submitting it as having come through the congressional staff. That's blatantly wrong and illegal as hell. But it would be a long tough litigation to prove without more evidence than you have now. By circumventing the due processes of government they've created grounds for the claim of invalidity; illegality."

"Corruption," Boyd offered.

"Yes." The lawyer agreed quietly. "It's supposed to be just a discussion group now, but we know laws were broken in the past. Polk is an example of that. It was 1975, Viet Nam was imploding, there was a lot of fear, and some Air Force general officers got cute with their personnel system. As far as I know, it stopped after Polk."

"Why tell me this?" Boyd asked simply, shaken by the gravity and aware of the power he now wielded with this knowledge.

"You've only scratched the surface, Boyd. My friend at Justice told me that three or four years ago some of the militia movements began to coalesce, to share printing and mailing facilities, some right wing talk shows got money to go national, and people started paying attention. The usual suspects, the John Birch Society, the NRA, the militant zionists and Cubans, weren't involved. Big money has been showing up in right wing political organizations, big money. And, now we have a presidential election year. Last winter some underground organization used a computer network to help the Florida DEA roll up the distribution network of the Mexican drug cartel. The militia movement made a lot of friends in Florida. We can't figure where all that money is coming from."

"I saw Freeman and his assistant collect thousands of dollars in one night," Boyd said.

"Chicken feed. Add a zero and you're still short of what they're getting. No, Boyd something else is happening, and you've gotten closer to it than anyone. It could be foreign money, but our most dangerous adversaries don't have that kind of cash. It could be the Russian mafia, or some international crime syndicate. We're stumped, and now we know that they know about Delano and if they use that for cover, our whole government will be on the defensive because so many of the big dogs are in Delano. We need to find out what this Freeman guy is up to. With regard to his allegations about Delano, it's the devil you know versus the devil you don't know."

"Sir, it comes back to Polk."

"Yes, what was he thinking, associating with militia groups? Idiocy! Every military officer knows better than that. They must have had something on him; blackmail."

"Sir, put yourself into the shoes of the other pilot, the guy who wasn't Polk, and also wasn't who he used to be. He can't go back, and the future is an empty lie, and on top of that, Freeman is there and he knows everything. Carmella De Beauvoir said he was tormented. I think he was trying to be honorable, to prevent Freeman from spilling the Delano secret, and was tormented by what he couldn't stop Freeman from doing."

"OK, that sounds reasonable. What is Freeman doing?"

"Sir, I've met Freeman twice now. He's intense, and he's worried that you're right on his tail. If he knew how far we are from knowing anything about him I'm sure I'd never see him again. Whatever it is he's doing, he's still doing, and I'm pretty sure it isn't anything like what it looks from here. He's too smart to show his cards."

"And, whatever it is, he's been at it for years," Ames said, lips pursed. "Well, we aren't going to figure this out here. Ames stood and came around the desk offering his hand, the meeting at an end. "Captain Chailland, thanks for coming to Washington, now go back to Colorado and find Freeman."

CHAPTER FIFTEEN

"You didn't bring your dog." Colleen said, a week later as she let him in. She was always on the offensive.

"He doesn't like Chinese food," Boyd said, setting down the bottle of wine he had brought. The decision-making process had delayed him for half an hour at the liquor store. "I figured you for a beer man," she said as she took the wine and opened the refrigerator, revealing a twelve pack of Coors Light. Boyd felt better already.

They had talked several times since the militia meeting and at lunch the day before she had invited him over to taste her specialty, oriental cooking. She dressed southwestern and looked hispanic from the back, but when she turned, Boyd was confronted with eyes green as the hills of Eire.

"This is not the neighborhood I'd expect an English professor to live in," Boyd said following her into the living room with a beer.

"Those ivy-covered Tudor houses near the campus are way out of my price range. Junior faculty salaries are an insult, and there are lots of English majors looking for work. Besides, I wanted some extra room."

"That's what really surprised me, the two-car garage converted into another room. A roommate? Storage? Dogs? Tropical fish?"

"Martial arts. My mother enrolled me in karate when I was six. In graduate school I couldn't afford a gym or karate membership so I worked out in a friend's garage. Some of the other junior faculty drop by and we run through our kihon."

"Hmm. I'll mind my manners."

"It's not like the movies. Karate is very spiritual. It's about balance, both internal and external. We don't go around breaking boards."

"Unless you get mad."

"You don't get mad, that would show loss of control."

"Oh." Boyd finished his beer, and Colleen rose and led the way to the kitchen.

"Was your father some kind of Air Force big shot to get you into the Air Force Academy?" Colleen asked, sipping a glass of white wine and turning up the fire under the wok, which was already hot. The food was cut into pieces and arranged on the counter.

Boyd's laugh was spontaneous and deep. It seemed like everything she said was designed to inflame or insult him, yet it was always delivered with a warm smile and in a completely conversational tone. "Dad was a disabled farmer. No one in my family was ever in the military. My football coach in high school contacted the academy about my going there," Boyd said, now more amused by her lack of tact than irritated.

"Oh. A jock. What did you play?" she said as she threw the first of the spices and oil into the Wok. Steam and fragrance rose immediately.

"Tight end," Boyd said, watching her throw various things into the wok, culminating with a bowl of fish cut in cubes from the refrigerator. He'd been worried it was to be a vegetarian endeavor. "Remember the game with Army in '04?"

"You scored the winning touchdown?" she asked, rhetorically.

"No. I knocked the defensive end on his ass and the fullback cut down the outside linebacker. I rolled over and hit the inside linebacker as he came out and the halfback walked over untouched."

Colleen put a lid on the steaming wok, now apparently complete, and bent over to open the oven. She wore tight white jeans with a tooled leather belt and silver and turquoise buckle. With high heels and her knees straight, she bent low to pull a pie out of the oven and turn it off. Boyd almost didn't see the pie.

"Is that an oriental pie?" he asked, recovering.

"That's a blueberry pie. They're in season now and you can only take this oriental stuff so far. There's ice cream in the freezer."

"Could we start with this?" Boyd said, bending down to smell the fresh, steaming pie.

"No! I've been cleaning vegetables and fish all afternoon. You have to eat that first and make me think you like it before you can have any pie," she said with a laugh, taking the wok off the fire and spilling the contents onto a serving platter.

Boyd lingered by the pie. Carrying the platter with the fish on it she bumped him with her body and pushed him toward the dining room. Her fragrance was spicy and oriental and seemed to fit with the smell of the food in her hands. She returned for the rice and the wine bottle. She brought Boyd another beer.

The fish was covered by a thick, dark delicious sauce. The vegetables were crisp. Boyd's portion disappeared soon after Colleen took a first, critical taste. She refilled his plate and was soon just watching him eat.

"Do you always eat this much?" Colleen asked after he finished the third plate.

"I run thirty miles a week and lift weights every third day. It gives you an appetite. I'm just a growing boy."

"You are indeed. There aren't any like you around here."

"I've spilled all my secrets. How about you? How did you become a feminist?" Boyd asked, slowing down to finish his beer and take stock of her answer.

She related an academic sojourn that went from English undergraduate major to a masters in political science and a PhD in women's literature. She had followed her various academic interests through several universities and had taken the job at Colorado because they offered her a tenure track and the most money. Intellectual life around Boulder was known for its liberal bent and she found kindred spirits there.

"I still don't understand why you were out at John Rigdon's ranch at a militia meeting," Boyd said, doing some challenging of his own for a change.

She smiled, looked down at her wine, then up at him, "I'm writing a book."

Boyd laughed, that made the most sense of anything he'd heard in the last week.

"Don't laugh. Every English teacher in America is writing a book. I didn't want to write one of those, 'Taut emotional thrillers' set in a respected but shabby Midwestern liberal arts college that revolves around a new Romance language professor who exposes the pretentions of academe."

"I'd certainly rush out to buy that one."

"It's almost a formula. The editors at the big publishers print a couple every year, hoping they might catch on. They never do."

Boyd finished his beer and went to the kitchen for another. When he turned from the refrigerator she was smiling at him.

"You're laughing at me. You don't think I read, is that it?" He said, crossing the portal from the kitchen to the combined living room and dining room. His shadow in the flurorescent lights behind him in the kitchen fell across Colleen. The corners of the shadow, formed by his shoulders, were like a teeter totter on either side of her head rising and falling as he walked to her.

"No. I smiled at my good fortune. I wanted some action in my book, something more interesting than faculty infighting."

"Do I look like action?" He challenged, sitting down and leaning back in his chair.

"It's not the shoot 'em up action I want. It's energy, potential energy, to borrow a term from my chemistry colleagues."

"So, am I to be the villain in your book?"

"At first that's what I wanted, a villain from the right fringe, but the issue isn't that simple."

"Well, an academic with a lick of sense. No, it isn't simple. If the UN really does have designs on John Rigdon's land, whose side are you on?"

"The UN isn't going to take John's land," She dismissed him with a wave of her hand, and her eyes wouldn't meet his for a moment.

"So you bought a gun?" He said, to let her off the hook.

"Yes. I started by buying a gun. I was really trying to find a way to go to one of those militia meetings. John Rigdon made it easy. The militia is a lot like the people's revolutionary movement in Central America, naive, passionate, disorganized. There is energy there. I'd hoped to try to capture it somehow with some characters. You ready for some of that pie?" Colleen asked, abruptly picking up the plates and heading for the kitchen.

"You bet. I'd almost forgotten." Boyd followed closely with the glasses and silverware. He began rinsing the silverware and putting it in the dishwasher. "You being an English teacher, what do you read, just for yourself?"

"I like Shakespeare. I think he was a hack writer at the time, turning out popular plays based on historical events, such as Richard III and Julius Caesar. He had a knack for the human condition, and his dialogue is much copied, so we see it as very good. I like Octavia Butler and Rita Mae Brown. They're women writers of equal talent. I'm a professor of literature first. My focus on women is only a part of that. How about you? What do you read?"

"Clancy, Clive Cussler."

"Of course."

"Ross Thomas, Elmore Leonard, and a lot of military history. I read anything I can find about fighter pilots."

"Professional pride?" She asked, neutral in her expression.

He nodded. He wasn't willing to lay all that out just now.

"Are you in Colonel Freeman's organization?"

"I just met him a couple weeks ago. I'm on the accident board investigating that plane crash out at Buckley. The general who was killed was an old friend of his."

"I think Freeman is a nut. John Rigdon thinks he's Abe Lincoln and John Wayne rolled together," she said as she put the last glass into the dishwasher and closed the door, turning the dial to start it.

"I wonder, what if he's right?"

"I checked out some of the web sites he mentioned in his pamphlet. They're there, like he said, and some of the information is just what he said, but I didn't feel there was anything conclusive there about the United Nations. He's twisted it around, I think." She didn't sound entirely convinced.

"I'm a bit surprised to be here," Boyd said. "I thought you feminists hated the military."

"We just believe in standing up for the rights of women. We're not against the military or for lesbianism, or communism, and we have no stand on abortion. At least I don't. I want the world to know and appreciate women's literature because it's good."

That seemed to be a dead end. Boyd sat looking at the top of his beer, wondering who Freeman was. Colleen was looking at him.

"Want to see my dojo?" She asked, rising and leading the way to the former garage door. Inside was a simple room with cheap carpet over a concrete floor and a woven mat in the center. There was a mirror on one wall and a large poster of an old karate master.

"You must be good," Boyd said, looking around.

"Want to wrestle?"

"Wrestle?"

"Yeah. I used to wrestle my brothers all the time. I'm good." She said, the seriousness of the preceding moments gone.

"You'd have to be good," Boyd said, hoping she meant to really try him. She was fair-sized for a girl, maybe five seven, and no more than 140 pounds. "No karate."

"Ok. No karate, punching, biting, arm locks or full nelsons. Anybody down cries uncle, fight's off."

"You're serious."

"You bet. Kick off your shoes and get ready." With this she removed her necklace and shoes and watch.

Boyd quickly removed his shoes and watch and began to circle her, catching the spirit. She clearly meant to have a real contest. For several minutes they circled, feinting, grabbing at each other to obtain that first hold, nervous giggles and challenges gradually faded.

Catlike she dropped to one knee and grabbed for his leg for a take down. Surprised by her quickness Boyd was able to avoid the grab by kicking backwards, removing the leg from her grasp. The maneuver put all his weight on his other leg and left him off balance. She stood, very close to him now, and grabbed him by the waist. She arched backward and his feet left the floor. Amused, he relaxed a moment to see what she thought she could do with this move. It was a mistake.

"You're too easy!" She hissed as she arched, twisted a quarter turn, and dropped him onto his back, with her atop.

The wind went out of him as he slammed onto the concrete floor. She straddled his hips and attempted to pin his shoulders, all her weight holding him down.

Now the advantage shifted considerably. Boyd grabbed her under her arms and flexed his abdomen and hips, throwing her backwards over his head. She landed on her butt with a loud thud that rivaled the one when Boyd had hit the floor. The air went out of her. Boyd rolled over and grabbed her shoulders pulling her backward to pin her.

Thinking he had her now, Boyd relaxed a moment before finishing her off. She bent at the waist and her knees flew on either side of his head, grabbing him. She twisted at the waist and Boyd fell to his side on the floor. Another twist and he was supine again with her thighs on either side of his face. He rolled face down and grabbed her around the waist. Her thighs flailed on either side of his head as he released an arm to get a hold a little higher, then the other arm a little higher. Her struggle was useless as his weight was now on top of her and she was no match for his strength. The next arm hold brought him to her breasts, where he lingered to rub his face over them in a triumphal gesture. She was now giggling. The next hold had them face to face and he pinned her, now no longer struggling. He squeezed hard, letting her feel his arms and shoulders and the strength that was there but had not yet been used on her. She squeezed back, and then their mouths came together in a long kiss, punctuated by more squeezing.

Panting like winded dogs they rolled apart, eyes locked as they quickly removed their pants. Colleen pushed him back again, forcefully. After wrestling with her, Boyd was not surprised by this move.

He lay flat and she covered him, naked thighs brushing his as they kissed again. After a time, her hand found his penis between them, and she arched her back and her knees grasped his hips giving her the angle and leverage to force it in. This was her show, and he lay still.

During the next kiss her muscles relaxed and he was all in. Astride and in control, she leaned back, pulling up on his shirt. He removed it and her eyes hungrily flicked over his chest and shoulders, then her hands, then her mouth. Her tempo increased and she sat up, eyes on Boyd. With her climax she lurched forward and shoved her hands under his back and squeezed again, finishing with a series of fast pelvic thrusts.

"Wow! You really do like to wrestle." Boyd said, amused at feeling like a woman must feel after being jumped by a sailor who'd been at sea too long.

"There's always been something about grabbing a muscular man that just sets me off. I never grabbed one like you though."

"I hope that's a compliment," Boyd said, gently rolling her onto her back and looking down into her eyes, already beginning to shudder.

CHAPTER SIXTEEN

Pulling into the parking lot at Culpepper Aviation, Boyd saw the old pickup truck that had been there the week before. In addition, there was a shiny new black Chevy Camarro convertible with the top down.

"Boyd. Good to see you," Ben said, munching on a plate of fried chicken surrounded by mashed potatoes and gravy, and collard greens. He was seated at one of the desks in his office. Sitting on the adjacent desk was a middle aged woman with steel gray shoulder length hair. She wore a smart business suit. Ben turned to her, "This is Boyd Chailland. He's from down at Buckley. Boyd, this is Henrietta Flick. She sustains me," he said with a grin back at Henrietta.

"Your appetite is your most endearing feature," Henrietta said to Ben with a smile of appreciation, then turned to Boyd. "Ben tells me you're investigating a plane crash."

"It's been depressing. Such a brilliant career and then he dies on a routine flight back home," Boyd said, walking across the room, watching Ben shovel down another mouthful of potatoes. "So many details to follow up on. I'd rather be dropping bombs down on the range," he added, looking down at the food. It was just at lunch time. "Say, are those collard greens? I haven't seen those for awhile."

"Sure are. Got some more. Want some?" Ben said, opening a tupperware container on the desk to reveal another large portion. "Henrietta does greens better than almost anything," he said, smiling at Henrietta again.

"Well, just a taste," Boyd said, taking the spoon and scooping up a bite. Bitter and coarse to the mouth the whole thing was steeped with the smell of smoked ham. Boyd flashed back to his crippled father proudly displaying a pot of the cooked greens in their little house. He'd smelled them cooking as he walked down the dusty road even before he reached the cool shade of their big oak. In his mind he bent over to smell the steaming pot and saw the smile of satisfaction that came with his nodded approval. He hadn't cared for them that much then, preferring the hamburgers cooked down at the teen hangout. Now, he'd swap anything he had for a pot of those collards and a talk with the old man who had made them.

"Mighty fine," he said, meaning it. Ben scooted over to make room for Boyd to pull another chair up to the desk. Henrietta beamed at the positive effect her cooking had on these two men.

"Another Southern boy. Does the Air Force recruit anybody from up north?" Henrietta said.

Boyd could detect traces of her drawl, probably from Texas.

"Well, another payroll looms. I've got to get back to the office. You boys enjoy your lunch," she jumped down from the desk, her eyes sparkling, and headed for the door.

"Drop by for a beer later," Ben said, washing down his last bite of chicken with a hefty gulp from a large glass of iced tea graced with a sprig of fresh mint.

Henrietta looked back over her shoulder at Ben and nodded as her eyes met his. With a wave she was out the door.

With the last bite in his mouth Boyd looked up to see her gray hair flying in the wind as she accelerated out of the drive and onto the county road. He'd noticed the wedding ring and remembered Ben had said he wasn't married.

"Married to George Flick. They own a chain of funeral homes in Northern Colorado. George shakes hands and looks doleful, Henrietta keeps the books," Ben said, sensing Boyd's unasked question. "George went fruit last year. Came out of the closet, as it were, with a whoop and a yell for all to hear. Ran off with a high school art teacher. Henrietta ran the office with her usual aplomb for two weeks until he returned, sheepish but happy at last. She's a most agreeable companion. Invariably in good humor and with a nicely rounded behind," Ben said, smiling with happy satisfaction. "She brings me lunch on Wednesdays. It's part of the reason I'm going to need a larger flight suit."

"Interesting arrangement," Boyd said, thinking it must have its share of odd moments.

"Ah yes," Ben said, leaning back in his chair and chewing on a toothpick, eyes out the window on the settling dust in the parking lot.

"I have news about General Polk," Boyd said, changing his tone to one of seriousness. He walked to the door of the hanger and looked to see if there was anyone there.

The King Cat smelled hot and the outer hanger door was open. The smell of agricultural chemicals was even stronger than before, but there was no person there.

Returning from the hanger and sitting on the desk, Boyd related the story about the assumption of Trus' identity to manufacture a general officer. He withheld the information about the Delano Society.

"So, Trus has been buried by the shifting sands of the Sahara all these years while I was mad at him? Damn! I should have figured that out. He wouldn't have just walked away from his old friends. Not Trus. It makes sense now," Ben said, smiling, and wiping the last remnants of the chicken grease from his hands and mouth. Boyd had told him only that the Air Force had seen fit to use Polk's identity for its purposes and not the whole story. Ben knew better than to push for details. They didn't matter anyway. "Damn." The smile got broader as he realized the weight of years of doubt and disappointment was lifted from his shoulders.

"I thought it was the least I could do for Polk. At least now two people remember him and know what happened to him.

Two who care, anyway," Boyd said, feeling good about what he had done.

"Come on, I'll show you my spouse, Ben said, jumping up and grabbing keys from the top of a file cabinet. This, as fine as it is, is just my business," he said, patting the King Cat as he walked around the huge crop duster, and opened a door to the other side of the hanger. " This is my love." Boyd had assumed the second door housed another crop duster or parts. When he walked into the hanger he got a bigger jolt than when he'd first seen the King Cat.

Its aluminum skin gleaming with a sheen brighter than on its first day off the assembly line, a fully restored P-51 Mustang, the fighter that dominated World War II, was the object of Ben's affection.

"Wow! I've never even seen one of these up close," Boyd said, walking over to the aircraft and touching it.

"I bought it while I was still in the Air Force. While I was down in Georgia, an old warbirds enthusiast had two of them and more money than flying skill and flew one into the dirt. The widow wanted her money out of the other one as quick as she could. I got it for only twenty grand. It's worth fifty times that now. Where else can you get that kind of appreciation on an investment that's been as much fun as this one?" Ben said proudly, patting the four blade metal prop.

"Do you fly it?"

"Sure, whenever I get the money together for gas. It takes the profit from a week of crop dusting just to fill the tank; a hundred and eighty gallons. At four bucks a gallon wholesale, that adds up."

"It must cost a fortune just to maintain."

"It does. I do air shows and that covers routine maintenance and some insurance. I have sponsors. The Commemorative Air Force helps out with overhauls and coordinates bookings for the air shows."

"What's it like to fly?" Boyd asked, walking around, touching the wing.

"The biggest difference between this and a jet is instant response. Even with your F-16, when you hit the throttle you have to wait a second or two for power. With this, it's just like hitting the accelerator on a fast car. If you're only going a hundred and twenty knots and hit the throttle it'll roll you over," he said, making a rolling motion with his right hand demonstrating a counterclockwise roll. "The torque of that engine is something to feel; a 1500 horsepower, inline V-12, Rolls Royce/Packard Merlin, the highest product of the art of piston engines."

"As far as the flight controls, it has no hydraulic boost," Ben said, walking behind the wing and laying a hand on an aileron. "You just pull and push fore and aft and right and left on the stick and the ailerons and elevators move. Just like in your jet, you don't use the rudder much here. Too fast. Mostly use it on landing and takeoff. Get into a fight with another plane and you get tired pretty quick. I worked out with the guys in the A-7 before the Colorado Guard got F-16s. She's not as fast but she turns quicker. I can hold my own," he said, prouder yet.

"So you do aerobatics at air shows?"

"I used to, but I'm too old now. I used to do a simulated dogfight with a T-6 painted like a Japanese Zero but that got too hard too. Still, no air show is complete without a Mustang so there's no problem with bookings."

"I always liked that part of the air show, even when the Thunderbirds or the Blue Angels were flying."

"Ladies and Gentlemen, look to your right for a special treat. It's brought to you by Jones Brothers Ford right here in Des Moines, where you can see the newly redesigned Ford Mustang. From LaSalle, Colorado, is Ben Culpepper flying his completely restored P-51 Mustang, Shady Lady!" Ben used his best announcer voice to recite his standard introduction.

"Oh, that's so cool."

"I come in from the right at about 400 knots and 500 feet off the ground in front of the stands, then climb up to three thousand feet while the announcer talks about the Merlin engine and some of the lore and history, then I do an Immelmann loop and come screaming back down at the stands and pass off to one side, come back with a roll, and then an 8 point roll and a final fast pass and then land."

"I'll bet you draw a crowd."

"Oh yeah; can't beat the ladies off with a stick."

"You old dog. After I left last week I felt really bad that you were just pining away up here after your retirement. Hell, you've been having a ball," Boyd said, looking at the airplane and thinking about Henrietta.

Henrietta pulled into the drive at 6:30 to find the back hanger door open and the P-51 rolled partially out onto the ramp. Boyd's lanky frame was leaned against the prop looking up at Ben seated on the wing with one hand over his head, fingers together and pointed down at the other hand flat in front of him.

"….and Erich Hartmann told me this himself, at an air show twenty five years ago. He was here from Germany promoting his book. He shot down 352 allied planes in World War II with a Messerschmitt 109. He'd passed through a formation of B-17s, busting one in the process and pulled up beneath them and was climbing back up for another pass when he looked behind him. Two Mustangs were diving down on him, having followed him through the bombers. They were closing fast with full power from their dive. He was climbing so he was much slower, a sitting duck. They were abreast, apparently expecting him to make a quick turn when they started firing. Whichever way he went, he was a goner. Usually they would come with one to the side and a little behind and if they'd been like that then, we'd probably never have heard of Eric Hartmann," Ben was saying, not yet acknowledging Henrietta's approach.

"So, what did he do?" Boyd asked impatiently.

"He dropped his nose just a bit, not so they'd notice, but enough to get a little speed and be a bit more level. Just as they started to fire he pushed the stick forward with all his might, the nose dropped, he got about four negative Gs, and the plane slowed like he'd slammed on the brakes. With the speed from their dive they were by him before they could do anything. He rolled his wings and was now in a dive above and behind them, with them wondering what happened. He dove in on one to within about fifty feet and just touched the trigger. The 20 mm cannon in the Messerschmitt's nose blew the wing off the Mustang. He rolled left to find the other Mustang in a hard left turn trying to get away. He brought his nose inside the Mustang's turn and kept it there, closing the gap. They were now a couple thousand feet lower than where they'd first jumped him and his dive gave him power to match the Mustang's larger engine. When the Mustang crossed his nose, he touched the trigger again and the Mustang exploded. One B-17 and two P-51s in 90 seconds. It ain't the machine, it's the man," Ben said, ending the story and looking up to see Henrietta walking across the ramp.

"Still on World War II, with Korea, Viet Nam and the Persian Gulf wars still unfought? My, it's to be a long night," Henrietta said as she approached, still in heels from the office.

"No, Ma'am. We fought those already. We're just gettin' to the 'Big One'," Boyd said, slightly startled. He'd been fascinated by Ben's story.

"We're pretty much done. I had to hear about Boyd's exploits in the skies over Iraq. He wanted to hear about 'Nam. Then we got into great pilots and exploits and that naturally led to Erich Hartmann. But now you're here," Ben said, jumping down from the wing of the Mustang. He and Boyd pushed the warbird back into the hanger and locked it up while Henrietta returned to the car and deftly slipped into slacks and loafers.

During dinner at The Farmer's Inn, a Mexican restaurant just down the road, Henrietta told stories of her grandfather, a barnstormer in west Texas during the depression. She'd been fascinated by biplanes since watching him fly over her father's house and do a roll on her birthday in the sixties. When she'd first seen Ben fly over her house in Greeley she followed him back to the hanger.

Bulging with beans and good humor, Boyd found his way back to the farmhouse in time to feed Eight Ball before falling into a dreamless sleep.

CHAPTER SEVENTEEN

"I thought you were going to try to sell me something," John Rigdon said, opening he door of his modest ranch house a few miles from the range where they had first met.

Set on a hill with a 180-degree panorama of Colorado's front range from Pike's Peak to Long's Peak, the house was fenced from the black cattle gathering toward a pond in a draw a half a mile away. Boyd had called to ask for a meeting, explaining who he was. Being in the Air Guard made him an immediate insider as far as John was concerned.

"Since the oil came in I've been a popular guy with the investment brokers. Everyone wants to make me rich."

"No, I'm just trying to find out a bit more about your militia and some of the things Colonel Freeman talked about last week."

Mounted elk, mule deer, and mountain sheep dominated the living room, and an adjacent den had a bear rug, complete with head, facing the television.

"Got that antelope right here on the ranch," John said, approaching the mount nearest the front door. "He's the state record from '04. Stalked him for two years. I'd see him in the summer, but couldn't find him during antelope season. Finally just walked to that ridge over there about a mile and spent the night in my down bag. Sure enough, the next morning, he must have seen the truck back at the house, there he was." John proudly walked around telling each tale as he got to the trophy.

"I used to do some bird hunting, back in Missouri," Boyd said, admiring some quail mounted in natural surroundings in a glass case.

"One of my neighbors has deep water rights. He irrigates a section of land for corn. Pheasants are thick out there. Come back in November I'll show you some shooting. Let me show you something here," John said, taking a key ring out of his pocket and opening a glass-front gun case. He took out a rifle that might have lain across John Wayne's saddle in any of a dozen westerns. "That's a Winchester '92. Been in my family since it was new. That's all my grandfather would use hunting. Said if he couldn't bring down a deer or antelope or an elk with that, they were welcome to their freedom. I got the antelope with it."

"Thirty-caliber?" Boyd held the lever action carbine, pointed it out a window and put a pigeon sitting on the barn in the open site.

"Yeah. You can get some heavier loads for elk. Still need to be pretty close though. Not like a lot of guys today; sit on a ridge with a nine-power scope and a 7-mag and knock off anything in the valley, three hundred yards away. With this, you have to learn to move quiet."

"Got a pretty good crowd at the meeting last week." Boyd handed the rifle back to Rigdon.

"Lot of heavy hitters came out from Denver to hear Freeman speak. The commander of the Colorado Unorganized Militia arranged the visit out here to avoid the media. We can control who gets in here better."

"Is he pretty well known?"

For a moment, as John was locking the case, a cloud crossed his face, a whisp of mistrust. He looked at Boyd, then pulled out the key and put the ring back in his pocket.

"You got your military ID?"

Boyd produced his military ID card. Rigdon looked briefly at it and handed it back, satisfied.

"Why do you want to know?"

In fifteen minutes, as they walked around the two trophy rooms, Boyd related the surface picture of the accident, Polk, and some of what Freeman had told him about Polk's political work before his death. They ended up looking out a large picture window at the front range, cattle making their way to water on a hot afternoon across three low ridges to the west.

"The feds have gotten real sensitive about anything to do with the militia movement. We've been told to watch for infiltrators. Hell, I'm sure we have a couple already. Freeman is pretty well known. Real secretive. Shows up, gives a speech, maybe shows a film of General Polk, then he's gone. We don't know where he lives, and the address on all his brochures is a post office box in Dallas."

"So, what's he trying to accomplish?"

"He's the closest thing we have to a national organization. We'd be a real target if we had offices somewhere, so guys join his party to have some way to affect the political process, at least that's what I felt when I gave him money."

"Does he get many donations?" Boyd asked, following John out onto a back patio.

John took the cigar out of his mouth and looked straight into Boyd's eyes. "He got ten thousand dollars here the other night."

"This is called the Wattenburg Field," John said, slowing the pickup a couple miles from the house and pointing at a small oil pump, its weighted arm pumping a dozen times a minute. "It stretches from Wattenburg just west of here all the way to the Nebraska line. The oil is down three thousand feet, so the wells are pricey to drill. The formation, Kodell, is really a sandstone layer. You fracture the rock and the oil leaks out. It's not a way to get really rich unless you stumble onto an area where it's already fractured, which mine wasn't."

"So, you own the whole thing?"

"Oh, hell no. I couldn't think about drilling one of these wells. They run a half a million bucks apiece. The best one I got only gives thirty barrels a day. No, the deal is, some investors drill the well. I put up the mineral rights and get a share of the oil, then I get some more for letting them have access to the tank." He pointed to a hill where a silver tank sat, a well-used dirt road snaking toward the county road in the distance.

"Still sounds pretty good to me," Boyd said, enjoying the ride. The grass was green in a wet mid-June and the rolling hills looked like a herd of buffalo or a band of Arapahoe could come galloping over at any moment.

"Another problem," John interrupted the silence. "For every barrel of oil, we get two of saltwater and a few thousand cubic feet of gas, which we can use to power that pump, or pipe to a gas transmission company. We can't burn it off like they used to. All that costs money," he said as he put the truck into gear and they bounced forward.

"I can see why you might have been sensitive to Freeman's talk about the UN."

"You're goddamned right!" John turned toward Boyd, took the cigar out of his mouth and stabbed the air with the stub of his right index finger. "If those UN guys think they got some right to call the shots around here, they can come by and haul off some saltwater, then mend some fucking fences, make a tax payment or two, shoot a coyote, dig a well, and patch the road next time it washes out. Then we'll talk about your ecosystem!"

CHAPTER EIGHTEEN

Congressman Roscoe Kelly had personally scoured his files, at home and at his Capital Hill office to purge any mention of General Trusten Polk, and had found nothing. He'd also looked for any paper that connected him to his friends Carl and Ralph, again nothing. The pang of anxiety he'd felt upon hearing of Polk's death had become acute when he'd been briefed by a junior member of Delano that the accident board had learned Polk had been a fake created by Delano and that the story was going to get out. The brief had occurred as the two men walked across Independence Avenue between the Congressional Office Building and the Capital; outside, no chance of bugs or eavesdropping.

"Idiots!" He'd responded to the young congressman bearing the message. "Leave it to a bunch of brass hats to get us all in trouble."

The younger man returned to the Congressional Office Building chastened by the fire of the powerful man's wrath, and Kelly continued on to the Capital, mulling the new information.

Kelly was sure he'd have gotten the chairmanship even without Delano help; the solid support in his Boston district was built on a reputation he'd built over a lifetime of politics. He was a natural in the bare-fisted politics of Boston, and well connected to those who made the city great. Loyalty, his father had told him a hundred times, is what makes a man. "Pug" Kelly had been a fisherman, and Roscoe's favorite memories were of him and his father out on the ocean. Kelly's Wholesale Fish Company moved most of the catch from the Boston area throughout the city and beyond, and Pug was a well known fixer of disagreement and conflict that affected the docks and all who worked there.

When Roscoe was ten, Pug went to jail for six months for taking illegal bets on horse races. He'd taken the fall as a common bookie because he refused to rat out the Boston mob, who ran the whole racing syndicate.

"What's a working man to do, wants to put a bet down on the ponies?" Pug would say. "Huh? Got the racing form at the corner news stand, got the horses and jockeys in the paper every day; a guy can't sit down over coffee in the morning and handicap a race?"

Roscoe saw no harm in a working man making an off-track bet on a horse race, and he remembered how Pug's loyalty had been repaid. A man showed up at the door one night, the week Pug went to jail.

"You Pug Kelly's boy?" He'd asked.

"Yeah."

"Give this to your mother. Don't open it." The man had said, and handed him an envelope. That cash paid their rent. Coal showed up in their coal bin every month; groceries were delivered prepaid.

Roscoe was proud to honor his father with the Pug Kelly Memorial Bridge, paid for with taxpayer dollars on an earmark appropriation out of the highway fund. It wasn't a big bridge, and the old bridge over the creek his father had had to cross every day going to the docks needed replacing. There'd been some labor problems with the bridge, something about scabs working for a sub-contractor, and it had delayed things for more than a year, substantially increasing the cost. He'd finally had to call on one of his father's old friends to intervene and smooth things out. The old friend agreed that it was important that a working man like Pug be memorialized with a bridge; after all the fat cats had plenty of bridges named after them. Roscoe promised to write stronger wording into future projects guaranteeing participation only by Boston union labor. The bridge was finished.

Ralph and Carl were not registered lobbyists, just lawyers with a prestigious law firm. Roscoe didn't know if that was good or bad; lobbyist visits were logged by both sides so everyone knows who talked to whom. He'd met some people through his friends, people in the banking industry. Not a crime, he was a banking expert, and how can you maintain expertise in an industry as complex as banking if you don't talk with bankers?

Still, Roscoe Kelly was worried. He decided he needed to call some people in Boston, some old friends, people he could depend on. Loyalty makes the man.

CHAPTER NINETEEN

"Chailland buys a round!"

It was the first thing Boyd heard as he entered the hall on a drill weekend Saturday afternoon, unzipping his G-suit. It had been a tough flight with eight dive bomb passes and four strafing runs followed by an air-to-air refueling and then half an hour of air combat maneuvers where he was against two other F-16s. He'd been up for over three hours and to compound it his air conditioner had gone out. At altitudes above twenty thousand feet it wasn't too bad, but down where it wasn't so cool, the sun shining through the canopy made it quite warm in the cockpit, especially wearing all the flight gear. Even his G-suit was wet with sweat. The thought of a cold beer, even if he had to buy for the house was appealing.

"Why the round?" Boyd asked, stepping into the pilot's lounge.

"Rule number seven. Girlfriend called," A pilot pointed to the "House Rules" on the wall as he opened the Coke machine and pitched Boyd a Moosehead, its green glass attracting just a slight sheen of condensation in the dry mountain air.

Boyd was quite familiar with the house rules, posted in most pilot lounges outlining conditions necessitating the buying of a round for the house. They all start with, "Hat on in the bar." Myriad minor infractions and irritations, such as having to borrow money or get change were included and, like most pilots' lounges, if your wife or girlfriend calls, you buy. The last rule was, if you read the rules, you buy.

"I didn't know I had a girlfriend," Boyd said, taking a twenty and stuffing it in the coin box of the machine.

"Colleen Chamorro. Number's on the board," the other pilot said, raising his beer in unison with the others in a toast to Boyd's girl.

"So what does a fighter pilot do on Saturday night?" Colleen asked when Boyd called.

"Oh, usually drink some beers with the guys then go to the club and drink some more, then go out and eat somewhere."

"What if it's not a drill weekend?"

"Run 10 miles then throw a couple steaks on the fire."

"A couple?"

"Well, Eight Ball likes a steak now and then. Especially T-bones. There's that nice bone to chew on the rest of the night,"

She laughed. "I think you and Eight Ball are too much alike. I need to meet this dog."

"How about tonight?" Boyd asked, thinking about Colleen's breasts gently swaying as she pulled her leg out of her jeans the week before.

"I'd like that. Should I bring something?"

"I'll get the steaks if you'll bring some salad," Boyd said, enjoying the stir of several appetites.

"You never get away from airplanes, do you?" Colleen said, standing in the shade of a scraggly elm in Boyd's backyard, looking north at a half dozen airliners lined up and descending for a landing at Denver International.

"I hope not," Boyd rubbed Eight Ball's ear and finished off a Moosehead.

Colleen and Eight Ball had hit it off from the start, but then Eight Ball hit it off with everybody. Sometimes Boyd wondered if he even had a threatening growl in him.

The shade from the elm lengthened to include the wooden back steps and they sat there, Colleen with a glass of white wine and Boyd with another Moosehead.

"I've always been a pacifist. I've demonstrated against every war since I was in the first grade. I've been arrested six times at Rocky Flats. I've never even known anybody who's been in a war. Aside from your obvious charms as a man, I am fascinated by what makes you do it. Is it the money? Do they pay you guys great piles of cash?" Colleen asked, after a pause of several minutes while they watched the planes and the sun sink closer to the mountains. "If my question is offensive, I'm sorry. You don't have to answer."

Boyd was silent for more than a minute. Not only had he never been asked that question, he'd never even thought of what he did the way she seemed to see it.

"I guess to understand me, you'd have to know the airplane. It's the pinnacle of man's development. The conception, design, engineering and manufacturing of the airplane makes any of man's other devices pale by comparison. The fastest sports car is a slug. The electronics in the latest stereo or video set are obsolete. The newest skyscraper is boring. In my Falcon I do things every day you've never even dreamed about. I could be over those mountains in a minute from here. I could do a loop over that thunderstorm over there," Boyd said, pointing to a late afternoon cumulonimbus to their north, dark and foreboding. "In an airliner you can look out and see a little segment of sky. From the front seat you have the full panorama of earth and sky and clouds. A city from fifty miles out is a blanket of sparkling diamonds at night. You can see the origins of rivers from the air, little changed by man in spite of two hundred years of earth moving. When it's cloudy and raining down here, it's still crisp and clear up there, above the clouds. Down here, I'm limited to the capabilities of my flimsy body. Up there I can accelerate to the limits of human endurance with the flick of a wrist. The engine under me pulses with life and a power equal to a freight train." Boyd stopped, sensing he might be waxing a little poetic. Colleen looked intrigued so he continued.

"They don't let just anybody strap one of these things on and go for a ride. You have to be good just to get asked to try out for the team. Physically you have to be perfect to begin with, eyes, ears, health; no defects. You have to be top of the heap academically. Flight training takes a year. Many don't make it. Of those who do, they are divided into the 'heavy' drivers – that is transports and tankers and airliners – and fighter pilots. Then it takes another two years before you are proficient in a modern fighter. The fighter jocks are sharper, faster, smarter and more aggressive. Not reckless, though. If you don't plan your missions just right, and fly with just the right mixture of aggression and precision, you're out; in a flash. It takes longer to plan a mission than it does to fly it. And, it takes a lot of man-hours of maintenance for every hour I spend flying. There are a lot of people backing me up. They do it because they love the plane as much as I do, and I feel them watching whenever I fly. I'm the lucky one."

"You're also the one who dies if something goes wrong."

Boyd nodded, pursing his lips and said, "Yeah, that's part of it. Dying isn't my goal certainly, but when it happens to a fighter pilot, it's fast. The fact is, most fighter pilots live to be old men. In the event of a major war, like World War II, the first ones up would get thinned out pretty quick. Each one of us thinks we are a little faster, a little smarter, and it won't happen to us. It's an acceptable risk."

"How about those people on the ground who are dying as a result of your bombs and guns. What about them?"

"I trust the people who send me out. The people who plan the missions and select the targets. I know the criteria they use and effort they go to so they can be sure we won't harm non-combatants. In the Persian Gulf they showed us pictures of the target and pointed out where the civilians would be. They had already figured what the ordnance we were going to use would do and how to minimize the effect for the civilians. When we got to the target, it was just as they said, every time. It's hard to have a lot of sympathy for an artillery battery that's shelling a city or our troops. You put the pipper on 'em and push the pickle." When Boyd said this he turned to look at Colleen, looking to see if she disagreed or thought somehow the logic there was faulty. She held his gaze for a moment and then looked down with no comment.

"Then there are the guys you fly with. I've already told you they were extraordinary individuals from the beginning. It's a team sort of thing. We have a common love of the aircraft and of flying and share that experience. We compete fiercely in practice, constantly striving to be the best and stay the best. The guys at the bottom of the list just don't get to stay. When you fly close formation you have to trust the guy on your wing, just like he trusts you not to fly into him or do some unexpected thing. Competition, trust and pride, not a bad basis for friendship."

"Still, wouldn't it be better to direct all that energy toward ending the need for war. It seems such a waste," Colleen said, still soft and thoughtful.

"When you pacifists and World leaders end war for all time, we'll stand down and become airline pilots, gladly. But it would be a shame for you to disarm us in the hope that our enemies will behave themselves and then when the Huns are at the gates and the women and children are being raped and pillaged and you cry to the heavens for assistance and God responds by saying, 'I gave you bright-eyed young men with the strength and the will to defend you and you spat on them and sent them away. Perish for your stupidity!'"

Colleen laughed at Boyd's interpretation of God's voice. His chin was down on his chest and his words were low, slow, and ponderous. He emphasized the word "spat" with a juicy punctuation that sent droplets flying into the dirt before them.

"Do you suppose that's what God would say?" she asked, questioning his interpretation.

"That's what happens when you are on the losing end of a war." It seemed the inquisition was over.

"Before the pillaging starts, let's eat," she said, looking at his hibachi.

Boyd rose and quickly built the charcoal into a mound and doused lighter on it. Colleen went in and began preparing the salad she had brought and they each refilled their drinks. Eight Ball, sensing the meal was at last at hand thoroughly checked the back yard for intruders by sniffing around and checking every quadrant.

Two thick T-bones hit the grill just as the sun dropped behind Long's Peak. Boyd had bought three but Colleen begged him to just cook two. She vowed to share hers with Eight Ball.

"How is it with the military getting smaller? Is that causing you warrior types any problem?" Colleen asked, matter of factly after they had started eating and Boyd had opened another beer. Boyd sensed the tension remaining from their earlier effort to understand each other.

"That's why I'm in Denver." Boyd laid down his fork as if the subject had ended his appetite. "They decommissioned my squadron. All of us had to find other jobs. I was lucky to stay in a flying job. Most of the guys got out or are flying desks, fooling themselves that a cockpit is in their future. The flying business is grim – guys in mid career are being told they aren't needed any more. Just like that."

"That's good, though. Not for you personally, of course. I've hoped to an end to warfare since I was a kid. Maybe I'm really going to see it."

"That's the 'end of history' drill. You think that just because you can't see the next enemy there isn't one there. Do you really think the Bosnian Muslims and the Serbs are going to bury the hatchet? How about the Pakistanis and the Indians, or the North and South Koreans? Will the Chinese and the Japanese ever be friends? They've been enemies for more than a thousand years. There are a hundred dictators on the continent of Africa right now. Iran has a nuclear weapon. Where are all of the nukes the Soviets built?" Boyd was getting steamed now. It was bad enough to see good men lose careers, and to almost lose yours in a downsizing, but to have civilians want to fire all the warriors was annoying in the extreme.

"I know it's wishful. But a world without war would be a better world for all. There are plenty of airplanes to fly without having to drop bombs. Do you carry nuclear bombs on that thing?" She asked, her tone no longer as soft as before. Nukes were her raw nerve and Boyd knew it.

"Thing?"

"Sorry. Aircraft."

"No. The Falcon is a tactical weapon. Nukes, if used are better delivered by other means."

"Tactical?" She asked, wanting to know the terms, gearing up for other questions. Several glasses of wine had loosened some inhibitions.

"Tactical means close to the front lines of a conflict, and more related to conventional weaponry. Strategic suggests strikes on an enemy's command, control, and communications center, manufacturing or homeland." He knew the homeland part was a mistake the moment he said it.

"So strategic means take out the women and children?" She said, no humor there.

"Look. There is no sense in this. I admit war is evil. If war comes to us, we have to have somebody ready to send out.

This whole thing is too close to me right now to debate. You have a more intellectual viewpoint. For me, it's all tied up with who, what I am."

"Intellectual viewpoint!"

Boyd flinched. He thought she was going to come right out of the chair for him.

"My mother raised me on a grade school teacher's salary. I never met my father. He got that patriotic disease. He became passionate about politics, and his homeland, and got into a boat and sailed off to liberate Nicaragua from the Sandanistas the year I was born. We never heard whether he was killed or died in prison. There was no glory. There were no medals. There was no telegram from a grateful nation. Daniel Ortega is still the president of Nicaragua, and as far as I am concerned, he can stay there as long as he pleases. You men get all excited about heroism and your goddamn wars. Sure, you go out with a loud bang and a trumpet fanfare. We quietly starve with our children back on the home front. If war ends, and it can't happen too soon, we, the women of the world will end it." Tears were on her face and defiance in her eyes.

Boyd wished he were someplace else. He stood, walked around the table picking up the plates. Eight Ball got excited as Boyd threw two mostly uneaten steaks into his bowl and carried it out to the back steps.

Colleen dried her eyes on her napkin.

Without realizing what he was doing Boyd returned to the kitchen, opened the refrigerator and took out the glass water bottle he kept there. Putting it to his lips, he tipped it up and drank half in three huge gulps. Wiping his mouth on his bare arm, he took a deep breath and looked at Colleen, then at the ceiling, took another deep breath and said, "You're right. I got into it through athletics. I learned the skills and the culture and I'm good at it. I've made the decision to consciously and willingly die for my country if called upon and now the country seems to think that's somehow a crime."

"Do you want to die for your country?" Was her simple response.

"No," Boyd said, realizing he had capitulated and wondering why. Agreeing to not wanting to die for one's country now seemed almost a violation of a code of honor.

"I'm sorry I ruined your supper. A fine man like you deserves his pride. My politics aren't mainstream and I shouldn't force them on you," Colleen said. She began clearing dishes from the table.

"I'm not sure who was forcing their viewpoint on whom. We're like fire and ice. Incompatible. Dominant in our own element."

Colleen stopped clearing and smiled, "That was literary. You might have a poet in you." She finished the dishes with Boyd's help, found her purse, said goodnight, and left.

Boyd found himself sitting on the back step talking to Eight ball at about the time he had expected to be making love with Colleen.

"What do they want from us?" He asked, finishing the last of the Mooseheads and heaving it across the fence into the field. "Is there something wrong with being strong?"

Eight Ball panted and swished his tail in the dirt, eyes on Boyd waiting for his next words.

"What are warriors supposed to do when there isn't a war?" Boyd knew the answer.

CHAPTER TWENTY

"Boyd, something's up with my ranch, with the deed at the County Clerk's Office." John Rigdon called the next Monday morning.

"Something? Something what?"

"I went over to Kiowa, the county seat, just on a whim. I keep the original deed to the ranch locked up at the bank, of course, but I wanted to see what was recorded with the county. Francine Whitman, the county clerk was there, an old friend. She found the deed, the original recorded from 1872, and it's there and perfectly legal. But, just in the past week a request for an official copy of it came from something called MERS, the Mortgage Electronic Registration System."

"What's that?"

"That's what I said. Francine said mortgages are not always recorded at the county clerk's office, like they have been since the beginning of the United States, now there's this corporation that handles all the steps of a mortgage transaction electronically; no paper, no recording, no county tax stamp, no trail of ownership."

"Is that legal?"

"Apparently. Now somebody has asked to have a copy of my deed. She says they do that when there's a mortgage in the works; to know the exact location and size of the land."

"You taking out a mortgage?"

"No."

CHAPTER TWENTY ONE

"Sixteen Sixty Lincoln Street, Suite 1430; be there before noon and bring your military ID and passport."

That's what Dan Ames had told him after he'd called his office at the Pentagon. He'd told Boyd to call him if he found anything. Two secretaries, an assistant, and finally; Ames came on the line.

"Oh, shit!" Ames said after sixty seconds of John Rigdon's story. "Oh, shit, oh shit!" There was a long pause, then, "Oh shit. That son of a bitch!"

"That bad?"

"Boyd, that's the mother lode of trouble. You don't know. Oh, the mother lode." More silence.

"What should I do?"

"Where are you?"

"At the base, Buckley."

"Stay there, I'll call right back."

And he had, in half an hour, with an address and the admonishment, now familiar, not to talk to anyone. Boyd had been intensely annoyed, feeling he'd been brushed off, until he got to the office.

"You're not being arrested," Marv Crowder quipped as he inked Boyd's fingers and pressed them onto the fingerprint card. "It's part of the appointment process; got to do it before you get your badge. Don't get to do this much here at the Denver field office, usually you get sworn in at the academy, but the boss in Washington said do this today, so here we are."

"You already got your mug shot," Boyd said, amused at the fuss, and deeply reassured that someone was now paying attention to what he'd found. He wiped off the ink and followed Crowder down the hall to his office.

"We need a witness in here," Crowder announced, and his secretary jumped up and followed them into the Agent in Charge's office where there was an American flag. "Raise your right hand."

Boyd moved in front of the flag, facing Crowder and raised his hand.

"I, Boyd Edward Chailland, do solemnly swear that I will support and defend the Constitution of the United States against all enemies foreign and domestic; that I will bear true faith and allegiance to the same; that I take this obligation freely, without any mental reservation or purpose of evasion; and that I will well and faithfully discharge the duties of the office on which I am about to enter. So help me God."

Boyd was rewarded with a handshake, and handed a badge.

"You are now a Special Agent of the United States Secret Service, congratulations."

"Can I flash this if I get stopped for speeding?" Boyd quipped, looking at his shiny new badge and thinking back to the small town cop in his home town who gave him a speeding ticket as payback for Boyd taking a girlfriend from him a dozen years before.

"Depends on why you're speeding, but that's a good question. Let's go over what you're authorized to do as a Special Agent." Marv motioned toward a seat as he returned to his desk and the secretary left. He pulled out a laminated sheet and read from it. "You're authorized to carry firearms, execute warrants issued under federal law, make arrests without warrants for any offense against the United States committed in your presence, or if you have reasonable grounds to believe that a felony has been committed. You can offer and pay rewards for services or information leading to the apprehension of persons involved in the violation of the law that the Secret Service is authorized to enforce. You can investigate fraud in connection with identification documents, fraudulent commerce, fictitious instruments, and foreign securities."

"I thought the Secret Service protected the president."

"We do, but we started out chasing counterfeiters, way before there was any other federal police authority, and that's still a core responsibility. As part of the Department of Homeland Security we safeguard the nation's money, and that includes electronic commerce; credit cards, money transfers, money laundering, and this new Mortgage Electronic Registration System that seems to be involved in something out in Elbert County. We also safeguard the President and Vice-President and their families."

"Well, you move fast. I just heard about this mortgage thing this morning," Boyd said, turning over his badge.

"Quite extraordinary, I've never gotten a call from the Director before. I thought it was a joke at first. He said you'd be here before noon and if you were late not to leave for lunch until you got here."

"I was really pissed. I called the General Counsel to the SecDef this morning and thought he was blowing me off."

"Apparently you've stumbled onto something that falls into the responsibility of the Department of Homeland Security. As a military guy you've probably not been aware of how territorial the federal government is. Turf is money, power, opportunity, and it's guarded jealously. You may be DoD, but you're on Homeland Security turf. Now, you're both. When the Director called this morning he said the Sec-Def was authorizing your transfer to us in a dual role. Your pay and allowances will come from DoD as before, but you'll report to me here, and be under the authority of the Director, who reports to the Secretary of the Department of Homeland Security; a cabinet post."

"That all makes sense, but what if this guy I've met is tied up with some foreign government or international cartel?"

"Then you're on FBI turf. That happens, especially where there's money laundering, usually one agency is designated lead and the rest just collaborate. We're lead for now."

"Ok. what do you know about Colonel Freeman and the Patriot Party?"

"Nothing."

Boyd put the badge away and pulled his chair closer to Marv Crowder's desk. "Are we secure here?"

"We run it for bugs once a month, the staff are all cleared to the equivalent of your Top Secret."

"This is a shaggy dog story; it meanders on and on, but it seems to promise a big punch line," and Boyd told the story from the plane crash on.

"Hmm." Was all Marv said during the hour the story took, beginning to nod enthusiastically toward the end.

"So, John Rigdon seems worried about his land, and when I told Dan Ames at the Pentagon, well, here we are. I never heard of this MERS thing."

"Fascinating story. You've been leading an exciting life. You've wrapped this thing up in, what, a month?"

"About that, but it isn't wrapped up. Not at all."

"Well, here's what I know. The Mortgage Electronic Registry System, MERS, is beginning to look like an invitation to fraud that may dwarf anything we've seen before. For generating fraudulent cash it sure beats the hell out of some guy trying to fake twenties with a printing press in his garage. It started out fifteen or twenty years ago with the big mortgage lenders complaining about the red tape of having to register all mortgages with the local county clerk. That involves a lot of worker bees at the local level and makes each mortgage an individual, unique thing. It makes it hard to combine a lot of them into a big security that can trade between large financial institutions. Congress drafted enabling legislation, slowly over a decade, that allowed a "modernization" of the mortgage industry. Electronic mortgages have made it easier to package loans into securities that are sold to banks. That securitization has put a lot of money into the system. Some claim that easy money caused the housing bubble that burst, causing the stock market crash in 2008.

"The bigger problem occurred when the banking industry and the government tried to clean up the housing mess; many – billions of dollars worth – of the mortgages in those mortgage-backed securities that have been guaranteed by the government are fraudulent. Many that utilized the MERS system weren't executed in a fashion that local authorities will recognize as valid, so they can't foreclose on the property, but worse than that, billions of dollars worth of mortgages are entirely fictitious. That means there never was a mortgage, just an electronic record that looked like a mortgage in the MERS system. At the height of the boom interest rates were low and mortgage-backed securities seemed to offer a safe, higher than market rate of return. Banks all over the world couldn't get enough of them. Now, in the aftermath, we're finding a tangled web of mortgage makers, mortgage lenders, mortgage consolidators, and securities traders that have been forming, consolidating, disappearing, and popping up again. It's impossible to trace some mortgages back to any legal action, or to know who got the original money, or to understand for sure if fraud was committed and if so, who did it. It's so big, and so ugly, we're trying to keep a lid on it until we can sort it out. If people knew how bad it really is there might be a panic, a run on the banks in anticipation of a general default on debt."

"Whoa! All this is kind of out of my league."

"Well, not really. You just turned up what appears to be mortgage fraud in progress. We always come in after the deed is done and try to sort it out after the fact. Now we can watch it happen. This is a rare chance."

Boyd nodded, beginning to feel confident about his role.

"Fraud always comes down to people, and people have lives, and that's how we catch crooks, by finding out about what they love. Love trips people up. Even if a crook doesn't love another person, they love money, or gambling, or fast cars. Freeman loves something or somebody, and he showed himself to protect it."

"Hmm. Interesting concept."

"Find out what Freeman loves and we can catch him."

CHAPTER TWENTY TWO

The Lear 35 is the perfect aircraft for the pilot executive who needs to fly in and out of someplace and leave no trail. He could have taken his Gulfstream, but people notice the Gulfstream, it has an air of ostentation about it. There are thousands of Lear jets in the United States, nobody notices them. Fast, reliable, and easy to fly, a Lear 35 isn't as nifty coast-to-coast as the Gulfstream, but it will get you from Keokuk to Chicago and then to Nashville on a tank of gas, then back to Dallas in time for dinner.

The colonel watched the miles tick off on the auto pilot and rehearsed what he needed to do in Washington. A mid-level executive at Washington Headquarters Services; a career civil servant, had been passed over for a promotion he'd felt was his. Instead, a black female got the job and became his boss. He was furious, and vented to a friend who reported it to the colonel; always on the lookout for the disgruntled. Tonight they were to dine in Alexandria, and discuss how Carl Story might help the Patriot Party to restore the old values to America; the old values where promotions were made on the basis of merit and not political contacts.

Carl Story was a Contracting Officer's Technical Representative supervising renovation contracts for the 114 properties WHS manages in the district, suburban Virginia and Maryland. Tonight Colonel Freeman would ask him to download his boss's emails; to document that her promotion was the result of political connection and not merit. He would download it onto a flash drive the colonel would give him at dinner. Of course, Carl would check it before inserting it into the DOD computer, and it would appear to be blank. It wasn't blank. It would insert a BOT into the database that would find the email accounts of dozens of senior military officers in addition to the SecDef and some congressmen and insert messages sent to and received from General Trusten Polk during the past six months.

Pretty simple, the colonel had been persuading people to do his bidding for years; his mind wandered back. It was like a bolt the first time he'd heard the word "sociopath" in a high school psychology class. Some people see all their fellow humans as prey, to use without remorse for whatever purpose they desire. That was him! He saw others like him, and recognized they were even less trustworthy than he was, because most of them couldn't reason beyond grasping what they wanted as soon as they saw it. These impetuous ones were destined to spend their lives in prison, preying upon each other. There was another subset of sociopaths, the patient ones.

His first caper was when he was 15. Gangly and awkward after an adolescent growth spurt, he'd been embarrassed by four upper class boys in front of a girl he liked. He waited. Months later, after Christmas vacation he heard these same boys had some cherry bombs and were going to bring them to school and each light one exactly at noon and throw it into the center of the common area for a "noon salute." It was harmless, adolescent acting out; and an opening. He had cherry bombs too, most high school boys in Louisiana in the 1960s could lay their hands on cherry bombs and he had two in his sock drawer. He tested his plan with one and brought the other to school on the day of the noon salute. Ten minutes before noon he entered an upstairs boy's restroom and went to the back stall. He lit a cigarette, common practice at the time, and stuck the cherry bomb fuse into the other end, then duct taped the cherry bomb to the bottom of the toilet tank, then went out to the commons to watch the fireworks.

Gathered with friends he was there when the four scofflaws lobbed their salutes and then ran into the building to hide, though the entire student body were witnesses as the four detonations reverberated off the school's brick walls. A minute later a dull thud was heard from upstairs. That cherry bomb shattered the toilet tank, flooding the bathroom, and opening the float valve ensuring a steady, unstoppable flow of water until the janitor shut off the water to the whole school. The principal's office on the first floor was under that toilet. The four miscreants who threw the cherry bombs took the fall for the fifth one and were expelled, and one who had already had some minor brushes with the law was labeled incorrigible. He got his GED at the state reformatory.

Nobody ever knew where that fifth cherry bomb came from.

"We better get one of those sandwiches before Jerry eats them all," the colonel said, recovering from his reverie and sending the co-pilot back for lunch. The Mississippi River wound beneath them as he thought ahead to his impending check in with Nashville Center, then his mind wandered back to his Pantheon of heroes.

Bernie Cornfeld; his first hero. He'd heard of Bernie while he was in college. Bernie manipulated the new concept of mutual funds to build a fortune with International Overseas Services, then skimmed the profits and sold the whole thing to another patient sociopath, Robert Vesco, who blatantly looted the company and fled to South America. Both of them lived out their lives dodging prosecution and enjoying their wealth, and neither spent a day in jail.

"Beep" Jennings and "Wild Bill" Patterson, took a small shopping center bank and made it a major nationwide force by making risky loans during the Oklahoma oil boom of the early 1980s. Nobody before Penn Square Bank had successfully bundled risky loans from the oil patch into commodities that big banks could trade; and they did it skimming profit from the making, bundling, selling and reselling. Their cowboy wildcatter's flair amused some Chicago bankers who bought way more than prudence would allow. When the oil boom ended, Chicago's Continental Illinois bank went belly up in the first Federal Reserve bailout of a "too big to fail" bank. Today the Continental Illinois Bank building, right across the street from the Chicago Federal Reserve, has a tacky plastic sign on the first floor identifying it as, "Bank of America." The colonel knew that, somewhere in Oklahoma, are guys on big ranches with thousands of cattle and scores of pumping oil wells that got their start soaking up some of that loose credit. Jennings and Patterson, the patsy enablers for the smart money, went to jail.

Marc Rich found his opening in the oil embargo on Iran in the 1980's. He was already an international commodities broker and understood all the nuance of that trade. He partnered with the Iranians and later Saddam Hussein to sell their oil, avoiding the blockade. In a delicious irony, Marc Rich bought Iranian oil at $12 a barrel and sold it to refineries in south Texas for twice that during the energy crisis of 1983. He was indicted by federal prosecutor Rudolph Guiliani for illegal oil trade and tax evasion. He fled to Switzerland and managed to evade extradition for years; years when he bought ships and profited by evading every embargo imposed by the US government. He bribed a US president, got a Presidential Pardon and returned home worth upwards of a $ Billion.

Sholom Weiss, a rabbi well known in the securities business, kited a check to buy National Heritage Life Insurance Company, then used the assets of the company to cover the check. He looted the company with the help of lawyers, businessmen, and the Gambino crime family. With $450 million gone, he was arrested. At his trial he was obnoxious, insisting everyone was at fault but himself. What chutzpah! Claiming he was wrongfully accused the whole time, he jumped bail and disappeared leaving a trail of wild parties with dozens of young prostitutes in luxury hotels across the world. They caught him in Austria, with great difficulty. He'd spent half of the $450 million he stole. It turned out he wasn't even Jewish!

They caught Whitey Bulger, too. Whitey was a Boston mobster who colluded with the feds to roll up his rivals, got rich then ratted out the FBI and disappeared. He stayed gone for fifteen years, but they caught him living the quiet life of a pensioner in Los Angeles. With his history as a rat, life will not be good for Whitey in prison.

Bernie Madoff and a dozen other schmucks didn't have sense enough to run and got to do the "perp walk," shackled on national television, then spend whatever money they had on lawyers before finally going to prison forever. How stupid not to have an exit plan? How stupid to have one and fail to execute it in time? He knew he could never just run; they'd find him. They found all those other guys, every single one. Some weaseled out of jail time, but none disappeared for good with their loot.

He would. And, he'd settle some old scores in the process.

CHAPTER TWENTY THREE

"Don't get any of that stuff on you. If you do, wash it off right away. It' just a herbicide, but who knows, it might make you sterile or something!" Ben shouted from the cockpit of the King Cat, engine cranking up again.

Boyd had signed on to be ground crew on a Saturday to spell Ben's regular helper who was taking a much needed day off. It was spraying season and every day counted. He had just pumped 500 gallons of water mixed with herbicide into the fiberglass tank in front of the cockpit. He disengaged the locking mechanism on the hose and pulled it away from the prop wash, which was blowing debris back out onto the grassy pasture from which most of it had come. Ben gunned the engine and the big plane rolled across the grass toward the end of the 2,000 foot asphalt strip. As he reached the end he turned the plane and applied full power simultaneously. The deep throated roar of the huge radial piston engine as the plane passed Boyd was worth the drive up from Denver. Ben stayed low after taking off to gain speed then pulled up almost vertical as he reached the highway and achieved the couple hundred feet of altitude he needed to fly to the field he was spraying, just out of sight over the horizon. Boyd recoiled the hose and re-read the caution statement and instructions on the drum the herbicide had come in while waiting for Ben to return.

Boyd was inside washing his hands when he heard the King Cat fly over again and land. He was uncoiling the hose when Ben motioned with a horizontal flick of his wrist across his throat that he was going to kill the engine and quit.

"Got it all sprayed. We'll just leave what's in the tank until tomorrow. I need to change the oil when it cools down some and make some calls. See if anybody else has noticed unfamiliar flora in their corn," he said gaily as he stood and turned his broad behind toward the ladder Boyd was bringing up. They both had a Coke while Ben called a few farmers to line up spraying jobs for Sunday morning.

"The attitude indicator, compass, altimeter, and airspeed indicator are all pretty standard. Over there you have RPMs, oil pressure and temperature gauges. There's no assist on the stick, but it's not that tough. The throttle is on the left, just like in your plane. The spray is the one below and behind it. Don't forget you have to adjust the fuel mixture. The higher you go the leaner you want it, but you know all that." Ben was leaning over the side of the King Cat and Boyd was seated inside, his long legs jammed on the rudder pedals. He hadn't asked, but this was what he'd hoped for. They were waiting for the engine to cool a bit more before doing some routine maintenance.

"I've got insurance on this one. If you drive it into the ground, I'm covered. Also, if I can't fly for some reason, I could hire another pilot to keep the business going. The Mustang is only insured if I or a pilot approved by the insurance company is flying it, in case you were wondering," Ben said with a smile as Boyd climbed out of the seat. He'd hoped against hope to get a chance to get into either plane.

"I'd sure enjoy a chance to try it out," Boyd said, standing admiring the King Cat.

"Let's change the oil first. I think its cool enough now. You'll have about half an hour's worth of gas," Ben said, walking toward the storeroom where the oil was kept.

"Bring over that waste oil drum. Use the dolly in the hanger."

Boyd's heart pounded with excitement as they drained the oil from the drain under the big engine and refilled the oil tank behind the pilot.

"These wide thick wings provide enormous lift. No sense pushing the speed, stay under 130. If you get the RPMs up too high you just get a lot of vibration and not much more speed. Stall speed, loaded, with the engine running is 68 knots. Take-off speed is 70 knots loaded, may be a bit lower with no spray and not much gas. Just fly around a bit this first time, you can practice stalls and rolls some other time. If it does quit on you, just land straight in. The odds of hitting a tree around here are pretty slim," Ben said, making sure Boyd was strapped in.

"Make a couple fast taxis up and down the runway first to get the feel of it."

Boyd closed the canopy, actually wishing he could have kept it open, and called, "Clear!" Ben was well back and Boyd started the big engine. He rechecked the gauges and his controls again. Satisfied everything was going to work he eased the throttle forward and the engine came to life. The plane rolled forward and Boyd pushed the right rudder pedal and the plane turned sharply right. He adjusted the throttle several times on the way to the end of the runway, varying the speed. On his first fast taxi the plane wanted to take off at about 65 knots and Boyd almost went for it but wanted to do just as Ben had suggested. The second taxi he cut the power precipitously to check characteristics on landing. The third time he was up into the wind.

The larger stick in his lap was harder to get used to than the slower speed. He was accustomed to the small stick on the right side of the cockpit in his F-16. The vibration was much more than he was used to but not much different from other piston planes he'd flown. It was fun to laze along so close to the ground and not have to worry about what was twenty miles in front of you. Turns were awkward the first few he made as the control surfaces were enormous on these two huge wings. Soon he was effortlessly flying about and enjoying his Saturday afternoon immensely. He watched the fuel and returned for landing well before supply became a concern for the older pilot waiting on the ground.

"Well done. You landed just like an old pro," Ben said, bringing up the ladder after Boyd had killed the engine.

"When the Air Force finally kicks me out of the cockpit I'm going to come begging for a job. This is more fun than hauling trash," Boyd said, descending the ladder and using a common description of the life of an airline pilot.

"Doesn't pay as well. And it's seasonal. You can have all the women you want, but I don't suppose that's a problem for you."

"How would you get women in a crop duster?" Boyd asked, curious and amused.

"Before I found Henrietta I used to cruise the interstate, looking for women in convertibles. I'd just fly in front of them and do a roll or something and then head off at an exit. You'd be surprised how many would follow."

"You old reprobate! They ought to put you in jail," Boyd said, laughing and wondering if the ladies minded much after driving around the back roads to the hanger and seeing the macho King Cat land and a portly middle aged man jump out of the cockpit with an erection.

CHAPTER TWENTY FOUR

Boyd had planned, briefed, and led a training mission that included two groups of aircraft approaching the target from different directions and low altitude. They were timed to hit moments apart, drop their bombs, and make their way back home at low altitude. Eight F-16s had flown their mission on the smooth air of early morning and now at midday those pilots who had not gone home were watching thunderheads build over the foothills. The duty day was at an end.

Boyd changed into his running shorts and shoes and headed out to the back of the base to run and think. Jogging along the asphalt perimeter road at Buckley, Boyd let his mind go blank. As the sweat began to drip down the back of his neck and soak his shirt and shorts and the muscles loosened up from the tension of his mission that morning, Boyd's pace became automatic and comfortable. The effort was just enough to blot out mundane thoughts and allow his mind to focus. It was shimmering heat, dust, prairie dogs, grasshoppers, and quiet broken only by an occasional distant rumble. The rhythmic slap of his shoes against the asphalt was hypnotic. Who was General Trusten Polk?

Boyd thought about the personnel files, scrubbed clean by the United States government except for the one OPR written in green ink. The official photograph, done with great care and precision by an Air Force photographer, showing a four star general, looking very much the part. He reviewed his visit to the official residence, also scrubbed clean, this time by Freeman. The cryptic entries in the diary documenting meetings with people identified only by letters and numbers. The lack of personal effects, the sterility of the place was depressing. Was the evidence of who the general was removed with such skill that nothing remained, or was there so little of the general that there was nothing much to remove? Would; could, a man give up all that he was to assume a high post and just forget a childhood, family, friends, education for the chance to be powerful and wealthy? Then Boyd remembered the University of Texas alumni magazine on the table in the general's living room. Trusten Polk, the real one, had been a graduate of Oklahoma. Could the fake general have been from Texas? Perhaps that was the only link Freeman had overlooked.

It was still early afternoon. There was still time to call back to Langley and ask Wayne Herrera to find that Texas alumni magazine. Boyd reversed his course and was soon on the non-secure line to Langley.

"Major Herrera. Boyd Chailland. I was calling to ask a favor. I'm glad you're still there. Will you be aide to the new commander?"

"No. I have orders to Alaska. I'll be moving in a couple days."

"Alaska? Did you piss somebody off?" Boyd asked, he knew Alaska wasn't all that bad an assignment.

"No, it's actually a good assignment. I'll be deputy DO and flying regularly in the Eagle again. I'm quite happy with it. It's the assignment General Polk promised after the year as his aide."

"I'm still plugging away at this investigation. We've really hit a dead end. Let me give you my number here and when you get to Elmendorf, call me with your number. I know I'm going to think of something to ask as soon as you're off where I can't easily talk to you."

"Isn't that the truth."

Boyd gave him his number at home and at the squadron, then asked the question he'd called to ask.

"Where are General Polk's effects?"

"They're in storage. I supervised the move. The new commander wanted to move in. Can't blame him for that, the house is part of the job."

"You probably don't remember, but there were some magazines on the table in the living room."

"We packed everything."

"Do you think you could find them without too much trouble?"

"I know which box they're in. I'll get them tomorrow and send them to you, but you'll have to ask for them in writing. I don't want to be in a position of tampering with evidence."

"No problem. I'll request them officially today and FAX the request to you."

Two days later Federal Express delivered a slim packet addressed to the accident board. Col Bertz and Boyd opened it together and logged in the three magazines with evidence numbers. They would have to be examined only in the board room. There were two Newsweeks and the alumni magazine. It had no sign of an address label on it and it was six months old. It could have been left there by anyone visiting the general. Bertz called in some technicians from the board and they dusted the magazines for fingerprints, finding a few that seemed good enough to check. Bertz grew bored and returned to his office. After half an hour the technicians finished and let Boyd have the magazines. Boyd leafed through the alumni magazine and found nothing interesting so he laid it on the table and began reading one of the Newsweeks.

After ten minutes of reading the Newsweek Boyd glanced back at the alumni magazine. It didn't lie flat on the table like a new magazine but had been held open and the binding stretched so that the first twenty pages came up off of the rest of the pages by a millimeter or two. Boyd picked it up and opened it to the page it seemed to want to open itself to. It was a feature on the class of 1974 which had had its 35th reunion that spring. There were two pages of old snapshots sent in by alumni. There was a picture of the football game with Texas A&M; a shot of the graduation ceremony; the campus after a rare snow storm; and a picture of the ROTC cadets marching in review.

The picture of the ROTC cadets was on the right side of the open page and Boyd strained to see if he could recognize anybody. He couldn't. He got up and walked to the other side of the desk where there was a magnifying glass and returned.

Boyd was going to hold the magazine with his left hand and the glass with his right but just at the last moment before picking it up stopped to consider if he might disturb something by so doing. He looked closer at the magazine. Just at the point where his thumb would hold the magazine there was a smudge. He picked it up and looked with the glass. The paper was wrinkled just at that spot and pulled away from the staple. Someone had held the magazine at that place. Looking away from the right side of the page he positioned his thumb and then the glass at the most comfortable position to look closely at the right page. When he looked through the glass it was on the ROTC parade. The caption read: "Cadet Colonel Horace T. Swilley leads the Air Force ROTC in review for a visit by Brigadier General William Sherman Miles." With the glass, Boyd peered closely at the picture. Underneath the visor of the parade cap worn by the cadet colonel was the youthful visage of a man now known only as General Trusten Polk, and two rows back was Barney Freeman.

Sadness and empathy flooded over Boyd. He could see, feel even, the man sitting alone in the living room of a house meant for families and entertaining, looking at all that was left of his own identity. Promoted now beyond his abilities and cut off from whatever roots he may have had, Horace Swilley was imprisoned in the shell of Trusten Polk's identity. On the one hand the Delano Society called the shots. They made him and they promoted him, and they used him for whatever purposes they had, probably not much. He was made to be used just in case he was needed. Then there was the shadowy Barney Freeman in the background, the only living link to his real identity. He must have been calling some shots too. Why? What did Horace Swilley do for Barney Freeman?

It took only ten minutes to find the University of Texas Cactus Yearbook for 1974 and find the ROTC graduating class. Because of the Viet Nam war just winding down ROTC was a hard sell that year and the class was small; only a handful. Up front by virtue of his rank was Cadet Colonel Horace Swilley. Seated in the back row with a grin that, in retrospect seemed sinister, was a younger Barney Freeman. The yearbook identified him as Luther Dupree.

"Why yes, we have Mr. Dupree on our alumni list. You can reach him care of Dupree Aviation, Dalhart, Texas 79022. His telephone number is 806 259-XXXX." The lady at the alumni office in Austin cheerfully gave Boyd the information the United States government with the combined powers of the United States Air Force, the Justice Department, and the Secret Service couldn't provide. Boyd called the number.

"Dupree Aviation."

"Yes, ah, what services do you provide there?"

"You mean for transient aircraft?"

"Yes and locally."

"We have fuel, both jet and aviation gasoline as well as minor repairs for most types of aircraft. We have a six thousand foot cement runway capable of handling aircraft of any weight. Our cafe is open twelve hours a day. We have an aviation museum featuring vintage aircraft that is free to the public. We have agricultural spraying and a variety of charter aircraft including a Lear 35 and a Gulfstream III. We have meeting rooms completely equipped with the latest in audio-visual equipment large enough for meetings of up to one hundred people. We offer a free shuttle to our hotel in the city of Dalhart. We are located only five miles from the Dalhart VOR, which makes us easy to find. In addition to that, we have the best prices on aviation gasoline in the area." The answer to Boyd's somewhat open-ended question was delivered with practiced efficiency and with considerable pride.

"Wow! That's quite a lot for a small town airfield," Boyd said, appreciatively.

"Sir, it's not a small town airfield. Dalhart was a World War II bomber training base and the runway and hangers have been maintained," the lady said defensively as if correcting people's impressions of Dalhart was a daily duty she was getting tired of.

Boyd apologized and hung up. The Gulfstream and the Lear 35 answered the question of how Freeman was able to get around so quickly after the crash. How he could afford it was the next question.

Boyd called Dan Ames. "Dan, I've got Freeman's identity. He's Luther Dupree and he lives in Dalhart, Texas. He runs a fixed base operation there, and he has a Gulfstream and a Lear jet."

"Fast work, how did you crack that?"

"His yearbook. The real Polk was from Oklahoma, but there was a Texas alumni magazine in his quarters. Inside was an ROTC parade in 1974 and leading it was Polk, then known as Cadet Colonel Horace Swilley. Right behind him was Freeman. The government owes me twenty bucks for paying the Texas Alumni Association for a copy of the 1974 yearbook. Dupree's picture and name were in that."

"Luther Dupree, even sounds sinister."

"Those airplanes pretty much clinch it that he's up to something. You're looking at upwards of five million bucks for the Gulfstream if it's in any kind of shape and a million and a half for the Lear."

"He isn't getting that skimming money from the militia movement."

"No, not at all. Do you think you can run him down, find out some more about him?"

"I'm on it. I'll get back to you when I have something."

"I may run down there. Take a look."

"Good idea. Be careful."

Boyd now had Marv Crowder and the Secret Service backing him up, but he needed more. He needed an accomplice. He needed someone smart, single, and with a private pilot's license. Someone who would stand beside Boyd at the shootout at the OK Corral and take whatever was coming, as long as the trip getting there wasn't boring. He called Webb Collins.

"Boyd! You planning another trip?" Webb asked excitedly. Boyd could imagine his fidgeting on the other end of the line, always ready for an adventure.

"Not exactly, but, yes, maybe. We need to talk," Boyd said, mysteriously. He knew the hint of mystery would hook Webb.

"Now?"

"Yeah."

"Ok. How about my health club?.We can pump some iron and we'll troll for girls. There's always a bunch there," Webb said. Boyd was surprised to hear Webb lifted weights, he couldn't have weighed more than 140 lbs. He wasn't at all surprised about the girls.

The club was one of those ultra fancy affairs where you see mostly designer aerobics outfits lounging around drinking Perrier.

Boyd showed up with a jock, a pair of worn out running shoes, cut-off sweatpants from the academy, and a sleeveless black t-shirt a friend had brought back from the motorcycle rally at Sturgis, South Dakota.

To Webb's credit, he had on a t-shirt he'd gotten at the Bolder Boulder 10k run and some plain gym shorts. They looked around for a place where they could talk. The aerobics room was empty. Boyd checked out some gloves for the speed bag and began warming up on that while he filled Webb in on the Trusten Polk crash.

"So, the Trusten Polk in the crash was the ACC commander, but he wasn't Trusten Polk," Boyd said, working into a rhythm on the bag. "This guy I found, the one who wrote the OPR on Polk in Viet Nam, looked at his picture last week. He was sure it was not the same guy. Of course, it's been twenty years since he saw him."

"How did this fake guy get to be a general?" Webb asked the obvious question. He had started out jumping rope but was now standing in slack jawed amazement.

"Some people within the Air Force did it. After meeting that guy Ferguson, I'm beginning to wonder what their criteria are for general," Boyd said, leaving out the really big secret and increasing the tempo and the power in his punches. "There's more." He told him about Freeman/Dupree and his organization and what Dupree had assured him was an impending takeover of the United States, then about his becoming a Special Agent in the Secret Service, and finally about the Colorado Unorganized Militia and the apparent fraud in progress with John Rigdon's mortgage.

"Wait a minute. You want me to help you do what? You've already reported it to proper authority, been deputized, and have the full weight of the Secret Service behind you. What's to do?" Webb said, totally serious now for only the second time since Boyd had met him.

"The Air Force and the Secret Service told me to find out what I could about this organization and Dupree. I want to go down there to Dalhart and nose around. They know my face. I need an accomplice. We could fly down in a rented aeroclub plane. You have a pilot's license. We fly in, get some gas, nose around."

The response with Webb was the expected one. He lit up with a wide grin at the prospect of an adventure. Then he turned serious again for just a moment. "Why not just sit back and wait. Maybe nothing will happen?"

Boyd was warmed up now and beginning to sweat. Adjacent to the speed bag was a heavy bag. He moved to that and began to jab and weave. "Someone took the identity of a downed pilot, a good man, and let his friends think he was a shit for turning his back on 'em as he got promoted. With that war record they jimmied the Air Force promotions system and created a four star general. They're still lyin' about that, and they want me to help them cover it up. Someone else took the other pilot they made into a general and turned him into a traitor." With the word "traitor" Boyd hit the bag a sharp, full force left jab followed by all he could put behind a right to the center of the bag. The impact and the expelled air from his lungs was audible throughout the health club.

"And now he's dead too." Boyd hit the bag again.

"Yeah, " Webb seemed to be catching on.

"That son-of-a-bitch Dupree has money," Boyd said, punctuating with another full force blast to the bag, "Powerful friends," another blast. "Some tough security types, and he threatened me if I didn't help him change the government of the United States. He danced an Ali Shuffle then moved back in for a four punch combination. "They're all pushin', on the wrong guy."

Boyd danced back from the bag and turned to see he'd attracted an audience. Two girls were pretending to warm up and stretch in the back of the aerobics room. Boyd went back to the heavy bag and pounded it for another minute without saying anything, story finished. Now the sweat was spraying the bag when he hit it. He hadn't had an opportunity to really pound a bag for awhile and the savagery he released on it was a surprise even to him. He'd had some boxing as part of the overall physical education at the academy. With his size and strength that heavy bag was a natural for him, though he knew that in a real match a smaller, faster man could take him apart. He took a short break and wiped the sweat from his face and head and turned around to see the group of two girls had grown to five, not even pretending to be doing anything.

"Were you waiting?" he asked, pointing to the swaying bag.

"Oh! No. Uh, you go ahead," one said, embarrassed. They were a rainbow of colors in their spandex outfits and brightly colored shoes. Attractive all, they quickly busied themselves stretching and doing warm-up calisthenics.

Boyd stopped abruptly and walked to the weight area. Webb followed, chatting with the girls.

"Fighter pilot. Needs to stay in shape," Webb said, as if Boyd needed any more attraction for their audience.

Webb walked confidently to the weight bench and picked up a forty-five to put on the end of the bar. Boyd, surprised, matched it with one for the other end. Webb lay down and quickly hoisted it ten times. Boyd added a forty-five to his end and Webb did the same. Boyd lay down and hoisted the bar ten times. He heard a faint twitter from the door to the aerobics room as he finished.

"I'll need a spot on this." Webb said as he picked up a twenty-five to replace the forty-five Boyd took off. Boyd found another twenty-five and stood at Webb's head, ready to help if he couldn't quite get it back up to the rack. Webb picked it up and quickly dropped in to his chest and bounced it back up, extending his arms.

"Great! Now another," Boyd said, hands close to the bar but not touching it. Webb tried again but his momentum slowed on the extension and the bar stopped. Boyd was quick to grab the bar and assist enough so Webb could complete the press and get the bar back on the rack. "Wow. I never would have figured you could do 185. You must be a real gym rat," Boyd said, appreciatively.

"I've always been partial to the smell of old sweat socks," Webb said, looking over at the girls, inching closer into the otherwise empty weight room.

Boyd removed the twenty-fives and added back a forty-five and then a thirty-five and a 2 1/2 to each end. When he lay down, Webb positioned himself to spot and the girls moved into the room altogether. Boyd lifted the 300 pounds smartly and did one press quickly, then a second just barely. Webb moved to help but Boyd shook his head and dropped the bar to his chest for one more. Beaded with sweat and grimaced with pain Boyd's face showed extreme exertion. Just half-way back up to extension the bar's momentum had almost stopped.

"Ugghhyaa!" Boyd expressed the air from his lungs in a primal moan that reverberated off the mirror clad walls in the weight room and the bar raised to the level of his extended arms.

Webb grabbed for it and it slid back onto the rack.

CHAPTER TWENTY FIVE

From 11'000 feet Capulin Mountain looks just like what it is, a spent volcano. Surrounded by the red dirt that was its lava, it rises alone out of the high prairie of northeastern New Mexico. There are some smaller pyramids tapering down from the really big mountains in the Rockies just west of there, but nothing that could be mistaken for Capulin. It had been a wet summer and the grass was green and mostly covering the dirt.

"Really looks like cattle country this year. Last year when I came down here for my first cross-country after getting my license it was so dry it looked like Death Valley," Webb said from the left seat of their aero club Cessna 170.

"So you've just gotten your license?" Boyd asked, idly, watching the cattle and thinking about John Wayne.

"Yeah. If the guard just paid a little more I could afford to fly more often. I only have 125 hours."

"Doesn't bother me. I watched you figure the flight plan and the fuel and weather and I thought you were right on all the way. The biggest surprise I found was that an aero club would have a tail dragger. They usually get tricycle landing gear so you novices don't get the tail too light and dump the nose in the dirt."

"They've sure told me about that enough that I'll never forget it if I live to be a thousand," Webb said, changing the radio navigation frequency to Dalhart from Tobe in Colorado.

As the ground dropped away from the Rockies and merged with the Great Plains, the red dirt gave way to heavier grasses on the Llano Estacado, the largest mesa in the United States and the ancestral home of the buffalo, and the Comanche Nation. Today the dry red range land becomes circles of pivot irrigated crops and large expanses of winter wheat as you go eastward. By the time they had Dalhart in sight the terrain was almost exclusively farmed rather than grazed.

"Doesn't look like much from here," Boyd said, twenty miles out, surveying the grain elevators and commercial buildings in town. The runway at the Dalhart Municipal Airport looked wider and more substantial than one would expect for a small town. There were quite a few hangers about, but not anything really big.

With no tower to control their approach they were on their own to be sure they merged with any other traffic that might be in the area. They announced their presence and intentions to land on the radio and listened for acknowledgement from other aircraft. There were none so they did a downwind leg and low approach before going around again and landing.

"I'll hang back and stay with the plane while you walk into operations. If you see anybody that looks like Dupree, raise your right hand to your face, like you're flicking away a bug and I'll go back to the plane. His security man, Jerry, sticks pretty close to him. I'll just have to take my chances that if Dupree's not here, Jerry won't be either," Boyd said, as they taxied off the runway.

The operations building was red brick and of recent construction. It was about twenty thousand square feet with a hanger attached to it and another, larger hanger attached to that. The smaller hanger was just the size to house the Lear 35. The door was open and it was empty. Down the runway from this main complex were rows of hangers, probably rentals. There were several transient aircraft parked on the ramp with people standing around, adjusting luggage, and walking back and forth between the planes and the operations area. Outside the fence by the parking lot was a small cafe. The area around the field included a couple agricultural spraying operations and then just grass and a few trees. There were remains of an old tower, probably from World War II days, behind another row of hangers perpendicular to the runway.

Webb taxied to the refueling area and shut off the engine. A fuel service mechanic was already on his way. After the refueling process Webb and the mechanic walked back into the operations building with Boyd lingering behind, watching for Webb's sign. There was none and after they disappeared into the building, Boyd followed.

In the lobby of Dupree Aviation was a fully restored German Messerschmitt. Boyd stopped in his tracks, Webb was similarly frozen a few steps further into the building, just in front of the desk.

The bored lady behind the desk was patiently waiting for this reaction, probably repeated dozens of times daily, to pass. Even to the uninitiated it was a stunning sight. Painted light tan with the black cross with white background prominent on its fuselage and wing it looked very much the spartan, no-nonsense killing machine it was in its heyday, some seventy years ago.

Wordlessly Boyd and Webb walked to the velvet rope, there to politely remind enthusiasts to keep their hands off this rare treasure. A small sign identified it as a Bf 109G-1 Trop, from the Libyan theater of operations about 1943. It looked smaller than Boyd would have expected. It was certainly smaller than Ben Culpepper's Mustang. The six exhaust ports on each side reminded Boyd of the inverted V, twelve-cylinder, piston engine with supercharger and liquid cooling, state of the art for 1938. In the center of the three-blade prop was the barrel of the twenty millimeter cannon that had been in the inverted V of the engine block. Two smaller machine guns were housed just behind the cowling and just in front of the pilot. The canopy was painfully small and squared. The glass looked thick and awkward. Boyd wondered if someone his size could even get into one of these. He ached to try; to sit where Hartmann, Galland, and Marseille sat. To look out of that canopy and imagine doing battle with the dozens of fifty caliber machine guns firing from a formation of B-17s flying at 25,000 feet, or yanking and banking with Thunderbolts or Mustangs. Perhaps most exciting of all, it smelled of fresh gasoline.

"Does it fly?" Boyd asked, not turning around.

"Yes. Colonel Dupree flies it all the time. It's very valuable, you know," the lady answered, adding her unnecessary assessment of its worth.

Boyd circled the Messerschmitt at least a dozen times, trying to memorize each detail, appreciating the German mind for the lethal simplicity of its design, wondering how many of these remained in the world; probably not more than a dozen.

"Your boy Dupree is certainly not a starving revolutionary," Webb whispered when they were on the side away from the desk.

Feeling insecure in the center of Dupree's world, Boyd left by the side door and walked over to the cafe, leaving Webb to pay for the gas and nose around in the museum and offices. He scanned the area as he covered the few yards across the parking lot. There were a few cars, probably the staff. Parked by the first hanger was an ancient Mercedes Benz. A new Chevrolet suburban was parked in a space marked, "Reserved". That was probably Dupree's car, Boyd thought. It made him walk a little faster.

A fortyish woman with a faded uniform and a cigarette hanging from her mouth was standing at the counter watching a soap opera on television. She snubbed out the cigarette and smiled when Boyd approached. There were no other customers.

"What ya got to eat?" Boyd said cheerfully as he sat on a stool and swiveled to look back at the hanger.

"Peach pie is real good today; just made it this morning." The woman said as she handed Boyd the menu.

"Get many folks through here? I guess the business is pretty much just what flies in."

"Some days it's real busy. Other times, like now, I just sit and wait," she replied.

"Big planes come in here?"

"Colonel Dupree has that big Gulfstream jet. We see a few like that and then smaller jets. Lots of little planes like the one you came in on." She poured coffee and threw the hamburger he ordered on the grill. Apparently she was observant enough to know what happened there.

"So, who comes in on that big jet?" Boyd asked, idly, looking at a crop duster come in for a short approach and landing.

"There's a big meeting center in that new building there," she indicated a steel building added to the back of one of the hangers. "That's the headquarters of the Patriot Party."

"The Patriot Party? I've never heard of that," Boyd said idly, eyes still on the crop duster.

"It's a new thing. Mr. Jack Anders rents the building from the colonel, and hires the colonel to bring people in. It's been real good for business."

"I don't know if I've met Jack Anders."

"You'd know if you had. They call him "Blue" Jack, 'cause his eyes are so blue. It's creepy; they seem to look right through you."

"I guess a lot of the smaller planes stop for gas. That ought to be good for business," Boyd said, changing the subject.

"Oh yes, some days we see twenty or more planes like yours and then those two-engine ones and some jets. Its fun meeting all the people," she said gaily, turning to drop some frozen french fries into the fat. Her name tag said, Delores.

"Do they rent out that Gulfstream?"

"It's here most of the time. When it's gone, the colonel is usually flying it himself."

"He brings people in to meetings in town? Like business-men or something?" Boyd asked, managing a wide yawn.

"No. They always meet here. If they're going to stay he takes them down to the hotel he owns. Mostly they're gone that same day. Sometimes one or two will stay but they usu-ally go out to the colonel's ranch about twenty miles west of town."

"Who is this Colonel?"

"Why, Colonel Dupree. He owns all this. He's very import-ant; must have been a war hero or something. Military people are always coming by here to talk to him. Sometimes we even see Air Force planes. One time a four star general came in here and had lunch."

"What'd he have?" Boyd asked, taking a bite out of his hamburger and thinking of Horace Swilley's weak stomach.

"Soup." She said without hesitation.

"Where's the colonel now?"

"He was in here for breakfast this morning," Delores said, refilling Boyd's cup and not noticing the hair stand up on the back of his neck or see him stop in mid-chew.

Boyd munched his sandwich and ate his fries with furtive looks behind him. He made inane small talk and decided to casually walk to the men's room if he saw the colonel approach. Soon a loud noise on the runway heralded the return of the Gulfstream. Shiny and new, it taxied to the front of the operations area and the door opened.

A muscular blond haired man walked out of the door of the operations office to meet the guests. His tight fitting shirt revealed massive shoulders and upper arms as he greeted his dozen guests and escorted them inside. The passengers were mostly middle aged white men in various types of dress. None of them looked like they worked with their hands for their living. A couple lingered talking inside and emerged with the pilot, Luther Dupree.

"That's Blue Jack," Dolores said, indicating the stocky man now returning to the operations building with some guests. A moment later Webb stepped out the back door and walked casually over, hand vigorously rubbing his right ear the whole way.

"Why don't you go get a weather briefing and I'll get you a burger and some of Delores' peach pie and you can eat on the road," Boyd said before Webb could sit down. Webb shrugged, looked at the menu and changed the order to a chicken salad sandwich and sauntered back across the parking lot.

"Does he fly that Messerschmitt much?" Boyd asked, calm again, watching Delores make Webb's sandwich and finishing a piece of pie.

"Well, they roll that door open and bring it out about once or twice a month. Lately, it's been a lot more often. Dietrich has been adding stuff to it and the Colonel takes it up fairly often to try it out," she said, wiping a wisp of greying blond hair from her eyes with her wrist so as not to get any mayonnaise from Webb's sandwich on it.

"Adding what?"

"I don't know."

"Where does he fly it? Air shows and stuff?"

"No. He used to do that but lately he just flies around here. He likes to fly low so he goes out to his ranch and scares the cattle, I think," she said, laughing to herself at the eccentricities of her boss.

"Who's Dietrich?"

"Oh, he's the colonel's crazy mechanic. Colonel Dupree loves that plane so much he has a full time mechanic just for it. He won't work on anything else. He's an old man. Talks to himself in German," she said, smiling again thinking about the mechanic.

"Well, it's a German plane. That makes sense," Boyd said cheerfully. He had enough information for the moment, no sense pushing until she gets suspicious. He swiveled around on his stool and looked at the operations building. A large transformer was on the power pole behind the building. The wires into it were larger and recently installed, though they ran along the same poles back toward town. Three-phase power meant heavy-duty electrical loads like elevators, machinery, or computers. On top of the building was a small satellite dish, not the kind you get to watch TV.

The sandwich was made and sacked with the pie and Boyd was sipping his third refill of coffee before Webb reappeared. He came out the ramp door and hurried across the tarmac. He looked over at Boyd sitting in the Cafe and made a quick but emphatic nod toward the plane. Boyd paid up and stretched before opening the door.

"Say, we're going to Vegas. Wish us luck."

"I will. Put one down for me," Delores said, lighting a cigarette.

"That Jerry is a tense dude," Webb said when they were started up and taxiing toward the runway. "I stood around the Messerschmitt and listened to the colonel tell all about it and then took the tour of the warbirds he has in back. Then they all went down the hall to a meeting room there. Jerry stood by the door and tried to smile as each one went through the door. I just stood around like I was part of the group. He looked over at me and asked who the hell was I and I said I was just enjoying the tour. He knew who was supposed to be there and who wasn't. It felt real cold after that, so I split. I think he was looking for recorders. He wouldn't let them take anything into the room. No briefcases, cameras, or luggage. He locked it all in an adjoining office. It seemed routine to him, and nobody complained."

"What would he be bringing people in here in groups for?" Boyd asked, taking control of the Cessna so Webb could eat his sandwich.

"Did you ever get pitched by an insurance salesman?" Webb asked, wiping mayonnaise from his chin.

"Couple times."

"Dupree and that blond guy with the big chest both had fresh shoeshines. The smiles and the handshakes and the tour of the building had the feel of a sales meeting," Webb said, opening the top to his coffee and taking a tentative sip.

"Do you suppose Dupree and Blue Jack are selling Amway?" Boyd asked with a laugh.

Webb tensed with laughter and spilled a few drops of coffee in his lap. Then he looked up and at the compass and said, "You're off course. We're supposed to be on a 310 heading. You're at 270."

"Lady back there said Dupree has a ranch due west of here close to the New Mexico border. I thought we could just swing by there and see if we could find it. It won't put us off course but a few miles, Boyd said, continuing on his westward heading.

"I noticed they have three-phase power and a satellite dish. Did you notice anything inside that was unusual?"

"Oh, yeah. Computers; they have a whole room full of computers, and people to run them. They were whirring away. Several women talking on the telephone; with those headsets you use when you want to keep your hands free to write."

"How many computers?"

"A bunch of servers in their own climate-controlled room with a security entrance and then terminals in several other rooms. Half that building is offices and computers. The operations part is fairly small. The museum is in that hanger next door."

Boyd sat with the map folded in his lap and glanced at it frequently while he flew. Webb started in on the pie.

"This ought to be the New Mexico border about here," Boyd said, looking right and left for something to fly toward.

To the north was a rocky outcropping. Surrounding it was mostly range land, the pivots being more easterly. For lack of anything the other way, Boyd turned in that direction. East of the outcropping was a frame ranch house with a well-kept road leading to the paved road further north. There was a satellite dish and several trucks and a van parked in the drive . There was the usual corral and a barn and somebody was riding an all terrain vehicle in circles around the corral.

"Fairly prosperous for a marginal ranch, I'd say," Webb said, looking down at the vehicles and equipment sitting around.

"We're thirty two miles east of Dalhart and north of that little river over there, if we ever need to know," Boyd said, estimating the location from the map and the LORAN. They didn't circle the ranch, just flew by as if they were weekend fliers.

"Hey, that looks like a parachute!" Webb said, finishing his pie and washing it down with the last of the coffee. He pointed toward the low rocky hill that had attracted Boyd's attention at first. Just in front of the hill was a round object with white and orange panels. "Do you suppose somebody punched out?"

"That's a parachute, all right, but it isn't from somebody punching out," Boyd said craning his neck downward as they passed over the hill. "See how it's hung up by those poles? See the sand pit in front and behind it? You've seen that before."

"Yeah, that's a strafing pit. What would he be doing with a strafing pit out here? This isn't part of a bombing range is it?" Webb said, suddenly worried and looking around.

"Not within a hundred miles of here," Boyd said, looking at the map again. He was used to seeing those parachute targets on the bombing range. A parachute makes a fine target and the range officer maintains a microphone just under the target that picks up the supersonic noise of the bullets as they pass and counts the ones that are close enough to pass through the parachute, giving an instant score to the pilot. The hill made a backstop.

"You don't suppose our boy Dupree has the guns in that Messerschmitt, do you?" Boyd said, remembering what Delores said about Dietrich adding something to the aircraft that Dupree had to test.

Was it the ultimate rich man's toy, or something else entirely? Surely he didn't plan to pursue his revolution with one old airplane and a bunch of wealthy retired military men with right wing politics and a lust for action. They talked about it for the next two hours back to Denver, but the mystery remained.

CHAPTER TWENTY SIX

"I wrote a poem." Boyd said, shyly. He had called Colleen at the university in the afternoon.

"Hum. That should be interesting." She was polite, formal.

"Would you like to hear it? It's about clouds," Boyd said, expectantly.

"Does it contain the words white and fluffy?"

"Nope."

"Maybe there is more to you than I thought. Ok. Let's hear it," she said, challenging.

"Not so fast. A poet doesn't just throw out the sweat of his brow over the phone. There must be a mood setting."

"You're proposing a formal poetry reading, in the faculty lounge perhaps? We could make some punch."

"No. I was thinking of taking you up to about 10,000 feet over Arapahoe County and recite it to you while you watch a cumulonimbus build over Boulder tomorrow afternoon," Boyd said, confidently, the plan having been carefully laid the past few days.

"Not in your plane." She said darkly.

"No. I've checked out the aero club plane. It's a Cessna 170; much better for watching clouds."

"Intriguing," she said, thoughtfully.

"Have you ever flown?" He asked simply. He could tell she had taken the hook.

"Just airliners."

"You're gonna love it. I'll pick you up at your place at two."

The clouds built in the plains east of Boulder by early afternoon. It was warm and the plowed fields and pastures had absorbed the bright Colorado sunshine since dawn. The heat rose and finally produced an updraft a mile wide, drawing air from all directions. As this updraft rose to 20,000 feet it cooled, and moisture condensed, forming clouds. Still rising, but now carrying cloud with it, and drawing yet more ground level air into it, a mushroom cumulo-nimbus formed.

More than a mile away, but still too close, Boyd and Colleen marvelled at the boiling cloud, rising, expanding. Their little plane was buffeted by the surrounding turbulence at 10,000 feet as they circled.

"The power; I had no idea. What would happen if we flew in there?" Colleen asked into the intercom as she twisted and leaned forward to look up at the top of the cloud. Though fascinated by the whole adventure she had managed to maintain a businesslike demeanor. The headset, khaki slacks, and simple blouse gave her a professional appearance.

When she sat back up Boyd saw her erect nipples peering through the thin cotton blouse. So, she was enjoying the show. He'd heard how women would become sexually excited in a small plane, especially if they had never flown before.

"We'd be torn apart. Even the largest aircraft stay out of thunderheads. The turbulence can be incredible, not to mention the possibility of hail. You run into hail swirling around in there and it's all over," Boyd said, turning away, remembering the purpose of this trip and searching his shirt pocket for the poem. "I think poetry is appropriate at this point. I must confess, my cloud poem is still in the development stage, but I have, nevertheless, come prepared with a poem about flight."

HIGH FLIGHT

Oh, I have slipped the surly bonds of earth
And danced the skies on laughter-silvered wings;
Sunward I've climbed, and joined the tumbling mirth
Of sun-split clouds – and done a hundred things
You have not dreamed of – wheeled and soared and swung
High in the sunlit silence. Hov'ring there
I've chased the shouting wind along and flung
My eager craft through footless halls of air.
Up, up the long, delirious burning blue
I've topped the windswept heights with easy grace
Where never lark, or even eagle flew.
And, while with silent, lifting mind I've trod
The high untrespassed sanctity of space
Put out my hand, and touched the face of God.

Pilot Officer John Gillespie Magee, Jr.

As he read she looked from him to the cloud and back. At the end she just looked at him, silent for a minute or more.

"The bombs aren't even a part of it, then. It's flight."

"Bingo! Pilot Officer John Gillespie Magee, Jr. wrote that poem during World War II. He was killed just a few days after he finished it. His Spitfire was made to chase Germans, but when there were no Germans around he could fling his, 'Eager craft through footless halls of air.' What a kick!"

"It isn't just a kick. It's more," she said, looking back at the cloud then turning back. Ahead was the vast expanse of the eastern plains of Colorado in a vista that showed well the demarcation between the irrigated cropland along the Platte River as it gave way to the lighter green of the same buffalo grass that fed the vast herds of bison during the last century. Behind them the snow-capped front range of the Rocky Mountains loomed, and Denver lay, belching its brown cloud, just out her side window.

"How much is this?" she asked, resting her hand on the weight, eying the bench. It was later that evening, in the spare bedroom of Boyd's house where he kept his weight bench.

"Each of those big round ones is forty five pounds and there are two on each end so that's one eighty and the bar weighs forty five so it's a total of two twenty-five."

"Can I see you lift it?" Colleen asked, then added, "With your shirt off?"

Boyd laughed deeply, leaning back against the wall for support and looking at Colleen. "You naughty lady," he said, still shaking with mirth. He pulled off his shirt. Then he added, "I need to warm up a bit first; especially with a belly full of steak and beer." He dropped quickly to the floor and did a half dozen slow pushups followed by another half dozen quick ones, then did three where he pushed up quickly and clapped his hands before going down for another.

Boyd positioned himself on the bench and lifted the bar for three slow bench presses.

Colleen watched hungrily from across the room. She removed her halter top and nodded at him to do it again.

He complied, eyes on her, marveling at the contradictions of pacifist, literature professor, and horny bitch all in one fine package.

She approached the bench and kneeled at the end of it by his feet. She leaned up and grabbed the top of his shorts and slowing pulled them down while her eyes held his. Boyd's heart pounded with the exertion, the heavy meal and the sexual tension. He did three more presses while she unlaced his shoes and removed them and the shorts. He could feel the strength in his arms, augmented by the extra blood flow from lifting the weights. Her eyes scanned him up and down and then stopped, locked on his eyes as she stepped out of her shorts and kicked them across the room.

"Again," she said huskily.

He complied, eyes on her nude body, watching her watch him. With the third press she stepped closer and lifted her leg over the bench, straddling it. He set the bar back down. She scanned his upper body once more and then looked into his eyes as she lowered her torso onto his.

"Once more," she said as they touched.

Eight Ball stared at the two humans standing in the back yard nude except for their high tech running shoes. The lights in the house were all off and the lights of Denver gave the sky an eerie pink glow. The moon, Venus, Jupiter, and Mars were in the low western sky in an unusual and much publicized configuration. Airline traffic had stopped for the moment and the only noise was the breeze gently moving the leaves on the three or four sickly elms in the yard. The nearest house was two miles away and there hadn't been any traffic on the gravel road in front since before they ate their steaks. Boyd and Colleen each held a paper cup filled with ice cream, taking spoonfuls from the cups to their mouths without looking down. Their eyes were on the stars, and each other.

CHAPTER TWENTY SEVEN

Boyd waved at the secretary and scanned his ID badge to open the door to the back office area of the Secret Service office. He was a regular now, having been a Special Agent for all of a week. He'd briefed Crowder on Luther Dupree and his new accomplice Jack Anders the night he returned from the Dalhart trip. It was now the following Monday afternoon. The accident board had taken the morning, still caught up in dikes and turbine blades.

Marv Crowder heard him come in and was halfway up the hall to greet him, a sheaf of papers in his hand. "We hit paydirt! There's a mortgage in the system on John Rigdon's land."

"Crap!" Boyd said, he now considered John Rigdon a friend and was sorry to see him involved in this mess.

"Crap hell! This is the brass ring." Crowder closed the door and motioned for Boyd to pull up a chair. "Look at this." He spread the papers on the desk. "The Mortgage Electronic Registration System has assigned a Mortgage Identification Number to John Rigdon's ranch, and the ServicerID of the loan servicer shows that Boston Atlantic Fidelity is collecting the payments and forwarding them to the ultimate owner of the mortgage."

"But, there is no mortgage."

"There is a mortgage, for $5 million and its dated December of last year."

"Back dated?"

"Six payments have been made."

"Assuming there is a mortgage, and John didn't take it out, and John didn't make the payments, who did, and why? And, who got the $5 million?"

"This is scary," Crowder said, taking his seat and leaning forward. "The first fraud we discovered in the mortgage loan mess was where the mortgage makers made sub-prime loans and sold them to the big Wall Street banks at a discount and the banks bundled them in with solid, conforming loans and sold the package as AAA assets. Billions of dollars were made selling risky sub-prime paper as good loans. But that's not what's happening here. Boston Atlantic Fidelity is a small loan servicer in Boston with an incredible 99% on-time payment rate with loans they service. They are solidly in the cream of the crop of loan servicers and command top dollar when they sell mortgages; no discounts."

"A reputable company has John's mortgage?"

"An apparently reputable company; this is brilliant! If this is a fraudulent mortgage, it's a Ponzi scheme. Mortgages go bad when the payments aren't made, but what if the payments always get made? Nobody complains when one 360th of the loan amount plus a half a percent interest is made every month. If a loan servicer sends along that much every month the loan sits in a mortgage backed security for 30 years, so the homeowner need never know there is a fake mortgage on their property because nobody is going to foreclose; everybody is happy."

"How do they make money off that?"

"Let's say you buy a small mortgage company that's been around a few years and you create ten fake mortgages worth a million dollars among the hundreds of real mortgages made during the year. It only takes $80,000 to make a year's worth of payments on a million dollar's worth of mortgages; you sell the mortgages as good, current mortgages and keep the money. The next year you sell $5 million worth of fake mortgages; you need only $480,000 to make the payments on the mortgages from the first two years and $800,000 for the third year, but by now you've sold $16 million dollars worth of mortgages."

"Doesn't anyone look at the mortgages, individually?"

"That's what MERS eliminated, the due diligence of an investment banker going over the mortgages one by one, checking the county tax stamps and checking to make sure they had all been filed properly. It was a dull, tedious business and the bankers wanted something faster so they lobbied congress and got MERS."

"Wasn't there any pushback?"

"There must have been, it took twenty years."

"How does this tie in with what Dupree and Polk are doing?"

"The timing is sure suspicious. We're checking to see who the principals are in Boston Atlantic Fidelity. If this is what I think it is we might find Mr. Dupree has an interest. I'll bet they started out running a right-wing political organization, and then discovered the trove of personal identity information they had and got into identity theft. Only they leaped to the front of the pack with how they used the information. No tawdry credit card purchase, or fake bank drafts; that's amateur stuff. The mark is pretty quick to make a fuss when he sees something funny in his monthly statement. No, this requires an insider's insider to beat the fraud barrier at MERS; they claimed to be completely secure."

"Claimed?"

"There are fake mortgages in the system, we don't know haw many. We don't know if it's $50 million or $50 Billion, or more. We don't know for sure if Rigdon's is a fake. He told you he didn't have a mortgage, but people aren't always telling the truth about things like that."

"Dupree has a new Gulfstream aircraft; that's a $20 million toy. He didn't get that by skimming donations to a political party."

"Here's what scares me," Marv said, standing and looking out the window. "He's not hiding. Why isn't he hiding?"

The two men were silent for a minute.

"I have something else scary to share," Boyd interrupted their reverie. "I got Dupree's military personnel file. He's not a retired colonel; he was riffed as a major."

"Riffed?"

"He was separated by a Reduction in Force; it happens every few years during a military downsizing. They find they have too many mid-grade officers so they have a board and cut some of them. He was an instructor pilot in Mississippi, teaching cadets to fly the T-38. It can be quite a shock to suddenly be unemployed in mid-career. Imagine being Dupree and watching Polk rocket to stardom and then finding out you've been cut loose. You asked me to find out what Dupree loves, what drives him. I'm afraid it's revenge."

CHAPTER TWENTY EIGHT

Dawn on Saturday found Boyd back at Culpepper Aviation in LaSalle, helping Ben Culpepper reload the King Cat. On the third run he pitched up a cold diet Coke for Ben to drink while he connected the hose to the side of the big crop duster and turned on the electric pump to deliver 500 gallons of an organophosphate insecticide mixed with water. In five minutes the tank was full and Boyd disconnected the hose and caught the empty diet coke bottle as Ben dropped it down.

Ben gave him a thumbs up and a snappy salute as Boyd backed away. The big engine came to life, blowing debris around the hanger behind them and the plane taxied to the end of the field. As the King Cat cleared the trees at the end of the runway it turned right, toward town instead of left, toward the field he was to spray. Boyd watched, perplexed for a moment.

He saw the plane make a circle, gaining a few hundred feet of altitude, then turn back toward the field and fly along the county road. A quarter mile from the field Boyd saw the King Cat dive toward the road and then pull up and roll once before gaining additional altitude and heading east. Henrietta Flick's black Camaro came into view and turned into the drive.

"Quite the show off, isn't he?" Boyd asked with a laugh, opening the door for Henrietta.

"No. Quite the man," she said, raising her eyebrows and giving Boyd a conspirational smile. She had her hair up in a braid and was wearing a denim jumpsuit with a red belt and red leather western boots. This was Henrietta's idea of work clothes. "Got some lunch for you guys," she added, nodding toward a Styrofoam cooler in the back seat. Boyd reached in and picked it up. It had a promising heft. He turned to watch Henrietta walk toward the office. He made a mental wager with himself that when Ben came back he would shut down the King Cat and climb down to have a closer look at Henrietta in her work clothes. He was right.

During the break Ben unlocked a filing cabinet and got his books out for Henrietta, and when he and Boyd went back out to start dusting again she was deep into them. A few more runs and they were through for the day.

"When you make your calls today, you'd better call these three too. They really ought to pay something now. You're carrying them too long. I know most of them and they're not going hungry," she said, reading glasses perched on her nose like Boyd's first grade teacher.

Lunch was chicken and dumplings, fried okra and biscuits washed down with iced tea out of a full gallon jug Henrietta had brought along. Just as they were finishing, a shiny black

Cadillac pulled into the drive and a stately white-haired man got out. He was dressed in a linen blazer with summer-weight wool slacks and expensive loafers. Not a hair was out of place as he opened the door and walked in.

"George. Come in. We're just finishing some of Henrietta's famous chicken," Ben said with genuine pleasure as he crossed the room to shake hands. Henrietta smiled but remained seated at the desk where she had eaten a small amount of her own cooking. Boyd was surprised at the lack of awkwardness in this unusual situation.

"This is Boyd Chailland, a pilot friend of mine who's helping out with the loading today. Boyd, this is my old friend George Flick." They shook hands.

George seemed to be troubled about something but smiled amicably.

"Sorry to butt in, but I need Henrietta for a second. It's her weekend and we've just had a call," he said, most apologetically.

She rose and they walked toward the door, heads together, speaking in low tones. She nodded and took a piece of paper from him. He looked the quintessential funeral director, grey, composed, concerned, and in control.

"I'll go out about three. Don't worry. I'll take care of it," Henrietta said, looking at her watch and putting her hand on his back, as if to encourage him toward the door. He looked relieved, bent over and kissed her chastely on the forehead, then left.

"Poor man; he's been planning his weekend in Denver for weeks. Just can't relax," she said, returning to her friends but not to her carefree mood of moments before. She left soon after to make the arrangements for a funeral on Monday. Boyd and Ben opened the hanger and rolled out the P-51.

"I called the insurance company. They approved you flying it. Want to?" Ben asked, looking at Boyd with a big smile.

"Yes sir!" Boyd returned instantly. He'd not expected this, but was prepared with four hundreds in his wallet for gas, just in case.

Ben took a lot more time going over the instruments and emergency procedures than he had the King Cat. Being an older and far more unforgiving aircraft, not to mention several times more valuable, the Mustang required more effort to learn.

"The one thing you have to remember – and I know I've told you three times already, and you've probably read it too – Don't give it full power all at once on the ground or at an airspeed less than 130 knots. It will roll so fast you won't believe it and you don't have the aileron to correct for it. You have 1,500 horses there and the plane doesn't weigh 6,000 lbs. The torque from that engine is incredible. So, don't come in slow and get in a panic and hit the power to go around. Think," Ben said, standing on the wing.

Boyd was strapped in, having declined the parachute. He didn't expect to be shot at, and if the thing quit, his chances would be better landing in a field anyway.

"Don't get too low. This is not a big-winged crop duster. This is made for thinner air," Ben said with a smile, enjoying Boyd's excitement. "Get up about 10,000 feet. Do some turns and rolls and try some dives but hold on the loops for awhile. You don't want to stall this thing. It is very hard to recover when it stalls. It snaps right in a rough sort of roll and just keeps on doing that, losing five or six thousand feet every time. It doesn't recover just by letting go. Be careful."

When there was nothing left to say Ben climbed down from the wing and hooked up the auxiliary power unit to start the engine. The big four blade prop turned a few times then the engine coughed and spit out some black puffs of smoke and then it caught and Boyd could feel the aircraft come alive as the power of the engine and propellers rattled his very bones. He checked the gauges and adjusted his straps. Ben gave him the thumbs up after checking again externally. Boyd slowly eased the throttle forward and taxied down the grass to the end of the runway. There he rechecked his gauges and tried a slow run-up of the engine. When he was sure all was well he turned onto the runway and taxied down the length of it, achieving only fifty knots or so. He repeated that three more times before giving the plane take off power and lifting off. Airborne at last in a P-51!

The noise was worse than in any aircraft he'd ever flown. Ben had warned him about this but it was still a concern. Surely, he thought, pilots hadn't had to put up with this much noise. He'd worn his earplugs, and had the helmet too, but now he could understand why old pilots have trouble hearing everything their wives say.

Boyd found the response sluggish compared with his Falcon, but with a shorter turning radius than the T-38 he'd flown in pilot training. He gave it throttle and easily achieved 350 knots airspeed level at 10,000 feet. A tight turn took both hands on the stick, instead of just a flick of his wrist in the Falcon. He tried a split S and was gratified the way the plane changed directions and accelerated in a dive, good to have if someone was after you. Before he knew it, the allotted half hour had passed. He did a downwind leg and one low approach before throttling down and landing, smoothly.

"How was one of these armed?" Boyd asked, helping Ben roll it back into the hanger. Thunderstorms were threatening in the west.

"Six 50-caliber machine guns in the wings," Ben answered. "A lot of guys take the space where they were and add a fuel tank and a baggage compartment. I just left it the way it was."

"Fairly substantial firepower."

"The 50-caliber slug would go through any aircraft of its day, bombers included. It didn't have the explosive punch of the 20-millimeter cannon, but we didn't have to try to shoot down B-29s. In a dogfight with another fighter – which is what this was built for – you only have a second or two to do the job. Better to have six rapid-fire fifties to fill the sky with lead."

"What happened to the guns that were here?" Boyd asked, idly putting his finger over the plastic cap screwed into the port where the barrel had protruded from the wing.

"The government took the guns out before they sold surplus fighters. They didn't want somebody arming a revolution or an invasion with them. At the time they were fairly cheap. The engine is what people really wanted. That Rolls Royce Merlin engine has run many a racing boat and even a few dragsters. Really, it's what made the fighter what it was. When they originally designed it, back in the thirties, they had a smaller engine, and it wasn't any better than the other planes we had. The Germans and Japs both would have chewed it up. You know as well as I do, in a dogfight when you're really mixing it up in tight turns with another plane, it's power that makes the difference, either to get a kill or get away. There is no substitute." Ben gave a last shove to get the Mustang in the right position in the hanger.

"That's what makes the difference with the Falcon," Boyd said. "It's got a big engine and it's made out of light composite. The body doesn't weigh as much as your car. It'll turn all day and stay up." Boyd leaned against the side of the fuselage. He felt a bit reluctant to lean against the prop of a piston aircraft that was still hot. He'd heard stories of a cylinder just firing spontaneously and giving the prop a quick half turn.

"Could a guy get machine guns for a plane like this? I mean, are there even any in existence?" Boyd asked, coming back to the subject again.

Ben looked quizzically at Boyd and then smiled. "Anything can be had for a price. There are plenty of 50-caliber machine guns around. It's illegal as hell to own one, of course, but arms merchants sell them to anyone with the price. You could arm this plane in no time. If the Alcohol, Tobacco, and Firearms people caught you, they'd confiscate the plane – a fairly stiff penalty."

"Could you get the ammunition?" Boyd asked, thinking about Dupree.

"Oh yeah; 50-caliber ammunition is plentiful and cheap, not out in the open, of course. There are a few legal ways to get it," Ben said, pulling down the hanger door as the thunderstorm hit, blowing leaves into the stall with the Mustang. A bolt of lightning hit less than a mile away, punctuating their talk of firearms.

"How about 20-millimeter cannon ammunition?" Boyd asked, throwing down some kitty litter to absorb oil dripping beneath the plane.

"That's even easier than the 50-caliber. You know how many 20-millimeter cannon shells the US military must shoot off in just one month? Hell, there must be scores of manufacturers in the world. Of course, now you have an absolute illegality in even possessing one shell. If Billy Joe Redneck is bouncing down a back road with some 50-caliber ammunition in his pickup and one goes off, it really isn't much different from a deer rifle. But, if he has a 20-millimeter cannon shell and it goes off, it's going to peel open his truck like a sardine can, and maybe kill everyone in it…. What's this sudden interest in armament?"

Boyd enlarged on the story Ben already knew about Freeman/Dupree to include the Messerschmitt and the strafing pit.

"So that bastard has guns in his Messerschmitt? That would be a kick. I wonder where he got the plane. There are so few left, and the museums in Europe – especially in Germany – will pay almost any price to acquire one," Ben said with a grand smile, appreciating the pride of ownership of something so rare, and the fun of being able to actually fire a machine gun again in practice.

"On the surface it seems like just a rich man's toy, but there are some sinister elements to this I can't discuss with you. It's really for your own protection," Boyd explained, feeling guilty already.

"Oh, I understand. Still, it piques the interest. The Messerschmitt was a great airplane. Depending on which of the Daimler-Benz engines it has, it could have up to 1,500 horsepower, though the vast majority of Messerschmitts were in the 1,200 to 1,300 range."

"How do you know so much about the Messerschmitt?" Boyd asked as they left the hanger and entered the office. The rain was pelting the parking lot with big drops, suggesting that hail could start any moment.

"Air shows, books, museums, talking with other warbird enthusiasts. As we fighter pilots get older, we get more fascinated by the history of our profession, and those men and machines that are a part of it," Ben said, getting the keys for the Coke machine and opening it up. He tossed Boyd a Silver Bullet and took one himself. It had been a long hot day and both men were tired and thirsty. The two beers were gone in a couple long draws. Ben grabbed a couple refills. Then he added, "I have a confession."

"What's that?"

"I have the guns for the Mustang. They came with it when I bought it. I've never put them in, but they're back there in the closet. Just for completeness, I guess," Ben said wistfully.

"Wow! I don't suppose you tell many people that," Boyd said, realizing now, if there had been any doubt after flying the Mustang, how complete Ben's trust in him was.

CHAPTER TWENTY NINE

Boyd's bedside clock radio was set to a local radio station that usually came on with the national news, slowly piercing his consciousness: "Congressman Roscoe Kelly, Chairman of the House Financial Services Committee has been tied to mortgage fraud in Boston! The Boston Herald broke the story this morning that the SEC is investigating Boston Atlantic Bank for securities fraud in connection with its wholly own subsidiary, Boston Atlantic Fidelity. BAF is accused of selling a fraudulent $5 million mortgage bundled in with other agricultural loans to Deutsche Bank last month. William T. Hanrahan, a major stockholder in the Boston Atlantic Bank and a close personal friend and major financial backer of Congressman Kelly, has released a statement through his attorney."

"What?" Boyd responded sleepily. He looked at the clock; 6 AM. A moment later his telephone rang.

"Boyd, turn on your TV!" It was Marv Crowder.

Boyd fumbled with the light, and then found the remote.

"…and denies wrongdoing by his client and assures the many and loyal customers of Boston Atlantic Bank that it remains a rock of stability in the Boston and national economy. Furthermore, he adds that this irresponsible reporting of a routine inquiry by an oversight agency has blown this whole matter out of proportion. He is confident that..."

"Boyd! Did you blow the whistle about Boston Atlantic Fidelity?"

"No," still struggling to concentrate as he sat on the side of the bed.

"We just called the SEC three days ago."

"Wasn't me."

"My boss has been breathing fire through the phone line this morning, accusing me of leaking this to the press. This has hit big back east. Apparently Kelly has political enemies in Boston and they're all over him."

"Never heard of Roscoe Kelly," Boyd said, balancing the phone on his shoulder as he measured coffee into his coffee pot.

"You would have if you were a banker. He's the guy who pushed the MERS legislation through congress. We found a rat, just not the one we expected. Listen, don't talk to anyone about this. Don't let anyone at the base know you've had anything to do with this, and don't call John Rigdon. We'll get back to him when this gets clearer, OK?"

"Sure."

"Look, there's something else. Yesterday, late, I got a call. I'm getting transferred. I don't know when. It's a promotion, I think. Uh, you may be getting a new boss here."

"Something we did?"

"I hope not. Look, there's a battle going on in Washington. I haven't talked to my boss there twice since I've been here, two years, and now twice in twenty four hours. It's all behind the scenes, but I can hear it in his voice, he's scared. I'm still in charge here, and I'm telling you to run with this thing. Find out what you can as fast as you can."

CHAPTER THIRTY

"This is crazy! I can't believe I'm going off on an unknown venture with you two oddballs to the wilds of Texas," Colleen said as she dropped her backpack onto the back seat of Boyd's new Chevy half ton pickup. Boyd was on the other side trying to accommodate her suitcase next to his on the floor behind the front seat.

"Think of it as a patriotic adventure," Boyd said, checking once more to be sure everything was stowed and ready. "Webb's leaving this afternoon in the aero club plane and should get down there about the time we do. I figure we'll drive and won't have to rent a car."

"And we're going to Texas to do what?"

"Look, uh. I need to come clean on something." He pulled out his Special Agent badge. "I'm kind of a double agent, I'm still in the Air Force, but we found something funny on the accident board and I've been sort of deputized."

"Something funny? Oh, I get it. That Colonel Freeman," she smiled, seeing her initial suspicions about any right wing organization verified.

"Yeah, it's complicated. Freeman isn't his real name. I tracked it down, he's Luther Dupree and he owns an aircraft service and leasing company in Dalhart. We're just going down there for a couple days to, uh,"

"Spy on him?"

"Well, uh, yeah."

"OK." Colleen nodded, mulling this new information, then pointing to a small cooler between the front seats, she asked, "Beer?"

"They have beer in Texas, that's iced tea," Boyd said, getting in and adjusting the mirrors and seat belts glad she hadn't grilled him more about the trip. He had made a special trip to Greeley the afternoon before just to get a gallon of Henrietta Flick's iced tea. One must be prepared when one faces the unknown.

"You are a consummate persuader to get me to go to Texas instead of preparing my lecture outline for the first Literature of the Oppressed Minorities course I'm to teach in two weeks." Colleen said, stowing a briefcase under her seat as Boyd backed out of her drive in Boulder.

"That would include Jews in Europe, Christians in Arabia, and white males in contemporary American society, then," Boyd said, feigning fascination.

"No, dear," Colleen said, patient with his little joke. "That would include women, blacks, hispanics, and homosexuals in contemporary American society. I think we've had quite enough from the white males. I'm sure the libraries of our grandchildren's day will not be housing classic library editions of Mickey Spillane, Tom Clancy, or Elmore Leonard."

"They'll have Rita Mae Brown? There is one horny lady."

"You know Rita Mae Brown?" Colleen asked.

"Sure. You said she was one of the bright stars of women's literature, and, ever anxious to experience the best of the printed word, I found her at my local library. I must say, she's been a busy girl," Boyd said with a mischievous grin, pulling onto Interstate 25 and heading south.

"You men have detailed your sexual exploits since the dawn of time. Why should women be any different," Colleen said, slightly on the defensive for the first time in Boyd's memory.

"I don't think there is anything wrong with it. I was just wondering if she can type and pull the hairs out from between her teeth at the same time."

Colleen slapped him on the leg and looked out the window to hide her smile. She was shaking her head.

"See if I discuss literature with a fighter pilot again," she said, looking back at Boyd. His attention was directed to the road ahead as they approached the congestion of the Denver metropolitan area.

"Why are we doing this instead of the FBI? When you called the other night and invited me on this trip I accepted just for the lark of it. Is it serious.?"

"It seems there is some financial services fraud going on, that's Secret Service not FBI, so the Air Force had the Secret Service make me a Special Agent. Dupree has a well financed operation in Texas that has right wing political aspirations. Your friend John Rigdon may be a part of it."

"John is a simple rancher. He wouldn't have anything to do with something like that."

"You know he's involved. You saw him standing there with Dupree. And you know Dupree collected money that night. John himself told me it was over ten thousand dollars. What's Dupree doing with all that? But, there's more. Somebody is monkeying with a mortgage on John's ranch. We don't know yet who that is. So, something's up and we don't know who the good guys are and who the bad guys are. But, there's more, and it gets scary."

"That bank in Boston?"

"Forget you ever heard about that bank in Boston," Boyd said, looking Colleen in the eyes, beginning to wish he'd done this alone.

"This is big. Okay. I'll do my part. What is it?"

"When Webb was inside last week, someone opened a door right by where he was standing, waiting with the men who were there for the meeting. He got a look inside the office complex. They had several phone operators and one of them was speaking Spanish. We thought you might follow some of the office people and try to meet them someplace else and see if you could find out anything about what they do there."

"Do I speak Spanish?" she asked, hostile again.

"I'll bet you do." Boyd said with a pleasant, benign smile.

"Just because I have an hispanic surname, I'm assumed to speak Spanish?"

Boyd gave her a blank look.

"What if I only speak English?" She said, angry.

"Then we'll have to rely on your powers of persuasion in English; and that should be adequate," he said, unruffled yet, and beginning to enjoy grating on her feminist sensitivities.

"And my mother is Irish!" she said, angry beyond a mere debate.

"So was mine," Boyd said simply. The past tense in his statement stopped her, for the moment.

The sun rose on a dry Colorado August day. They sat in silence through Colorado Springs and almost to Pueblo. As the day warmed, the warm dry air coming in through the open windows began to make the prospect of something cold to drink ever more appealing. Boyd opened the cooler and produced the gallon of iced tea and two of those huge plastic glasses convenience stores sell soft drinks in. In addition there was a bag of ice and four fresh sprigs of mint. He offered a glass to Colleen.

"You thoughtful man. I would be delighted to help you learn more about Mr. Dupree's business in whatever language you need."

The trip over Raton Pass and then across the descending plains of eastern New Mexico, passing close to the spent Capulin Mountain, took a little longer by car than when Boyd and Webb had done it in the Cessna two weeks before. Boyd saved the difficult revelation until they were so close as to make turning back seem silly.

"Could you open that map there in the glove compartment?" he said, matter of factly.

Colleen found a map of New Mexico and another of Texas and inquired which one he meant.

"Probably need both. We'll be in Clayton in a few minutes. Look south of there to the Punta de Agua river. We need to find a road that will put us just north of the river on the Texas-New Mexico border."

"Why?" she asked, looking at the New Mexico map.

"That's where you drop me off," Boyd said, braced for the storm.

"Drop you off? I came along to drop you off for some hike in the boonies?" she said, too surprised to be as angry as she was likely to get momentarily.

"No!" Boyd said, glad to get this unexpected moment to explain. "Dupree has something funny going on at his ranch west of Dalhart. He flies an old World War II fighter plane out there and has target practice on his own private bombing range. In addition, a lot of people are staying out there, and there aren't any cattle. I'm going to spend one, maybe two nights out there to see what's up. You are going to go into town, check into the motel alone, shuttle me some food and water, and feather the nest for my return tomorrow or the next day," he said, breathless from saying it all in one sentence.

"Bullshit!" she said, throwing the maps onto the floor. Boyd had expected something a bit more eloquent from a professor of literature.

"Look, you're checking into Dupree's motel there in Dalhart. If he gets a wee bit suspicious and calls down there and hears a Boyd Chailland from Denver checked in, he's gonna know it's me. When he told me to keep quiet about what he told me about his Patriot Party he looked me in the eye with a cold stare that came from the gut. I don't know who our senior leadership in Washington think they're dealing with, but they haven't ever had a heart-to-heart with Luther Dupree. He is smarter and tougher than anyone I've ever met, and I've been in the smart-and-tough business. Whatever it is he is doing in Dalhart is bad. We want to see it from a distance and get out."

The seriousness and emotion of Boyd's retort took the anger out of Colleen and she recovered the maps and found a road.

"I'm going to sleep with Webb," she said.

"He isn't your type."

"Oh? How would you know?"

"When you'd do that trick you have of grabbing at his leg to get him to pull it back out of the way so you can dump him on his back and then jump on him with all that hair and tits; that'd be the end of it with him. The fight would go right out of him. You'd have him pinned so quick you wouldn't even break a sweat."

"You think you know so much," she said, attention back on the map.

A narrow two lane blacktop snaked across the open country south out of Clayton and intersected a similar road that took them east into Texas. As they crossed the border Boyd stopped the truck and climbed into the bed and then, carefully onto the roof to stand and look both ways with binoculars. He saw the rocky outcropping a few miles to the south. A gravel road left the blacktop and headed for it.

"The ranch is about ten miles down this road, and it's a dead end. Drop me off over there. Webb will be coming in about 4:30 this afternoon; quitting time. Wait for him at Dupree Aviation, but also keep an eye out for who leaves about that time. Maybe you can meet someone. Tomorrow night, after dark, bring me this filled with water and some food," he said, handing her an empty collapsible gallon jug. "Go down this road about two miles, no more. If anyone comes by while you're waiting, make out with Webb," he stopped the car and grabbed his backpack.

Inside the bedroll was his survival knife with its heavy leather scabbard. There was a nine millimeter automatic inside the pack. He left it there lest he alarm his companion any more than necessary.

The road was a ribbon of black, shimmering in the heat in both directions. Boyd kicked off the old running shoes he had worn driving and slipped off his khaki shorts. Standing on the edge of the blacktop in his boxers he opened the pack and removed Levis and put them on, followed by some light-weight hiking boots and the leather belt threaded through the scabbard of his survival knife. He re-packed the shorts and running shoes and shouldered the pack frame.

"There's some money in a bank envelope in the glove compartment. You and Webb should use it for all expenses. It's the money from my expense draw from the Secret Service. No sense using our money for this. When we finish here in a couple days we can spend the rest of it at the Broadmoor on the way back," This somewhat hollow sounding promise at the end did nothing to soften Boyd's sense of having pulled a fast one on Colleen.

"What if I stayed out here with you?" she said, hopefully.

"Maybe tomorrow night, if things look quiet over there tonight," he said, nodding toward the south.

"I thought you said you were coming back in tomorrow night?"

"Probably. Depends on what's out here."

She nodded, surprisingly agreeable and shifted into low. Boyd leaned into the window and gave her a chaste kiss. She threw her arm around his neck and pulled his head back into the jeep for one that contained considerable promise. He stepped back and she released the clutch and headed toward Dalhart.

It was a wonder the cattle found enough to eat to stay alive. Nearly every growing thing had thorns on it. The predominant growth was prickly pear and yucca, with some clumps of buffalo grass, now dried in late summer and scattered far apart. Boyd vaulted the fence and walked away from the road, to the west. As the sound of the car retreated he was left with just the crunch of his boots on the coarse, sandy ground and the buzzing of an occasional fly. After a mile he felt he was no longer visible from either road and turned south.

In less time than he would have thought necessary he encountered the rocky outcropping. From the ground it was far more impressive than from the air. A hundred feet high and composed primarily of large and small boulders pushing up out of the soil, it was a mile long and several hundred yards wide. The boulders offered constant opportunity for shade and sufficient cover to hide, even from the air. Boyd made his way to the top and surveyed Dupree's ranch. A fence line ran from the center of the rock north and south in both directions. Could someone have decided, long ago, this was to be the western edge of Texas and drawn the map accordingly? There was certainly nothing else of note to call a landmark. The ranch house was barely visible some five miles farther south. Midway between the two was a functioning windmill and a large stock tank. Scattered about was mesquite, which is a large evergreen shrub or small tree.

Directly east of the highest point of the rocks was the parachute, tethered to two sturdy poles. Both poles were thoroughly riddled with bullet holes. Climbing down to the site, Boyd encountered numerous chips in rock from rico- chets and long shots. It had not been necessary to put a sand pit to catch most of the bullets behind the parachute. The ground was soft enough to accomplish that on its own. Boyd inspected both poles for signs of anything larger than the 3.92 millimeter Mauser ammunition the Messerschmitt had most commonly fired from the light machine guns in front of the pilot. A 20-millimeter shell would have blown the pole down. Scratching around in the dirt behind the parachute he quickly dug up several spent bullets and saved them for whatever analysis might later be needed. He climbed back into the rocks and cleared the ground for several yards in all directions, making certain there were no burrows or holes under rocks for a rattlesnake to be hiding. He didn't want to wake up in the middle of the night and get a big surprise. West Texas is noted for cattle and cowboys and rattlesnakes; big ones. He stowed his gear in unobtrusive fashion among the rocks, then made two peanut butter and jelly sandwiches and drank some water. He lay in the shade with his head on his bedroll and was soon asleep.

The sun was low in the western sky and shadows were long when Boyd awoke from his nap. A red glow reflected from some clouds back over the Rockies gave the rocks and the sandy ground a different look. Boyd could see lights on in the ranch house. He preferred to make it there before dark. No sense risking stepping on one of those rattlesnakes coming and going. He put on a dark long sleeve shirt and a black baseball cap. He decided to leave the 9 millimeter on this first trip. It would look better if he actually met someone if he could pretend to be a lost hiker. He did take the knife and his Secret Service badge.

Approaching the house just as the western sky turned from midnight blue to black, Boyd stopped to listen and take stock of the situation. There was a spacious two story ranch house with a barn to the side big enough to have housed some horses and some machinery. He saw a corral on the other side of the barn but no sign of any animals. Behind the house was a shed with glass on the south side and a steeply sloping roof and a chicken coop that was also vacant. The yard was fenced with a typical barbed wire stock fence, down in a couple places where someone had apparently driven a car through it. A silver propane tank was just inside the fence. Several window air conditioners made a reassuring background noise. Across the drive to the house, barely visible in the moonlight and about two hundred yards away was a pole barn with open sides and a stage at one end, like a picnic pavilion. Beside it was a sturdy steel building about as big as a two car garage; both looked new.

Boyd approached through the backyard, his attention on the lighted window, from which he could hear voices and see figures moving inside. Halfway across the yard he froze, stopped by a smell that changed this situation completely.

"Dog shit!" he whispered to himself, lifting his foot to find the offending substance adhering to his boot. It was fresh and the size of the pile indicated he might be dealing with a substantial sized animal at any moment. He looked around to see a house or other place of habitation that might come alive. There was none. Maybe the dog was inside. He took two more steps and could clearly see inside the house. Three men sat at a dining room table while a fourth entered the kitchen and got a beer from the refrigerator.

Boyd took another step and brushed a clump of grass. He heard the faint sound of a chain tinkling from the barn and turned to see a German shepherd, alerted by the noise. For a moment they both stood there; the shepherd sizing him up to see if he were one of the men from inside; Boyd judging the distance between him and the dog and between him and the fence.

They both jumped at the same instant. With a growl the dog was in motion toward Boyd, head down and running all out. Boyd covered the ten feet to the fence in three strides then put one hand on the metal fencepost and lightly vaulted over. The fence was four strands of barbed wire reinforced every few feet with a vertical strand of thicker wire to keep it from sagging. This would not stop the dog. Boyd accelerated from the fence at full speed, faster than he'd ever run on the track or football field. As he ran he yanked the front of his shirt open, popping the buttons, and pulled out one arm, then the other. He heard the dog hit the fence and struggle to get through. He wrapped the shirt around his left hand and wrist while running at full speed. He heard the dog get through the fence and give another low growl as he accelerated. He'd evidently been trained to attack and not waste time barking.

Thirty yards from the fence and only fifteen yards ahead of the dog, Boyd turned and dropped to his right knee, drawing his knife. The dog covered the distance in three bounds and without hesitation went snarling for Boyd's throat. Just at the top of the arc of the dog's leap Boyd thrust out his left hand, covered with his shirt, and thrust it into the dog's open mouth. As the dog bit down Boyd forcefully rotated the palm down and guided the dog's momentum to his right side. As the dog's feet were off the ground he had no leverage to prevent this from rotating him face up. The dog's momentum hit Boyd's side as he snapped his arm down extending the neck and brought the knife across the exposed throat with all the force his flexed bicep could muster. He felt bone. Blood from the two carotid arteries and both jugular veins sprayed over Boyd's naked chest and arms. The force of the dog's blow knocked Boyd to his back as he started a second sweep of the throat. He encountered a gaping defect, the bottom of which was the front of the dog's cervical spine. The second swipe severed that and Boyd lay panting, listening to the dog's last breath gurgle through his severed trachea.

Boyd was angry at himself for not taking more time before approaching the house. He thought of Eight Ball as he rolled the corpse off of his chest and sat up. He was covered with blood, warm and sticky and strong with the scent of dog. Already there was a puddle congealing between his legs. The dog's head, tongue lolling passively, was attached only by the skin of the back of his neck. While contemplating this unfortunate turn of events Boyd heard the screen door open and someone come down the steps. Shielded momentarily by the chicken coop, Boyd dragged the dog and himself behind a clump of prickly pear and peered through.

"Goddamned dog must've run off again," the man said to the others still inside. He held a western style lever action 30-30 in his right hand and peered down the beam of a flashlight pointed out toward the barn and then out into the prairie. Its feeble rays could not bring enough illumination to bear on the prickly pear for the man to see what lay behind it. The light made a cursory circle of the area and was then switched off. "Every time a deer passes within a hundred yards he's off on a chase. At least he don't bark much," the man said, trying not to be too critical. The dog must have been his. He turned and went back inside.

Shaking from the excitement; half naked and bloody, Boyd decided to retire and regroup later. He carried the carcass of his recent adversary toward the stock tank 2 miles away. He stuffed it under a mesquite bush, hoping the coyotes found it before the men did. The tank was full and the water running at just a trickle as the windmill moved placidly with the thin night breeze. He tested the water and found it reasonably clean so he stripped off his clothes and jumped in. The cool water was refreshing as he stood in it up to his waist scrubbing the blood off his chest and arms. Regaining his composure Boyd floated on his back and watched the half moon light the western sky.

CHAPTER THIRTY ONE

A shadow passed Colleen's window at the Best Western in Dalhart just after she turned out the lamp by the bed. She dismissed it as a late arrival walking to their room. She was about to roll over and close her eyes when she looked back to the closed blinds and saw the shadow had returned. She watched as the shadow of a broad shouldered man lingered in front of her room. Was it Boyd?

The shadow retreated again and she waited. Impatient, thinking he might be getting something out of the truck, which was parked right in front of the room, she got up and went to the door. Leaving the security chain on, she opened the door a crack. It wasn't Boyd.

Right in front of the door, writing down the VIN number from the driver's side of the windshield was a large man with blond, almost white hair. He turned and she looked into the bluest, most intense eyes she had ever seen. A chill went down her spine and she closed the door, locked the deadbolt, and rushed to her cell phone to call Webb, who was in a room on the other side of the motel.

"Webb, get over here, now!"

"What?"

"There's someone outside my door!"

"OK, OK. Lock the door."

Two minutes later Webb knocked on the door, "Colleen, it's me Webb."

The blue eyed man was gone.

CHAPTER THIRTY TWO

It was barely after six the next morning when the Messerschmitt flashed overhead, not a hundred feet above Boyd, who had heard it coming and was crouching in the boulders. He peered from behind a boulder as the plane rose and circled to the south to make another pass. It had been repainted flat black. The Luftwaffe markings were still present but in subdued tones.

Boyd watched with mounting alarm as the old war bird climbed a thousand feet as it circled to the south and then back east before turning and dropping a wing and coming straight at him again. When he saw the plane stabilize in a shallow dive he knew he was in for a strafing run and curled behind a boulder hoping that crazy Dupree hadn't found a bomb someplace to try to drop out here. The clatter of the machine guns was actually reassuring. He could hear the bullets hitting the posts and the ground and the rocks around him, apparently Dupree had lost some of his accuracy as he'd gotten older. The plane roared over even lower than before, way below minimum altitude on any Air Force range. The throaty rumble of that big V-12 added to the prop wash to pierce the morning calm.

After the second pass the Messerschmitt climbed steeper than before and went further west, then began a dive at the farmhouse. Boyd wondered for a moment if he meant to strafe there but it was a dry run, just meant to wake the guys up. The plane rolled coming off the dry run and climbed back for another run at the range. Boyd pressed himself to the back of the boulder again. This time there was none of the clatter of the machine guns but two loud explosions in the dirt in front of the parachute followed immediately by the deeper reports of the cannon actually firing. The shells had impacted and exploded before the sound of their being fired reached Boyd. This was early in the run while the Messerschmitt was still half a mile away. The rest of the run was silent. This was followed by two more runs where nothing was fired. The plane turned toward Dalhart and Boyd was left in silence to ponder the meaning.

That they were 20-millimeter cannon shells was clear to Boyd, even without climbing down and examining the small craters left by their impact. It was also clear to Boyd that the cannon had jammed after firing the two shells. It fired several rounds a second and if you fired it at all you fired more than two rounds. They would probably make some adjustments in the firing mechanism and be back in a few minutes for another try. Boyd looked over at the ranch with his binoculars and saw no sign of activity so he stayed put. Within an hour the Messerschmitt was back for a repeat of the dry flyby and the machine gun pass. On the third pass three cannon shells came slamming into the pit in front of the parachute before the gun jammed. The Messerschmitt rolled in frustration coming off the target. Or did he see something? Boyd covered his head with the olive drab sleeping bag but the plane was headed back toward Dalhart.

Twice more the sleek black warbird made strafing runs with the cannon and each time fired no more than a few rounds before the gun jammed. By mid-morning he was through and Boyd was left in the intense heat alone. He got out his binoculars and studied the land around the house. A bus had arrived and dozens of young men milled about the common area between the house and the newer complex to the south.

At noon Boyd climbed to the top of the rocky outcropping and tried his cell phone. There was just enough service there that he could call Marv Crowder.

"Hey Boyd, how's the camping trip?"

"Hot and dry. What's up with your promotion?"

"Don't know. The Director said I was going to Seattle, the Chief Field Agent said to stay put and find Dupree; seems to be some conflict at the home office."

"Sure got some conflict with the Air Force. That Major General Ferguson that showed up to oversee the accident board a couple weeks ago disappeared the day I went to Washington. Apparently the new ACC commander kicked him back to NATO. We've had the ACC JAG acting as security for every meeting. Weird, a brigadier general is sitting outside the meeting room checking ID."

"We got Dupree's tax returns. Interesting guy."

"I thought that was illegal."

"Not when it comes to national security. Dupree left the Air Force in '85, used his GI Bill to get a masters in finance at LSU. He went to work at a Savings and Loan in Baton Rouge in '87. In '94 he bought into Panhandle Texas Savings and Loan and moved to Amarillo. It took him a few years, but by '99 he was reporting income in the million dollar range."

"That's the year Trusten Polk made brigadier general. When did Dupree get into the aviation business?"

"He opened Dupree Aviation in 2004. He still reports income from Panhandle Texas, and so did Trusten Polk."

"Got their hand in somebody's cookie jar."

"Yeah. I found your guy Jack Anders, too. Homeland Security has a file on him going back ten years. He's been busted a couple times for selling unregistered firearms; got caught with a machine gun, got his picture taken at a skinhead rally in Minneapolis, was photographed again in North Dakota at a militia field exercise where a surveillance team heard machine guns and explosions, probably dynamite. He was booted from the army on a bad conduct discharge. No jail time."

"Petty crook?"

"No, that's the background for a budding revolutionary. They don't rob banks, they trade in weapons and demonstrate, meet, and plot."

"Exercising their constitutional rights."

"That's what they would say. Anyway, we were watching him pretty close and he just disappeared about two months ago."

"Got a picture?"

"Look on your phone."

"Those are some blue eyes. Waitress said they call him Blue Jack."

CHAPTER THIRTY THREE

He was sixteen when he first whipped his father. It hadn't been delayed by any lack of trying; he'd endured broken teeth, ribs, and an arm. He first stepped in front of his mother and took the beating when he was ten. His father was a long haul trucker. To support his family, Lars Anders covered four thousand miles in a week of amphetamine-fueled driving. His truck, a shiny red Diamond Reo, was the envy of the other boys in the neighborhood with its chrome shiny exhaust stacks and high squared front. It represented conflict and pain for Jack.

A big, blue-eyed man with a weakness for everything, Lars would park the truck in the yard and stumble up the steps. He'd hit the refrigerator and grab a six pack, barely acknowledging his wife and child, and retreat to the bathroom. Jack's mother would rush supper, to have something on the table when Lars came out of the bathroom; something to blunt the first six pack before he soaked up the second. A period of normalcy would ensue, where Lars inquired about Jack's progress in school and happenings around town. When he was younger, Jack would be put to bed, to hear the accusations, the anger, the beating, then the fucking; loud and long. When he got older he would rise and insert himself, with painful consequences. The following morning would be apologies, promises, gifts, family outings. Then the cycle would repeat.

His high school football coach sensed Jack's anguish and tutored him in weight lifting and boxing. Jack responded by becoming a standout defensive lineman; big, strong and belligerent. One night, in his sixteenth year, Jack saw again the face of the devil. Contorted with a rage he couldn't control, Lars came at him as he had dozens of times before. This time Jack stopped him with a fist backed by 170 pounds of weight room muscle, and followed it with a well timed boxing lesson that broke Lars' jaw and three of his ribs. Lars had planted the seed of the devil in Jack's soul, and that night Jack felt it; felt that rage well up in him that he'd seen in his father.

Terrified of the demon he knew was within, Jack never touched alcohol. The army was an obvious choice, and Jack left home at 18 with a warning to his father that he'd be back. He was the top troop in boot camp, the honor graduate of infantry training; airborne by age twenty.

Army discipline kept the lid on a culture of angry violent men, and Jack saw that as the key to control. Purity. Purity of body; Jack neither smoked nor drank, ate no red meat, and worked out to exhaustion on a rigid plan of fitness and training. Purity of spirit; Jack was not religious in the organized sense, but he read the Bible daily, read self improvement books, and fastidiously maintained his personal space and possessions. Purity of association; Jack avoided those he knew carried the seed of the devil and later attempted to bring them into his world of purity and control. Purity of culture; Jack saw as evil anything that threatened to disrupt order and discipline.

In one of his military books, Jack Anders saw a picture of a German soldier from World War II. The man was draped with a bandolier of machine gun bullets, dirty and weary from combat, but his blue eyes pierced young Jack's soul; it was him. That young German had answered the call, offered what he had to defend his homeland. He was big, and strong, and Jack Anders was his reborn spirit. Later, Jack read *Mein Kampf*, Adolph Hitler's plan for German domination of Europe, and read his speeches. When the Internet became available, he downloaded the Leni Riefenstahl propaganda films of the 1930's. Purity was the key; purity of race, purity of habit, purity of spirit.

CHAPTER THIRTY FOUR

Webb cut the lights and let the Chevy truck coast to a stop exactly two miles down the gravel road. It was 10 PM and Colleen twisted forward and backward in the seat beside him to peer into the night. Even in the dim light of the enlarging moon they could see the rocky outcropping to the west. They were talking quietly about whether they should flash their lights or make some noise to alert Boyd when he walked up behind the truck. They both startled when they heard the crunch of his boots just before he spoke.

"I'm glad to see you guys," he said quietly, opening the door on Colleen's side and slipping an arm around her shoulders.

"We're glad to see you," Colleen blurted. "Blue Jack was outside my room last night."

"He was copying down the VIN number from the front of your truck. If Dupree's operation is as good as he brags it is, they know you're in town."

"Is that all he did?"

"He stood out there for a couple minutes. I saw his shadow on my window shade," Colleen said, shivering a bit.

"There are a bunch of young guys staying there," Webb added.

"That explains the bus full of guys that spent the day at the ranch. I heard shooting in the morning, sounded like target practice. During the heat of the day they stayed in the shade of a pavilion he's got. Suppose Blue Jack was in town last night doing a bed check?"

"Boot camp. Militia boot camp."

"Yup. Wonder how many guys they have. I called Marv Crowder today. He says they've been watching Blue Jack and he dropped out of sight two months ago."

"Boy were you right about Dupree," Webb said, excitedly, anxious to relate his adventure of the day.

Boyd reached behind Colleen's seat and hefted the water jug and began drinking out of it while Webb began to talk. He had considered going back to the stock tank and drinking that late in the afternoon after his water ran out.

"I talked my way into one of his sales meetings. It was almost like being in an Amway meeting. The pitch was exquisite." Webb said, turning sideways in the seat to face Boyd and Colleen.

"Hey, wait a minute. You guys bring any food. I don't listen too well on an empty stomach," Boyd said, wiping water off his chin. The jug was a third gone.

"But of course. And beer too, if you promise to mind your manners," Colleen said, grabbing a shopping bag from the back seat and handing it to Boyd.

"There's a gate open over here, let's pull the truck behind that brush. There's a rock to sit on back there about a hundred yards. We can go over there to eat. You guys eat yet?" Boyd asked, taking the bag and a Playmate cooler while Webb and Colleen gathered other items from the back.

Their repast included a half dozen burritos from a Mexican restaurant in Dalhart; not those dinky burritos some fast food places sell, but the ones made with fresh full-sized tortillas. There were tortilla chips and fresh salsa, spicy with jalapenos and cilantro. A foam container contained at least a quart of pinto beans boiled simply with salt pork and green chilies. The cooler held a half dozen silver bullets, packed in crushed ice. Webb carried the remains of Henrietta Flick's iced tea and Boyd's giant plastic cups. Colleen had brought a bedspread from Dupree's motel and Boyd spread it across a large flat rock, leaving room for the three of them to sit on or lean against it. They unpacked the food and drink and silently dug in. Boyd wolfed down a couple burritos and a quart of iced tea before popping a Coors Light and sitting down to watch Colleen delicately eating the beans out of the Styrofoam cup.

"What does that beer commercial say? 'It doesn't get any better than this," Webb said, chuckling at Boyd watching Colleen eat and her eyes locked onto his.

The moon lit their meal as satisfactorily as if they had had lights on. A night bird opened with a brief effort and then fell silent.

"Let's hear that story now," Boyd said, opening a third burrito and taking a more leisurely bite.

"That damn Dupree can charm socks off better than anyone I've ever listened to. You won't believe what he's selling," Webb said, putting down his cup to use both hands to better tell the story.

"How'd you get in?"

"I just went up to the lady behind the desk and said I was in the neighborhood again and I had talked to the Colonel over the phone and he'd invited me to a meeting they were having last week and when I got there my name wasn't on the list so they wouldn't let me in. She asked if I'd answered an ad and I said yes and she asked which one and I hesitated for a moment and said I couldn't remember which magazine it was in and she just filled in by asking was it the Air Force Times and I said yes and she said she could get me into the afternoon meeting. This time Jerry wasn't there."

"So? Was Dupree there?" Boyd asked, popping another Coors Light.

"Oh yeah. What a clever guy! The front of the room had a U. S. flag flanked by a Texas state flag and one for the Air Force. First he showed an introductory film in which he is introduced by General Trusten Polk, and Polk calls him a great American and a patriot to be looked up to by all Americans. Then he gets up and thanks all the 'good Americans' who have taken the time to come to this organizational meeting of the Patriot Party. Then he says a little prayer for the memory of a fallen hero, Trusten Polk! He tells how he and Polk had been organizing the Patriot Party for some time, on the sly of course, because active duty military officers are not allowed to participate in political activity. Polk was 'tragically taken' just at the point when they were ready to make a big move with the party."

"That sounds a little flaky to me," Boyd said, finishing the burrito and sliding a hand down into Colleen's back pocket.

"Oh, to hear him talk about the basic tenets of the organization you'd want to join it too. This looked like a group of recent retirees. He talked about strengthening the VA system and enlarging the benefits for retired military and a lot of that simple, 'good government' stuff he told you. Especially the part about getting the drug dealers off the street with simple straightforward law enforcement techniques made possible by a few changes in the laws guaranteeing the rights of the accused. When he said, 'drug dealers should have no rights,' he got a big round of applause."

"From how many people?" Colleen interjected.

"About twenty. The room was half full. Not bad for a Tuesday in August, a hundred miles from nowhere."

"How'd they get there?" Boyd asked.

"He flew in about a dozen. The rest drove. The pitch was to start this Patriot Party with a hard core of 'dedicated American Veterans.' He said we would lie low and wait for a major political moment to occur, which would happen in a few weeks. Then all the faithful would make themselves known by contacting local officials and elected representatives and insist on certain basic but simple changes being made. Printed posters and literature would appear all over the country at just the right moment. It would seem to be a massive grassroots movement and the timing would be everything. He said many 'well known public figures' had been planning this for more than five years and were just at the point of recruiting 'local leaders' when Polk was killed. Then he hinted that 'certain elements' had learned of their efforts and were opposed to them and it was possible Polk's death was not an accident. That caused quite a stir. Everyone knew who Polk was."

"Who is the 'certain element'?" Boyd asked.

"Someone asked that at the meeting. Dupree said something like, 'I can't mention any names, of course, but you know them. They always seem to crop up to stand in the way of any real reform. They always take the side of the minorities. They always want to weep for people in prison. You know the names.' and sure enough the crowd filled in half a dozen names. Dupree just gave an enigmatic smile and went on. Then he introduced Blue Jack Anders, Chief of Security for the party. Blue Jack talked about bringing some of the better disciplined militia units to Texas for training; to have someone to maintain order at rallies."

"So when did he ask for money?"

"Just at the end. He said the core of the organization was supporting it but the time had come to 'broaden the base of support' and that's where these guys could help by coming up with a couple hundred at least to pay printing costs for the big push in a few weeks. The checkbooks came out and he got what he wanted. It was as slick a fleecing as you ever saw."

"Were there any doubters?" Boyd asked as a coyote yipped back to the west. Colleen scooted a little closer to him and wrapped her arms around her chest.

"Not a one. They must have been screened pretty well. Maybe he had some shills in there to whip out the check-books first, to encourage the others to move," Webb replied, taking a big bite of beans and washing it down with a huge gulp of tea.

"You put something in the pot?"

"In cash. Not gonna give that guy my checking account number."

"Sucker."

"Who's the sucker, it was your money."

The first coyote was joined by one from the east and almost immediately a couple from the north chimed in. Boyd had seen dozens of the animals slinking about in the past 24 hours. No bigger than an average sized bird dog, they seemed content to keep their distance and just watch. The night before, he had lain awake listening and there was just a slight anxiety about their approaching while he slept. He reasoned they couldn't do much damage through the sleeping bag before he'd lay to with the 9 millimeter and waste the whole pack. They looked smart enough to know that. He smiled to himself at what Colleen must be thinking as she scooted closer and put one arm behind him and in his back pocket.

"I've got a job interview Monday," Colleen said proudly, filling in the silence after the coyote serenade.

"At Dupree's?" Boyd said with surprise.

"Webb pointed out the car of one of the clerical workers at a parking lot behind a fourplex in town. We sat there for less than an hour when she came out with a laundry basket. We followed her to the Sunshine Laundromat and gathered together some clothes for me to wash. I changed into some jeans and a simple blouse and hit her with my Nicaraguan Spanish.

"I knew you were the one for this job," Boyd said, proudly. He crushed the first beer and carefully replaced the can in the paper sack they had brought. He opened another.

"I told Rebecca I badly needed a job. I said I had worked in Miami for awhile since coming here from Costa Rica. She bought it and told me about where she works. She said she takes some calls in English but doesn't do well because the patriot types recognize her Spanish accent and freeze up. When a call comes in from one of their Spanish language ads, they transfer it to her."

"They have ads in Spanish? Why?" Webb asked, finishing the rest of the iced tea. Apparently he'd been so excited on the way out he hadn't heard her story.

"They have one that runs in the Miami area that says, essentially, 'Liberate Cuba! Expel the dictator Castro and unite with our friends and families in beloved Cuba!' She said her border Spanish was a hindrance but that was all they could find here. I should do better. They have enough calls for two operators."

"What's this guy's real politics?" Boyd asked nobody in particular, scratching his head and looking west at the moon rising in the sky. "He seems to change according to the audience."

"I think that's it," Webb said. "Whoever wants to change the status quo, Luther Dupree's their man. He's making a business out of revolution. And a fine one it is too. All his equipment is right up to date. No corporate home office has any better audio-visual setup than Luther Dupree's there in Dalhart," Webb said, sure in his conclusion, then added, "I'll bet he has a navy flag and a Marine flag and an Army flag and who knows what other flags in his back room. He just trots out whatever he needs for each pitch."

"So what have you found?" Colleen asked, standing up and stretching after sitting cramped next to Boyd for several minutes.

"He's definitely gearing up to do some serious shooting. He's got a 20-millimeter cannon mounted in his

Messerschmitt and he and his mechanic are working on getting it to work. I don't know where he gets his ammunition, but revolutionaries with money seem to be able to get anything."

"What does that mean?" Colleen asked.

"A 20-millimeter cannon is a fairly dangerous weapon. The Messerschmitt was never much of a ground attack plane. They designed it primarily to shoot down other planes. It was difficult to beat in World War II in that job," Boyd replied, his love of the breed carrying him away from the import of what he was saying.

"Could he shoot down a modern plane, like yours?" Colleen asked, worried.

"No. Not at all. I could spot him fifty miles away and powder him with a missile before he knew I was there. When I'm loafing along trying to conserve fuel I'm a hundred knots faster than his top speed in a dive. He can't be thinking about taking on any modern fighters. Even the F-100 Dupree flew when he was in the Air Force would fly circles around a Messerschmitt. It's just a relic of a bygone time."

"Maybe he means to strafe somebody. After all, that is what he's practicing," Webb said, soberly.

Boyd contemplated that for awhile, and then said, "It just doesn't make any more sense than the idea of trying to inflict damage on a modern fighter. Anything you could do from the air with an old fighter you could do just as efficiently from the ground with something else. Yet, a cannon firing four 20-millimeter shells a second is more than a rich man's toy."

"You find out enough, or do you need to stay out here longer?" Webb asked, finishing a beer.

"Tomorrow's Sunday, probably won't be a lot going on out here. How about I come in tonight, and then drop me off again late tomorrow night?"

CHAPTER THIRTY FIVE

GENERAL POLK A FAKE!

DENVER. The Rocky Mountain News reports that the accident investigation board looking into the death of General Trusten Polk in a fiery plane crash last month has learned he may have been an impostor. Air Combat Command Commander Charles Kreitz has declined comment beyond acknowledging that some irregularities have surfaced about Polk's background and are being thoroughly investigated. He assured the Rocky Mountain News that all board proceedings are being held in accordance with Air Force regulation and that the cause of the accident will be determined and any confusion about General Polk cleared up.

The headline of the USA Today in the lobby of the hotel caught Webb's eye and he picked up the complimentary copy just as Colleen rounded the corner to meet him for breakfast. Boyd had returned to the ranch the night before.

"Wow!"

Webb grabbed Colleen's arm and hustled her out the door to the parking lot. "Careful! Don't know who's watching. We're just tourists, remember?"

"Oh, yeah," she said, then nodded at the bus pulling out of the parking lot filled with even more young men than the day before. "Them too."

"Looks like it's starting," Webb said, sitting in the car reading the front page article with Colleen.

By ten all the networks were breaking the story. By noon television remote trucks had lined up outside the gate at Buckley. One cameraman with an Army Guard ID card was able to get through the gate and found Colonel Bertz eating lunch at the food court at the base exchange. Somehow, he knew just who he was looking for and where he might be.

"Colonel Bertz, is it true that General Trusten Polk was an impostor?"

All he got for the national feed was Bertz with ketchup on his shirt trying to get out of a side door, denying any knowledge of anything. That was all the media had at the moment so the network ran it. The effect was that there was a cover up in Denver; it was picked up by news media all over the world. By mid-afternoon the networks had their top reporters Denver-bound.

The staccato burst of machine gun fire caused Boyd to drop to the ground and hug it, thinking he'd been seen, even though he was still half a mile from the house and well hidden by mesquite. The first burst was followed by another a few seconds later and then a continuous fire. All were short bursts of a half dozen shots. The shots cracked in the morning stillness. Dupree had not appeared at dawn and Boyd had decided to walk over to the ranch and see what security was up to before breakfast.

The bus was back, and thirty men were lined up, shooting down a makeshift firing range with assault rifles. They wore desert camouflage pants tucked into desert boots and brown Under Armor t-shirts and floppy boonie hats. Walking up and down the line behind them was Blue Jack.

Boyd crawled closer, approaching from behind and to one side. They were firing at plastic gallon jugs stuck on sticks, each about chest high.

"Four shots! Any more than four and you're wasting ammunition! Short bursts! Don't spray it around like a hose. Aim, squeeze off a burst, re-assess. Got it?"

There was a buzz of, "Yes sir!"

"Try it again."

Boyd crawled closer. The smaller steel building next to the new pole barn was the arsenal. Through the open door Boyd saw a uniformed man counting out ammunition boxes and filling clips. Several assault rifles were laid out on the counter and a row of Remington firearms safes behind him.

CHAPTER THIRTY SIX

Retired General Branch McTiernan squinted at the television lights, his lens implants caused a halo around bright lights that obscured much of what he saw. It gave him a confused look just as the interview began. He hadn't been following the story about Polk and had agreed to be interviewed on short notice thinking the reporter wanted background on the end of the Viet Nam war.

"General McTiernan, did you know General Trusten Polk?"

"No, not personally."

"Did you give the order to put another pilot in his place after a plane crash in Libya in 1975?"

Shocked, the old man stuttered, mind reeling with recollection of a long held secret. "I was told to, uh…"

"Somebody told you to what?" The reporter pressed, sensing the defenses were down now.

Order was returning to the old man's brain; a calmness was spreading. He'd long known this day would come; needed to come. He had hoped it would come before his time was up. This reporter was well informed, knew the answer to the question he'd asked. That was why he was here. Many could give background on the end of the Viet Nam war; few could give what Branch McTiernan had.

"I was told to fly a young lieutenant to Libya on the fastest plane we had at the time; an F-111."

"Why?"

"The Air Force needed to groom someone who could become a congressman, a senator, maybe president. The Navy had heroes, the Army had heroes, we needed one. A war hero went down in Libya, a man with a bright record, and my boss, General Conroy, Air Force Chief of Staff, wanted a young lieutenant he knew to fill that identity."

"An impostor?"

"Yes. He was to be groomed for success."

"By whom?"

"The Air Force." The old man's heart thudded in his chest. He'd just trashed Rob Conroy's reputation. He didn't care; he'd never liked that arrogant prick anyway. Besides, he'd been dead for twenty years.

"Just the Air Force?"

"The Delano Society." Now it was out. What could they do to him, put him in jail? Hell, that would be better than the damn nursing home his son was contemplating. Leavenworth wouldn't be so bad; be around military types, even though they'd be criminals they'd be a younger set than at the nursing home. "I was in it," the old general added, eyes now clear and looking into the camera. "It's a group of senior leaders.

We got together every few weeks and talked over how to run the country."

"Run the country?" The reporter was shocked at his success.

"Yeah, kind of an end run around the friction of government; political parties, getting elected."

CHAPTER THIRTY SEVEN

WASHINGTON IN TURMOIL

WASHINGTON, DC. This center of government is all but shut down as allegations of corruption and treason resound. Several congressmen, including Roscoe Kelly (D, Massachusetts), the powerful former chairman of the House Financial Services Committee have been linked to the Delano Society, a secret organization of politicians, military and business leaders rumored to have been running the country for years behind the scenes. Speculation about the Delano Society and who might be a member has dominated the news and talk radio since the investigation into the mysterious death of General Trusten Polk discovered he was an impostor, placed into the identity of another officer by the Delano Society.

"This is Lester Holt at NBC News in New York. We interrupt this program to bring you breaking news. We are taking you live to the Pentagon in Washington, DC, and NBC Pentagon Correspondent Natalie Spencer. Natalie, what have you learned about an unprecedented action by the Secretary of Defense?"

"Thank you, Lester. Secretary of Defense and former congressman James P. Harrison has issued an order to all military units within the United States to confine themselves to their barracks until further notice. This action has been used in Third World countries teetering on the brink of revolution to calm citizens by reassuring them that they will not be subject to a military take over. No order of this kind has ever been issued in the United States, Lester, and it suggests that this crisis is more serious than anyone realized."

"Were there any additional details?"

"No, Lester, but armored personnel carriers are parked in the south lot of the Pentagon, and check points have been set up on surrounding streets and at the Metro stop at the Pentagon City Mall."

"Incredible. Thank you, Natalie, and now we go to NBC Political Affairs Correspondent and host of NBC's Meet the Press, David Gregory."

Webb and Colleen sat in the motel coffee shop, morning paper spread out, flicking between the channels to get any crumb of additional information about the spreading crisis. There were few other motel guests as the bulk of the hotel was occupied by the ever enlarging group of young men coming into town, and they had all left at dawn in a bus.

"Better get to work. No telling what might be going on out at the airport," Webb whispered after they'd checked all sources and found nothing new.

Colleen nodded and finished her coffee.

Boyd was getting badly sunburned. This was his fourth day on the ranch and though he was under a mesquite bush it didn't afford much protection from the sun. At dawn the bus had returned, now full of at least thirty young men in the same desert camouflage pants and Under Armor brown T-shirts.

"Homeland!" They'd chanted during a morning run around a makeshift parade ground, carrying weapons at port arms, then raising them above their heads. This physical training went on for an hour, then they did close order drill for half an hour, inspected weapons, and broke for water and a talk by Blue Jack.

Boyd rolled behind the bush and retreated a few yards before standing and walking toward the stock tank to cool off. When he returned they were firing on the range again; disciplined now, firing short bursts of four shots. After a while they cleared their weapons and marched out into the brush for some small unit tactics, rushing objectives and heaving dummy grenades. As the day got hotter they broke for water and gathered in the pole barn, sitting around picnic tables while Blue Jack lectured. They had lunch, some more lectures, and then they sang a song and filed onto the bus back to town. From his vantage point it looked like scout camp, but with guns. Lots of guns.

Boyd checked his cell phone and found there was service near the house. He called Marv Crowder.

"Marv! There's an armed insurrection brewing down here in Texas."

"How many shooters you got?"

"Dozens."

"Hold that for now. We got bigger problems. Heard the news?"

"No."

"Someone leaked the SecDef's emails to Trusten Polk, implicating both of them in aiding and abetting state unorganized militia organizations and recruiting them to stand by as a kind of political goon squad."

"That's what I'm seeing; thirty-eight I counted this morning, drilling and firing on the range."

"The FBI has called the SecDef in for questioning and he's holed up in the Pentagon claiming it's all a political move to discredit him and his party."

"Holed up?"

"Tanks ring the building, just like Bolivia or Pakistan; protecting the military hierarchy while the civilians sort it out."

"Damn. Never thought I'd see that here."

"Me neither. Look, Homeland Security is in the same boat as Defense. Our secretary is rumored to be in Delano. He's not speaking to the press. He thinks it's us leaking all this stuff and he's livid. First he said he was reassigning me, then said I was fired and to clear out the office. Right after he called, the Chief Field Agent called me back and said to stay here and keep looking for Dupree."

"We found Dupree, why don't they pick him up?"

"You think you can do it?"

"Me?"

"You've got the badge."

"He's got an army down here. We're going to need a hundred men to round this bunch up."

"It's just us for now."

"How about using somebody local; the sheriff or maybe the highway patrol?"

"Right, some small town sheriff gets his dick shot off trying to bring in Dupree. No, stay put, watch the ranch, deputize your friends and warn them to keep their heads down. I've been in touch with some other agents, and some friends in Washington. This is sorting out to be Delano with their entrenched power base and those just outside the power circle. The political appointees are Delano and the permanent staff are not; it's the little people against the anointed ones."

"Isn't it always?"

"It may come to gunfire. The SecDef and some of the top generals have been swaggering around DC in armed convoys."

"We've got some armament issues down here, too. Dupree has the guns working in that Messerschmitt. He was out here the other night with a new pickup truck; a Ford 350 Dually, with an auxiliary fuel tank in the back, like farmers use to refuel their tractors in the field. I think he's got aviation gas in it and he's going somewhere. What's he gonna do with that thing?"

"Well, he's got the sky to himself, the Air Force has been grounded."

"That leaves Dupree's Messerschmitt the most powerful air force in America, and with that truck he can get it anywhere on the continent."

"Really?"

"Think about it. You stand down the Air Force, tie down the planes, close the hangers, send everyone home. Then, all of a sudden, you want to put some planes up. You can't, not for a day or so."

"Ha. You think the Russians are coming?"

"No. At the Air Force Academy we studied Clausewitz, the German general who laid out the principles of warfare. He said victory comes when you put overwhelming force at the critical point of your adversary's weakness."

"So?"

"What critical point could Dupree hit with an airplane that fires four 20 mm cannon shells a second, and follow it up with a hundred trained fighters armed with automatic weapons and hand grenades?"

"I hadn't seen it that way. Well, it won't be the Pentagon or the White House, they're ringed with Abrams tanks."

"Look, this is getting weirder and weirder, but maybe we need to start putting something together. I'm going to betray a confidence, and I want your word you won't let anything to happen to my friend."

"OK."

"Ben Culpepper, the crop duster up in La Salle, has a P-51. It works, I've flown it, and he has the guns for it."

"You're not serious?"

"What's going to happen tomorrow? We've been getting a bombshell a day, and the more threatened they are the more the powers that be in Washington hunker down. They're paralyzed. We need to get some muscle down here."

"Let me see what I can do."

"Betrayed! The citizens of the United States have been betrayed by a cabal of elected and unelected criminals! Criminals who used the resources and good faith of our nation for their own enrichment! They chose power over duty, money over integrity, and ten of them, United States Senators, are absent from this chamber today! Where are they? What are they planning? Do they intend to fight? Fellow Senators, and citizens watching in homes throughout America, we stand on the brink of chaos. Our nation is riven by greed and back room dealing, and the only path forward is to tear out this cancer and return our nation to the sacred roots of our constitution!"

"This is Brian Williams and welcome to the NBC Nightly News. You've just seen live coverage from the floor of the United States Senate as senators debate what action to take in light of the disappearance of ten senators, accused of being members of the Delano Society. A similar hearing is taking place in the House of Representatives where the Speaker has called for a joint meeting of the House and Senate later today; an extraordinary move seen only in times of extreme crisis.

"Now we take you to another breaking story. We go to Norfolk, Virginia and our reporter Gretchen Hempster at the Norfolk Navy Base. Gretchen, what have you discovered?"

"Thank you, Brian. Behind me the Norfolk Navy Base sits empty. Yesterday three aircraft carriers, the USS John F. Kennedy, USS George Washington, and the USS Harry Truman were moored here, along with an array of support ships. Today, as you can see, they're gone. We've been told that leaves were cancelled and sailors recalled quietly over the past week, and last night, they all shipped out."

"Amazing. And where do your sources say the Atlantic Fleet has gone?"

"Well, Brian, just beyond the empty docks there is the North Atlantic, and they're out there someplace."

"Thank you Gretchen for that in depth report, and now we go to Knob Noster, Missouri and Gary Stanley of KSHB, our Kansas City affiliate."

"Thank you, Brian. In the top secret world of the B-2 stealth bombers deployments are a closely held secret. These aircraft come and go on a schedule that is never announced and always top secret, but never before has the entire wing with its support staff just disappeared. You can see over my shoulder there, empty hangers, and no movement. Whiteman Air Force Base seems to be a deserted ghost town. Brian, back to you."

"Thank you Gary, and now to New Hanover Township, New Jersey and our own Lester Holt at Joint Base McGuire-Dix-Lakehurst. Lester, what have you found?"

"Brian, as you can see behind me, there is a massive logistical movement going on here. This is the Air Mobility Command's east coast embarkation point, and it is busy. Twenty Air Force C-17 transports are lined up being loaded with supplies, while another dozen of the giant Lockheed C-5 Galaxies undergo last minute maintenance prior to loading. In addition, the entire 108th Air Refueling Wing of the New Jersey Air National Guard departed here yesterday for parts unknown. Military movements require lots of stuff; supplies, fuel, munitions, and this is where it gets loaded. Brian, something's up."

"Thank you Lester, and now here with me in the studio is NBC Military Affairs Consultant General Barry McCaffrey. General, what do you make of this?"

"Brian, I wouldn't normally seek, or release if I found out information about deployment of military forces, but in these extraordinary times, when the threat seems to be coming from within, I think Americans need to know where their armed forces are located. Today, I made some calls. The Atlantic Fleet is dispersed in the Atlantic, most ships are steaming in the vicinity of the Azores. Also deployed to the Azores are three Air Refueling wings, two wings of F-15 fighters and the F-22 wing from Langley Air Force Base. In addition, the 82nd Airborne is deployed there. My sources didn't say, but I'm guessing that's where the B-2 bombers went as well, as the security of all those resources is about as air-tight as anyplace on the planet. We have amended our mutual defense treaty with Iceland, and the ramp at the all-but-abandoned Keflavik Air Force base is busy with fighter aircraft, refueling, and transshipment of supplies to Europe and beyond. Our base at Mildenhall in the United Kingdom is a hub of activity with C-17, and C-130 aircraft as well as several F-16 wings. The 109th Air Transport Wing of the New York Air National Guard, the Raven Gang with their specially outfitted C-130 transports used for polar research and supply has transported units from the 10th Mountain Division to Thule, Greenland, and I expect to see the ramp there filled with most of our operational B-52 bombers. The B-1 bombers, extensively used in the Iraq/Afghanistan theater of operations are now nearly all at Al Udeid Air Force Base in Qatar. We have an enormous base there Brian, and additional units of the 1st Cav Division from Ft. Hood are streaming in to man the armor we've recovered from Iraq. Several fighter wings are en route there and to our base in Kuwait. The Pacific Fleet is leaving San Diego at this moment, and a tanker refueling bridge is set up over Hawaii so that transport aircraft can leapfrog the fighters deploying to Guam with their support personnel."

"What is going on?"

"Brian, we have the most powerful military force the planet has ever known, and there seems to be big trouble with our governance. In times of crisis you can hunker down, consolidate, or disperse. If you hunker down or consolidate you run the risk that one side in the conflict for control of the government will use your own resources to tip the balance of power, or that some adversary will use the confusion to act. If you disperse your power, essentially creating a frame of force around the United States you can protect the nation from within and without from bases that were built and maintained to support a global footprint."

"Incredible. And sobering. Thank you, General McCaffrey. And now, back to debate in the United States Senate."

WALL STREET JOURNAL

PAYBACK TIME!
LONG KNIVES ARE OUT FOR DELANO

NEW YORK. Political score settling is taking its toll as elected officials and senior Civil Service executives turn on their former masters, the elite political appointees who head most federal agencies. Some agencies are entirely in the hands of the rank and file, while others remain firmly controlled by their appointed leadership. Conflict is turning to violence in several agencies...

CHAPTER THIRTY EIGHT

BANK OF AMERICA NATIONALIZED!

WALL STREET. The Secretary of the Treasury announced today that the federal government has nationalized Bank of America, Citicorp, Goldman Sachs, and other large investment banks to stop a run on the U .S. banking system. Revelations yesterday exposing widespread fraud in the Mortgage Electronic Registration System have caused the stock value of these banks to plummet to depths not seen even in the 2008 panic. Because they hold large amounts of mortgage- backed securities, and an unknown number of mortgages in those securities are entirely fictitious, investors and depositors are scrambling to get their money back. Calling for calm and assuring the public that the federal government now stands behind all mortgages made in the United States through the new law pushed through both houses of congress last night and signed by the president today, he assured people their money was safe.

In a related story, Congressman Roscoe Kelly, author of MERS has been arrested fleeing his office in the Congressional Office Building and charged with bribery and insider trading. The powerful former Chairman of the House Financial Services Committee was caught exiting a back door into a car driven by a well known Boston mobster. A briefcase containing $200,000 was recovered in the car. The FBI was tipped off that Kelly was going to make a run for the safety of his home district to avoid arrest in the District of Columbia. The cash was held by the FBI as evidence.

"This is Lester Holt at the NBC News Headquarters at Rockefeller Center in New York interrupting this program to bring you breaking news. A large truck bomb has exploded in front of the Federal Reserve Bank Building in San Francisco. We are going live to our NBC affiliate in Oakland and reporter Harrison Springfield. Harrison, what have you learned about this massive bomb blast?"

"Thank you, Lester. A 20-foot U-Haul rental truck with an apparent fertilizer bomb has blown the face off the venerable old San Francisco Federal Reserve Bank building, killing at least a dozen people inside and on the street. This eerie replay of Timothy McVeigh's assault on the Federal Building in Oklahoma City has people wondering if right-wing militia organizations are involved. We have cell phone footage taken moments after the blast showing the awesome power of an estimated one ton of ammonium nitrate fertilizer and diesel fuel. The marble columns of the landmark building were sent tumbling down the street here like bowling pins."

"Thank you Harrison. We'll be back later for more details of this breaking story, but now we're taking you to the White House where the President is about to make a statement from the Oval Office."

"Ladies and gentlemen the President of the United States!"

Tall and somber, dressed in a dark suit with a subdued red tie, the President filled the screen, sitting motionless behind his desk. He peered intently into the lights for several moments, and then began, "My fellow Americans. The turmoil in our banking system is at an end. Congress has passed and I have signed into law the nationalization of the large investment banks. This has been made necessary by widespread fraud in the mortgage lending system. For too long we have tolerated predatory lending practices and lax oversight of collateralized debt obligations. Your small home town banks, which have been and remain the honest bedrock of American finance can be relied upon to make good their obligations and continue to loan money to worthy projects within their communities. These larger investment banks, now a part of our federal government, encouraged speculation and arbitrage in mortgages and destabilized the market for collateralized debt. That has come to an end. The shareholders of these banks will receive payment from the federal government in accordance with the actual value of the assets of those banks after a thorough audit."

"On another matter, rumors circulating in Washington and elsewhere that there has been some sinister organization, the Delano Society running our government are entirely false. This is an election year, and though I am not in any sense casting any blame in the direction of the Republican Party as such, it has come to my attention that certain elements with right-wing sentiments have been spreading these rumors."

"Sounds like Khadafy, Mubarik, Assad and all the rest when the people were at the gates," Webb said, feet propped on the coffee table in Colleen's room at the motel.

"No, Webb. Sounds like a statesman taking charge of a destabilized nation. A nation destabilized by fraud and collusion."

"Destabilized by something," Boyd said. He'd come in after four days on the ranch to nurse a sunburn and rest up. He took a pull on his beer and grabbed some more chips.

CHAPTER THIRTY NINE

Hyde Fleetwood taped a security code into his I Pad and entered the main Patriot Party database from his office in the command center beneath the Gulfstream hanger at Dupree Aviation in Dalhart. Unconsciously he pulled up his shirtsleeves that kept falling down over his bony fingers as he taped another security code to bring up the weapon he'd been working on for the past year, and took another pull from the Diet Pepsi that kept him going during his marathon work sessions. Sometime this week Dupree was going to get a call and Fleetwood would have two hours to launch the weapon. It was ready now, he could do it right now, but Luther had said timing would be everything and Luther had a way of being right. Fleetwood was tired of Dalhart and ready to move on with his new life.

Six years he'd been in Texas. Six years would not be penance enough to live down the scandal at MIT; he'd never get a job in academia again. The dean had warned him twice, but that fresh-faced sophomore with the innocent eyes and the desperate need to pass Database Fundamentals was just too tempting to pass up. Prior slip-ups had established his reputation, so students came to him and offered what they had, what they'd never offered before, offered to him, Professor Hyde Fleetwood, PhD. They caught him in the men's room the third time and the dean fired him that afternoon. Disgraced, he'd hid out at home for a week, crying, crushed. Then, Luther Dupree had called and offered him a job; a very interesting and challenging job.

"What do you know about banks?" Luther had asked over coffee when they'd first met.

"Nothing."

"They use computers."

"Everything uses computers."

"Is there any difference between, say, the university computer system that keeps track of the payroll accounts and the computer system that keeps the checking accounts at your local branch of Bank of America?"

"None."

"Could you get into such a system?"

"I do it all the time."

"And they can't tell you've been there?"

"Not unless I want them to."

"You want a job?"

"I don't want to go to jail."

"Neither do I."

And so, he'd moved to Amarillo and moved into an office at Panhandle Texas Fidelity Mortgage. Dupree was already running a Ponzi scheme creating fake mortgages, but the process was cumbersome and relatively dangerous.

"The first one I tried, back in Baton Rouge when I worked at a local mortgage company, could have put me in the pen," Dupree had confided their first week together in Amarillo. "I'd made hundreds of mortgages and thought I knew everything there was to know about mortgages, so I put together a fake one and tried to sell it to a servicing provider, intending to make the payments and keep the principle. They sent a photographer out to the address to take a picture. It was a vacant lot. Instead of calling the cops, they assumed it was sloppy paperwork and sent it back to me with a letter telling me to get it right and send it back through."

"Seems prudent enough," Fleetwood had said.

"You can't do fake mortgages at that level, plain and simple. You have to get to the servicing provider level," Dupree had said, getting up from his desk at Panhandle Texas and pouring them both another drink. "I went to MBA meetings for a decade. I'd go to committee meetings, hang around the exhibit hall where suppliers and venders hawk their products, but mainly I'd sit in the bar and drink with people. I'm a crook. I met other crooks, but I wanted one smart enough to see the long view. It took awhile. Willard Hudgins and I bought this mortgage servicing business three years ago. We can slip an occasional fake into Fannie Mae but we have to be really careful. Their system is based on the first six months of payments; if they're made it's a good mortgage, if not, not a good mortgage. It's the servicing provider that sends the homeowner their statements, and initiates foreclosure if they don't make their payments. The eventual owner of the mortgage isn't involved until it gets to that stage."

"I don't know anything about mortgages," Fleetwood had said.

"The feds just passed a law, mortgages are going paperless. It's all going to be on a computer."

"What's in it for me?"

"How much money do you want?"

"A lot."

"Give me a number."

"Just like that?"

"Just like that.

Fleetwood didn't need to crack into MERS, Panhandle Texas Fidelity was already part of the system and authorized to submit paperless mortgages. He explored their database and, with Dupree and Hudgins inserted mortgages into it to check their verification processes. Later, they inserted mortgages and followed them as they were bundled with other mortgages for sale to the big investment banks to aggregate into collateralized securities which were sold all over the world. Soon they were submitting fake mortgages at will and pocketing a fortune. Then Fleetwood put together a proposal to the Boston mob, to show them how they could profit if they bought into a mortgage service provider on the east coast. He set up the process at Boston Atlantic Fidelity, leaving a hole in their security so he could access it from Amarillo whenever he liked. Then Dupree had taken him to Dalhart and introduced him to Trusten Polk and the Patriot Party. He collated the demographics of all the contributors, explored their personal finances and identified the ones ripe for a fake mortgage they'd never know they had. He cracked the Department of Defense email database in Washington and read the encrypted emails of the SecDef and others.

Then, one day it all came to a halt.

"Shut it all down," Dupree had said about a year ago, walking into his office in Amarillo.

"All what?"

"Everything. Quit making bogus mortgages and start planning your retirement."

"I'm ready."

"This is the new you," Dupree had said, and dropped a passport on his desk. With it were a driver's license, Social Security Card, and credit cards.

"Just like that?"

"No, don't leave just yet. There's one more job. I need you to move up to Dalhart for a few months and build something that will distract the feds for awhile. Then, we all run at once."

CHAPTER FORTY

The vig on Luther Dupree's empire was $700,000 a month; the payments on $100 Million worth of fake mortgages. Cheap. Many U. S. corporations, states, and cities have been doing the same thing for decades; legally borrowing more money than they could ever pay back and making the vig by borrowing more money. The federal government has done the same thing and makes the vig by printing more money. The line between fraud and business as usual is so very thin, but everyone has to pay the vig.

This was all OK. He'd seen the basic template for a Ponzi scheme in graduate school and it had taken a dozen years to find a way to do it safely. Poor, lonely Horace Swilley, then known as Colonel Trusten Polk, had called during this time. It was a voice from his past. They'd met and renewed their friendship and Polk had spilled the whole story. How to use insider knowledge of corruption in government? Oh, let me count the ways!

Luther Dupree chuckled as he watched the hapless Roscoe Kelly on the news leaving the federal courthouse in Washington, disheveled and bewildered. The news went on to the president's address, but Dupree chuckled again, mind still on Kelly. The path to his downfall shone clear a decade before. Patience. Planning. It's not that hard when power corrupts a fool. He'd met Kelly only once. In his brief walk to the man's office he'd seen an ego pumped beyond control by years of political power. He'd seen hubris as Kelly told him how he'd come up "the hard way" in Boston politics. Dupree was delighted; politics means unions, rackets, the mob. The Boston mob; his kind of people. Of all the Delanos Dupree had met, and he'd gotten around to most of them with introductions by Polk, Kelly was the most vulnerable. And, Kelly was Chairman of the House Financial Services Committee! What luck, the biggest fool in Washington writing the rules for the nation's money supply.

After their brief meeting Dupree called upon Paxton Baggs, a powerful Washington law firm and purveyor of access to government. It was costly, but by dinner the next night Paxton Baggs had found two charismatic lawyers with the right stuff for Roscoe Kelly. Money flowed to Paxton Baggs, friendship flowed to Roscoe Kelly. Already a member of the Mortgage Banker's Association and a diligent student of the mortgage process, Dupree wanted to help the MBA streamline the process of mortgage lending. Dupree was able to gently guide Kelly along the process of getting MERS through congress unencumbered by the restraints registered lobbyists must observe. A chance meeting after dinner at the Yacht Club with a database encryption expert extolling the security of electronic systems, some bankers celebrating a successful catch after a fishing charter on the Chesapeake and mentioning some ideas for making non-conforming loans to lower income borrowers – that's how influence is used. A complex, fully integrated electronic mortgage system emerged with the energetic public support of the Mortgage Banker's Association and their paid lobbyists and with behind the scenes non-public and thoroughly illegal gentle guidance by Luther Dupree. MBA lawyers wrote the first draft of legislation, a common practice in Washington, and Kelly's committee hashed out the details. Over drinks afterwards Kelly unburdened himself of the confusing testimony and acrimonious debate in closed door committee meetings. Frank talk with his trusted friends Carl and Ralph often helped him to see the logical path to a workable system.

The Boston mob was not that hard to infiltrate; Dupree started at the top. For a cut, Dupree offered to show them how to make serious money with bank fraud. He helped them get rich, and Roscoe Kelly got tokens of appreciation, political support, and the friendship he valued so highly. All of it was tied to bank fraud. Kelly never knew. That clumsy $5 million mortgage on John Rigdon's ranch was made to be found, to double-cross the Boston mob and incriminate Roscoe Kelly. That was the trigger he needed to blow the lid off the Delano Society.

Dupree poured himself a bourbon and thought back to his days poking around in the Delano Society with Polk; the early days as his scheme first hatched. Corruption in government is always the same. It starts with a necessary lie, then the cover up of the necessary lie, then the conspiracy of those who know about the cover up. Conspirators bond with each other, for protection and for mutual advancement. Conspiracy is corruption, and it enlarges as more people find out about it and want a part of the action. Corruption casts a big shadow, enabling people like himself to hide and use its power. Corruption in government leads to violence as people find out they've been cheated and try to overthrow the corrupt ones, who try to protect themselves. How far would it go here, in the United States? Dupree didn't know, but he had some gasoline yet to throw into the fire.

CHAPTER FORTY ONE

Boyd was back out at the ranch on Friday August 9th. It was late and the shadows were lengthening as he returned to the stock tank. The sound of the water running at a trickle into the tank was too much to resist. He stripped off his clothes, being careful to fold them and tuck them next to the tank should Dupree come suddenly overhead. Naked, he balanced on the edge of the tank and fell face first into the clear water. Floating on his back in the stock tank he reviewed this whole crazy summer, beginning with the trip across the Midwest to Colorado with Eight Ball in his old truck, then the crash where two pilots died a fiery death and Boyd still didn't know if it was an accident or at the hand of either Dupree or some oddball conspiracy in Washington. He made a mental note to check with Moses as soon as they got back to Denver to see if the x-rays and microscopic photographs of the turbine blades were back from the lab.

Blue Jack now had nearly a hundred trainees, and was helped by a dozen fellow drill instructors. They'd worked out and drilled most of the morning, then fired on the range most of the afternoon, sung that song what was now haunting Boyd's memory trying to recall where he'd heard it, and boarded the buses for Dalhart.

What possible target could they be planning to attack that could not be attacked easier with some other weapon? A Messerschmitt would have to be the absolute highest profile way there was to harm something. One look at it and anybody, even if they'd never seen one before, could remember enough to identify it later, and with only a half dozen or so left flying in the whole world, it would only be hours before the police would be at the door of Dupree Aviation.

Was that it? Was this an elaborate ploy to bring the cavalry to the door of Dupree Aviation? If so, why was Blue Jack training an army to protect it?

Refreshed after half an hour, Boyd climbed out of the stock tank and air dried for a few minutes before putting his clothes back on. He was waiting by the road when his Chevy truck coasted to a stop just at the appointed hour, after the sky had turned completely black. The moon was low in the eastern sky, and three quarters full.

"Where's Webb?" Boyd asked, knowing the answer already.

"Oh, he had a headache. He was flying all day," she said, turning to get the sack of food from the back seat. She had handed Boyd the water already and he was gulping it down.

Boyd spread the blanket on the same flat rock they had used for a table nearly a week before and asked, "Well, what's for dinner?"

"We had a choice of chicken fried steak, the fare from half a dozen national chains or going back to the Mexican place," Colleen said, teasing him with the full white paper sack. It had no brand names on it.

"I'm so hungry, it all sounds good to me," Boyd said, trying to get close enough to smell the sack for a clue.

"We couldn't make up our minds so we got chicken fried steak and chili rellenos."

"Sounds like a sloppy mess, but I'm game," he replied, opening the first of several Styrofoam containers as she removed it from the sack. It contained a large pool of white gravy flecked with black pepper. One end had a mound of mashed potatoes as big as a softball and the other had a chicken fried steak as big as Boyd's hand. "Oh Texas!" he said, taking the proffered knife and fork and sitting down.

"Walking around in the boondocks must be good for you," she said, sitting down with a plate of chili rellenos and demurely taking a bite while watching Boyd plow through his food. He paused long enough to fill one of his big cups with ice and water and then resumed eating.

"Well, what happened today?" he asked, taking a long pull on the water and looking at Colleen.

"Webb flew around all day. Told the people at Dupree he had some business calls to make. He was in and out of the office during the day. No one seemed to pay much attention. He said he stopped at a small airport on the other side of town and they told him Dupree has been here about ten years but just started really showing signs of wealth in the last five. He got the Gulfstream last year. They don't like him much because he gets all the business in the area."

"He runs a pretty good operation. What did you find out?"

"It's bizarre! I don't understand this thing at all. As you know, they hired me right away on Monday, the interview was a formality. The lady who did the whole thing asked me to read something in Spanish and then asked Rebecca, the girl who told me about the job to come in and talk for awhile with me. They didn't ask for references or anything. The pay borders on insult, but for someone with no sign of education or job skills and no references, it is probably more than just enough to survive."

"What do you do?"

"That's the funny part. Rebecca, the girl we met last week, showed me how to talk to people using a more or less scripted spiel and then ask them to contribute money to the cause. We get bonuses for generating contributions above a minimum level. Anything over a hundred dollars on the first call and I get five dollars. It's different today. All day long people scurried in and out of the telephone room in a big rush. They were using our phones to call contributors to get additional information. I even heard them calling banks and verifying accounts and trying to get balances. It seems like they are coming to some kind of a deadline."

The coyotes started right on time. This time the chorus was from the north, and closer than the night before. Colleen seemed not to notice and continued her story.

"There wasn't much business in Spanish today. I only talked to one man, from Los Angeles, who was interested in some people down in Mexico fighting the government. He didn't want to donate any money. He was calling to see if we had information about his brother. I filled in answering the other phones, which were busy. They have an ad in Soldier of Fortune Magazine asking for ex-military members to join the Patriot Party. They slant it toward finding more about the MIAs from Viet Nam and to give America a more upright posture in the world today."

"You've even got the buzz words down. Those haven't exactly been concerns of yours over the years," Boyd said, teasing her.

"No. I've fought on other fronts, but today I played right along. Whatever this turns out to be will be worth my effort; I'll be back to feminist causes after that. But, listen, the other ads were even better. From Ducks Unlimited, some kind of hunting magazine, there were calls on an ad for the Patriot Party appealing to people interested in fighting against gun control legislation. I've never even met anyone opposed to gun control legislation, and today I must have given that spiel two dozen times, '…to assure law abiding Americans continue to have the right to own and bear arms.' They gave money too. I got a $50 donation and a couple of twenties and all on credit cards," she said, taking another bite of her chili relleno, now cold.

"I wish I could have heard that. If they'd have had any inkling they were talking to a Jane Fonda clone they'd have sent you something besides money," Boyd said, chuckling.

"I'm not a clone of Jane Fonda or anyone else! You just use her name because she was outspoken about her views, and I am too. I don't have quite the pulpit she does. My views are my own, and any alteration is for my own reasons and through no coercion from you or anyone else," she said, realizing at the end she was being baited.

Boyd finished the chicken fried steak and then a plate of green chilies stuffed with queso fresco cheese, breaded and fried and covered with green chili sauce. The cheese was no longer melted, but the heat from the chilies was intact.

"These must be those Hatch chilies from New Mexico," he said, halfway through, waving a hand in front of his face as if to cool off his lips. He opened the Playmate cooler and extracted a Silver Bullet.

"They're good, wherever they come from," she said. "Well, what did you discover today? Surely you didn't just sit out here in the wilderness and contemplate the cosmos."

"This guy Blue Jack has an army out here."

"And in town; he's got all the motels booked full and we had to wait half an hour just to get into that Mexican place to get this food."

"Revolution is better than tourism, I guess," Boyd said, finished with the first bullet and reaching for a second.

"Shouldn't someone be doing something about all this? Are they just going to let these fanatics take over Texas?"

"I've been checking in with Marv Crowder every day, he says he's on it."

"What if he isn't?"

"Hmm."

Boyd lay back, and together they looked at the stars, countless in the clear Texas sky. The rock was giving back some of the heat accumulated during the day and the warmth was comforting with just a touch of chill in the late night air. After a period of silence Colleen's breasts swayed in the moonlight as she sat up to remove her bra. She tugged at Boyd's belt and he obliged by opening it and his jeans. Persisting, she tugged at his shorts and he lowered those too, still supine on the rock.

"It comes slowly out of hiding," she giggled gazing down at Boyd's midsection. "So eager, so trusting."

"Is that poetry?" He asked, pulling the jeans down further now that all attention seemed to be on him.

"I'm paraphrasing a poem by Sharon Olds. She thinks it looks like a slug."

"Slug? She thinks this looks like a slug?" Boyd asked, holding the object under discussion.

"She's referring to its changing size and shape, and the noble, trusting, arrogance of it." Colleen said, bending to brush dry lips over the crown. Then she sat again and began to remove her shoes.

"I wouldn't take off my shoes if I were you," Boyd said, seriously. "There are more thorns per square foot here than any place I've seen. Let's get in the truck."

He stood and gathered the remains of their dinner stuffing it into the sack, then hopped to the truck with his jeans around his ankles and lowered the tail gate. He hopped up sitting bare assed on it and pulled off his boots. Colleen brought the bedspread from Dupree's motel and threw it into the back as she joined Boyd on the tailgate.

"There's something about that open sky," she said, breathless after they'd embraced sitting on the tail gate. She grabbed Boyd again, falling back into the truck bed and wriggling out of her shorts.

Boyd rolled onto his back, but Colleen rolled off and moved to the side of the truck bed, resting her elbows on it and offering her backside with an enticing wiggle. He rose and covered her.

"You gonna howl at the moon?"

"I hope so."

CHAPTER FORTY TWO

Boyd awakened to the snort of a horse. It was dark with just a hint of light in the eastern sky. He looked around. A horse stood a few yards from his sleeping bag, in the saddle sat a grizzled cowboy in jeans and western boots. He was pointing a Winchester lever action rifle casually at Boyd. Beside the horse stood a blue heeler, an Australian cattle dog panting in the cool night air.

"Don't pull out that pistol you got there," the man said. "Hate to have to blow a hole through ya."

A rustling noise behind him caused Boyd to turn. Two more horses stood in the gathering light of dawn. On one was seated another cowboy, a lean gray copy of the first, and on the other sat Blue Jack.

"Didn't need the dog to find you," Blue Jack said. "You left tracks between here and the house that a cub scout could follow. You Air Force types must not practice evasion and survival."

Boyd didn't respond. He slowly raised his hands, mind rushing to find a way out. Not much chance; three guys on horses, and that dog.

"Smart move. Don't get yourself shot just yet," Blue Jack said, then pulled out a cell phone and spoke into it. "Bring up the truck."

A pickup rattled across the desert from the house trailing a cloud of dust. Blue Jack dismounted and handcuffed Boyd, leading him to the truck while one of the cowboys kept a gun on him. The other gathered his gear and threw it into the back of the truck. Boyd was handcuffed to the toolbox bolted to the truck bed for the ride to the ranch house.

"I'm just lost," Boyd said, giving the story he'd concocted if he should be found. He was sitting in a kitchen chair with his hands handcuffed behind the back.

"Right," Blue Jack said, pacing in front of him. "You've been out here a week snooping around. I got the VIN off the truck you bought in Denver just before you and your girlfriend and that doctor from Buckley came down here and checked into the colonel's motel. You've got a Secret Service badge in your pocket, an M9 in your bedroll, and a cell phone with the Secret Service office in Denver on the call list. Now, fess up and give us some reason not to shoot you."

"Federal Marshals on the way."

"Hmmph. Nice try. We're watching their emails. Homeland Security is not on the way."

"You sure?" Boyd countered, thinking maybe some offense would work.

"You're not catching up on the papers, are you? Secretary of Homeland Security fired your buddy in Denver, Crowder

I think was his name, and closed the office there last night. Papers are saying this whole government crisis has been coming out of Denver. Buckley's been locked down."

"OK," Boyd said, trying to keep the shock off his face.

"OK, what?"

"OK, you got me. Now what?"

"Tell me something I don't know."

Boyd's mind was blank; defeated. To use a fighter pilot saying, he was out of options, air speed, and altitude.

Crunching gravel outside diverted attention as they all turned to look out the screen door. A black Cadillac Escalade coasted to a stop and Luther Dupree got out and quickly took the three steps up to the door.

"Whoa! What have we here?" He stopped in the door.

"Found him camped out over by the range," Blue Jack said.

"That's Boyd Chailland, from Denver."

"He's got a Secret Service badge on him."

"Really?" Dupree seemed surprised. Maybe he wasn't the all knowing super villain he'd pretended to be. Boyd's spirits rose. "Bad news for you, buddy," he said, looking at Boyd. "Can't have you in town just now." Boyd's spirits fell again.

Three buses pulled into the drive and continued around to the parade grounds beyond the house.

"Get those guys occupied," Dupree said to Blue Jack as he nodded at the men pouring out of the buses. Blue Jack left, calling orders as he strode across the parade ground. Soon the recruits were doing warm up calisthenics.

"Watch him," Dupree said to the two cowboys, then quickly climbed the stairs to the upper floor.

They'd looked natural sitting on their horses, now they were uneasy; one leaning against the door jamb to the front and the other sitting on his heels with his back against the kitchen wall. Worn western boots, jeans, western shirts with rodeo buckles and sweat stained cowboy hats styled just so. Ranch hands, not revolutionaries.

"Death penalty for killing a federal agent," Boyd said. "You can run, but they'll get you."

They fidgeted.

"Or, you'd end up at Leavenworth. Guards'd put you with the hard asses."

Conflict and worry creased both weathered, beyond middle age faces.

Dupree came down the steps with a small gym bag and a briefcase. He brushed by them as if they weren't there and went into the living room. It was an old, comfortable ranch house, probably unchanged from before Dupree got prosperous and bought it for its remoteness at the edge of the Llano Estacado for his strafing range. He rifled through a desk in the front room and retrieved some papers, then rushed through the screen door and back to the Escalade, throwing stuff into the back seat. He returned.

"You guys clear out when Blue Jack comes back," he said, pulling a wad of bills from his front pocket and handing each a bunch of hundreds. "I'll be on a trip. This will keep you in beans till you can find something else. Keep the horses, keep the truck." He shook hands with each man after handing them the bills. "Good luck."

The cowboys looked relieved. Boyd's spirits plummeted.

Blue Jack returned, sweating already in the rising early morning heat.

"Getting 'em warmed up. We're gonna do some small unit tactics for the new guys."

"No. Keep 'em in the shade and hydrated. Give 'em that purity lecture again."

"We did that yesterday," Blue Jack looked confused.

"We got trouble in town; seeing him here fits. He must be with that guy who's been coming and going all week in that Cessna 170, cluttering up the air doing nothing."

"He's got a girlfriend too."

"We hired a Spanish speaker this week." Then turning to Boyd, "Your girlfriend speak Spanish?"

Boyd didn't know whether to deny or confirm, he just gave a dumb look.

Dupree frowned, walked to the door and watched the recruits now jogging around the track. He seemed to make up his mind and turned back to Blue Jack.

"Send half of 'em home, tell them to go to bed and get some sleep and be ready to roll in 12 hours, be ready with the rest of them to secure headquarters if I call. Today may be the day they come for us."

Blue Jack looked shocked. Push had come to shove. Years of plotting mayhem and revolution had come to this.

"What? You're not ready?"

"Well, yes, er, no."

"Look, it's in the plan. Without brown shirts, political muscle, we're just pissing in the wind here. We need muscle to stand up to authority, to show the country we're a force to be reckoned with. We're not gonna take on the U. S. Army, just some bureaucrats with a search warrant. We just need a show of power; to run 'em off. Then we send these guys back home with tales of how they stopped the feds, if only for a day or two. The next time we need 'em, they'll be an army."

"Yes sir."

"Oh, I almost forgot. I got something for you," Dupree said and strode out the door to the Escalade. He opened the back and lifted a wooden box with rope handles. It was heavy and Blue Jack descended the steps to help him.

Boyd stood half up and was able to slip his handcuffed arms up the back of the chair, but Dupree and Blue Jack were back in a moment carrying the box. They set it on the kitchen table.

"There's a crowbar in the back of my car," Dupree said.

Dupree stood in the door to the kitchen surveying the rest of the house, oblivious to Boyd. Boyd looked, seeing for the first time the momentoes and photos on the walls – pictures of the T-38, F-100, T-37 with snapshots and signatures. Dupree walked over and idly looked at some of them while he waited, then turned quickly away when Blue Jack returned and took the crowbar from him.

"This ought to put some spine in those guys," he said, prying to top off the box.

"Whoa! Grenades!"

"Yeah." Dupree hefted a hand grenade, tossed it in the air and caught it, big smile on his face. "You know how to handle these?"

"Oh yeah. Ranger school, we did a lot with grenades."

"Don't give 'em out till you get to town. Don't want one of those yokels to blow the side off the bus."

"Right, I'll put 'em in my truck."

Blue Jack left and Dupree, still oblivious of Boyd began walking around the house, as if he were looking for something. Boyd noticed a picture of a young woman on a table top, a house on another, and a photograph of an old couple. Then Boyd realized, this was Luther Dupree's home, and he was walking around looking at it as if for the last time. Whatever it was he was planning, it was now.

CHAPTER FORTY THREE

Colleen was taking a call when Dupree came in the back door of Dupree Aviation and rushed down the back hall to his office. He was carrying a gym bag and a briefcase. She finished the call and motioned to Rebecca and pointed to the ladies room across the hall from the call center. She finished there, washed her hands, dried them and just as she was opening the door a loud klaxon horn sounded outside. It sounded like a fire alarm. She opened the door and bumped into a man she'd never seen before. He had a panicked look on his face, and he had a gun. Their eyes met and he stepped toward her as she backed toward the ladies room. The door at the end of the hall opened and the man raised his gun, a small automatic and fired. The silencer muffled the shot, which was right in front of Colleen's face, but she felt the heat and instantly the smell of burning gunpowder.

The shot hit Jerry, Dupree's bodyguard square in the chest and slammed him back against the door jamb. Jerry fired back. His weapon, a S&W 4006 had no silencer and the thunder reverberated even as Colleen felt the first round hit the shoulder of the man now trying to push her into the ladies room and slammed him into the wall. The second round hit the metal door frame and ricocheted down the hall.

Colleen dropped to the floor and attempted her wrestling takedown maneuver, thoroughly surprising the now wounded gunman and he fell onto his back in the hall. Jerry fired again, narrowly missing Colleen's head and hitting the floor taking a large divot of concrete and vinyl tile. The man fired again and Jerry doubled over, hit in the abdomen.

"Bitch!" The man punched Colleen square in the face with his good arm and rolled out of her grasp, standing. "Ya got this coming!" Blood was running down his right arm as he attempted to raise the pistol to Colleen's face but could not. He transferred it to his left hand and pointed it right at her head.

The explosion deafened her, and she felt heat and shock as the man disappeared from her view. Looking up she saw him propelled backwards down the hall toward the hanger, a surprised look on his face and a bloody hole in his chest. A second explosion singed her hair and the man's head exploded. He fell into a bloody lifeless heap. She turned to see Luther Dupree with a Remington 870 12 gauge pump shotgun in his hand, chambering another round.

"Any more?"

She couldn't speak. She shook her head.

"You hurt?"

She shook her head again.

"Call an ambulance," Dupree said as he grabbed Jerry by the collar and drug him back into the office, shotgun pointed down the hall.

The klaxon, still blaring, was activated by a metal detector installed at the end of the hall to detect anyone entering Dupree's inner offices with a firearm.

"You have enemies, Mr. Dupree, to explain why you'd have an alarm like that in your office?" Lane Parker, the Dallam County Sheriff asked, standing in Luther Dupree's office. He was a small man with sun-damaged fair skin, western boots, hand-tooled leather belt, and brown "Sheriff's Department" uniform shirt worn over western-cut twill slacks. He was taking notes on an IPAD, which seemed incongruous with the long-barreled Colt revolver in his service holster; an icon of an earlier era.

"I do have some enemies. I've been involved with politics, as you know, sheriff. You've heard about our friend, General Polk up in Denver. They've found something that points to his crash maybe not being an accident."

"Really?"

"Yes, and now it seems to have come here. Poor Jerry, he took the bullet that was surely meant for me"

"Jerry, the man that was shot. What is his job here?"

"Personal assistant."

"He was armed?"

"Well, yes."

"Why do you need a bodyguard?"

"Like I said, I have some enemies."

"Determined ones, it seems," The sheriff looked suspicious. "So, you think this may have something to do with the national situation?"

"Well, possibly."

"The dead man, the one who triggered the alarm with the gun, has a drivers license from Boston. Why would he be here, in Texas?"

"Well, I don't know." Dupree looked away, face creased.

"Enemies in Boston?"

"I've done some banking business there."

"Banking business?

"Yes."

"How does banking lead to this?" The sheriff nodded his head at the still open door.

Dupree was silent.

"Miss Chamorro, what is your job here?"

Dupree's eyes bored into her from behind the sheriff as he turned to her.

"I've just been hired this week." She dabbed a tear and looked at the floor. "I just went to the ladies room, and…" She sobbed.

"Did you know the man that was killed?"

"No, but he spoke to me in very rough terms, and was going to shoot me." She sobbed again.

"Why was he going to shoot you?" The sheriff wrinkled his brow. As he did this he stood and stepped between Colleen and Dupree.

Colleen caught his eyes just as Dupree's view was blocked and opened her eyes widely for a moment, then resumed her frail, frightened look.

"I tripped him. He was pushing me into the ladies room."

"So, you fought with him?"

"Yes, just before he shot Mr. Dupree's bodyguard."

"So, Jerry Crawford was a bodyguard?"

"He had a gun."

The sheriff's cell phone rang and he opened it to a text message. He stared at the phone for a moment, and his demeanor changed. He thought for a moment, abandoned his query about Jerry's gun and turned to Dupree.

"Uh, we need to find a next of kin for Mr. Crawford, someone to notify. He's gut shot, as you know. Never know how that'll turn out. The ambulance will probably take him straight to Amarillo. Good thing he had that body armor; he'd be a dead man for sure. Well, I gotta be going."

Abruptly he moved toward the door, then paused and looked back. "We ought to be able to wrap this up pretty quick. You gonna be OK? Want me to leave a detail here?"

"Oh, no. I'm OK. Just, well, Jerry was a friend."

"Yeah, it's tough. I'm going to take Miss Chamorro out and let one of the deputies get her story. You sure you're OK?"

"Yeah, thanks." Dupree seemed eager for the sheriff to leave, and since that text, the sheriff seemed eager too. No more tough questions, he nodded to the door for Colleen to precede him.

Carnage. She hadn't seen it before, there had been too much going on, but now she saw it all at once. There was a pool of blood on the floor, bullet holes in the door, the ladies room door, the floor, blood splattered on the wall by the ladies room and pooled on the floor in front of it, and at the end of the hall by the exit to the hanger, that shapeless bloody mass that was the man from Boston. Colleen gagged on the smell of blood and gunpowder.

"Now little lady, you've been through a lot. Let's just get you out of here," the sheriff said, escorting her down the hall, stepping around the blood and bullet holes and shielding her from the corpse at the end.

"I'm a…" She stepped out into the sun and vomited in the parking lot right in front of the sheriff's car. There were three others, lights flashing, radios chattering, and a ring of Dupree Aviation employees, transient air passengers and crew, gawkers, and a television camera crew. "I'm a," gagging again, and furious with herself, she struggled to regain control.

"Yeah, yeah, it's been tough. I know."

Infuriated at being patronized, she did regain control just as he opened the door of the squad car and pushed her into the front seat; roughly, she thought.

"I'm,' she was cut off when he shut the door and walked to the other side, getting quickly in.

"Secret Service," he said, starting the car and backing out. "Need to move this.'

"You knew?"

"Yes. We need to get you out of here."

"But, you don't know. Dupree's got an army out at the ranch. They may be on the way right now."

"They are on the way right now. I've been watching them since they came into town; we have an undercover deputy with them. He just sent me a text." He backed out and parked the car away from the furor going on at the shooting scene. "It's my son, Deputy Cody Parker."

"With those Brown Shirts?"

"On the bus." The lines on that sun-damaged, cigarette-aged face that had backed down Luther Dupree, were now bunched into a mask of pain. "Governor Rick Perry called up the Texas State Guard this morning. A convoy left Amarillo an hour ago."

"How'd he know?"

"Someone in Colorado."

"What's going to happen?"

"Perry sent them up here to stop the bus and those guys on it. It's gonna get bad."

"Look, maybe I can do something. We're just on the verge of finding out what Dupree is planning, and my friend Webb Collins in still in there, and Rebecca, the girl that got me in. I need to go back," she said, the words tumbling out, her mind reeling as she struggled to focus on what she'd taken an oath to do. "And, there's an inner sanctum, a control center. They're about to do something."

"But you're just a deputy, brought on out of necessity."

"Yes, sheriff; necessity." She looked him square in the face. "Necessity."

He paused. "OK. You armed?"

No, but I'm licensed in Colorado."

"Can you handle this?" He took the side cannon he carried and handed it to her.

"Too big. Never get it back in there. What else do you have? Mine is a Beretta sub-compact 9 millimeter."

He looked around, then opened the car door and approached one of the other cruisers. He returned with a Beretta 9 mm automatic. "This is all we've got. It works just like yours, only bigger."

She took it. "Heavier. OK. Safety, magazine release," she worked the safety, dropped out the clip, pointed it at the floor and cleared the chamber, catching the round that ejected. "I think I have it."

"You've been taught."

"A good friend. NRA member." The irony of that caused her to chuckle, but John Rigdon was a good friend, and he'd spent hours on the range with her. She chuckled again, she'd bought the gun solely to meet someone from the NRA to be a villain in her book, and she'd met John, a kind gentle man. And that led to Boyd. A what? A man. And now she'd just lived through a mob hit, and survived by taking the kind of action that, somehow, she'd trained for her whole life. She'd imagined scenarios where she'd have to depend upon herself, and she had. She had, by damn, she had, and probably saved Jerry's life and her own. And she was now on the point, out in front of the team, with the nation in jeopardy. "I need to get back."

"OK. Be careful, the cavalry is an hour away." He opened the door and she walked back inside.

CHAPTER FORTY FOUR

Lt. Col Clay Reid bounced along U. S. 287 north out of Amarillo in a command vehicle of the Texas State Guard. He'd gotten the call two hours before, while he was mowing the lawn on a Saturday morning. Much like the call Boyd Chailland had gotten two months before, he'd had other plans.

"Open the armory…" The regimental commander had said, calling from Midland. "We're mobilized!"

"For what?" The chaotic national scene seemed far away, and the deployment of most of the Air Force and Navy to bases outside the continent didn't seem to pertain anything for their unit.

"There's an insurrection in Dalhart. Governor Perry has mobilized us to back up the sheriff of Darren County, maintain order, and prevent the loss of life and property. How many can you arm and get up there today?"

"Today? We usually have about a hundred on a drill weekend, but that was last week. I can start a recall roster. We'd be lucky to get fifty here by dark."

"Start the recall roster. Have them assemble at the Darren County Sheriff's office in Dalhart, arm them there. Make a security detail out of the first dozen that show up in Amarillo and start north with the weapons as soon as you can."

"Yes, Ma'am."

So, here he was in an old humvee with three of his neighbors followed by a deuce and a half full of weapons with another half dozen guys. Behind that followed three pickups and a Dodge Caravan; he was going into battle with two dozen members of the 2nd Civil Affairs Battalion of the 39th Composite Regiment of the Texas State Guard.

CHAPTER FORTY FIVE

A key turned in the lock to the steel-plated door guarding Hyde Fleetwood's command center beneath the Gulfstream hanger at Dupree Aviation. Already terrified by the gunfire he'd heard upstairs, Fleetwood cowered behind his desk. The door flew open and a disheveled Luther Dupree burst into the room carrying a 12-gauge shotgun.

"Today's the day. I just got the call."

"OK." Fleetwood sat up, pulled his IPAD closer and began logging in.

"Set it for 1800 hours; that's six o'clock local."

"That's more than two hours. You said it'd be two hours."

"Got some extra notice. That a problem?"

"No. But you said it would be two hours."

"Wait til four o'clock then."

"No, no; I want out of here. I'll set it for six. No trouble."

"Don't try to leave just yet. The sheriff is still here."

"The sheriff?"

"We had some excitement upstairs. Some guy from Boston tried to get into the office with a gun. He and Jerry had a shootout. There is blood and bullet holes all over up there."

"Oh, my!" Fleetwood put his hands to his ears as if he were trying to block the news. "Is anyone hurt?"

"Jerry's on the way to Amarillo in an ambulance; gut shot. I blew the hit man's head off," Dupree said, cocky with the adrenaline high of dodging death and still being on track with his plan. He moved behind Fleetwood and pushed his chair into the desk. "Deploy the weapon. Watch those security cameras up there, and call me on my cell if you see any trouble. I'll get Blue Jack in here from the ranch with a security detail. You should be able to leave in an hour."

Dupree rushed up the stairs but paused just at the door dialing his cell phone.

"Jack, I need you in town." He paused, listening. "Good, that'll serve as a decoy. Arm the rest of the guys and come in by the back way." Pause. "I don't care what you do with him; handcuff him to a water pipe. Just don't let him get away. Leave someone to guard him." Then he left, slamming the steel door behind him.

Hyde Fleetwood finished logging into his IPad, and then he typed in the security code for the Patriot Party database. He located the weapon he'd worked on for the better part of a year and entered a start time, then typed in a long code that he had written on a piece of paper in his wallet and the weapon was launched. He sat back and took a long pull from his Diet Pepsi and watched the security screens. He thought back to his days at MIT.

The university had surely missed the multimillion dollar contracts he'd routinely gathered from the Defense Advanced Research Projects Agency, DARPA. He'd worked for a decade in their Information, Innovation, and Cyber Division studying ways to crack opponent's data systems and protect our own from their hackers. The year before he was summarily fired he moved into the Weapons, Platforms, and Space division. He'd not thought of the cyber attack as a weapon as such, more of a process. That changed. His whole thinking had changed. DARPA wanted to develop cyber attack as a weapon that could be created with a specific system in mind and so needed to think in terms of target, delivery, and effect; just like a bomb.

For the first five years he'd been in Texas Fleetwood worked on MERS and mortgage fraud, and he'd become damn tired of it. Dull stuff, it was. Then Dupree came up with a real challenge.

"What would it take to shut down the GPS system?" Dupree had asked one day.

Now there was a challenge. Fleetwood had worked on parts of it and knew that the best and the brightest of America's technical minds had put together security to safeguard it; that the main control center was located at Schriever Air Force Base east of Colorado Springs; out in the prairie. They had every technical and cyber safeguard in existence deployed around the GPS system; no way to get in. Too remote to get anything close enough to blow it up, not dependent on outside power, obsessed with security. It was one tough nut to crack. Fleetwood got right on it.

Fleetwood had pored over the complexity of the system, admiring it the whole time. GPS is critical to life as we know it in the modern world. Without GPS there are no cell phones because they need its precise timing to coordinate inter-cell handoff to base stations. Credit cards rely on cell phone technology to verify accounts. All aircraft now depend on GPS to navigate across the country and to land, no longer relying on the old radar and approach control systems.

At its core, GPS consists of satellites circling the earth, emitting a radio frequency that is picked up by receivers on earth. The receivers triangulate three satellites to get a precise location. Those satellites are actually flown by Air Force space operators, making minute adjustments in location to keep the orbits just so. It's complex, and yet, it's simple. Fleetwood found the vulnerability.

The central control facility with all its processing function is secure, both physically and electronically. From that central control facility at Schriever the atomic clocks on the satellites are adjusted to within a few nanoseconds of each other so that their internal orbital models remain coordinated. Those adjustments are made by a Kalman filter; a complex algorithm that uses measurements collected over time containing random variations and other inaccuracies to produce very accurate predictions of satellite speed and location. That algorithm assumes a linear dynamical system, i.e., an orderly, predictable universe of numbers. Fleetwood found a way to present the Kalman filter with false data, to confuse it into alarming the space operators that the satellites were out of orbit.

He got into the system at the space tracking station at Thule, Greenland. It's an American Air Force base supported by a Danish base. It was part of the original Distant Early Warning system using a giant sophisticated radar tower to see Russian bombers or missiles approaching from across the top of the world. B-52 bombers used to be stationed there, but no longer. A satellite tracking radar, and space operators make adjustments to satellites on a polar orbit. Some data from there goes to Schriever. Travel to Thule is restricted to those with a reason to go, and a security clearance; no exceptions unless you happen to be on an airliner that gets into trouble over the North Pole, and then guards watch your every move. Six months before, Fleetwood explained the vulnerability he'd found to Dupree and said that he needed to get some-one to Thule to crack the base system. Dupree found a way to crack the base at Thule without going there.

A whole shipment of USB external drives from the central Army Air Force Exchange warehouse in suburban Virginia arrived in Thule, part of a much larger routine shipment. All the packages had been opened and the devices loaded with the same kind of virus that Dupree had used to plant emails in the SecDef's computer. It wasn't long before some airman at Thule bought a thumb drive from the exchange and plugged it into his computer and downloaded something while he was logged on to the main system, and the virus found its way to the satellite data bound for Schriever, opened a port and waited for a message from Hyde Fleetwood.

On August 10 at 2 PM Central Daylight time the message came from Fleetwood, and at 4 PM Central Daylight time the virus began inserting non-linear data into all the satellite position data gathered at Thule and bound for Schriever. Almost immediately a satellite was determined to be off orbit and was taken down from the system, then another, then another. By 5 PM less than half the satellites were considered reliable, and the system was in jeopardy. The Commander of Air Force Space Command, in an excess of caution, shut the system down to save it from whatever was pushing their satellites out of orbit. Then the aberrations stopped. It took two hours to bring it back up. A lot happened in the interim.

CHAPTER FORTY SIX

Boyd Chailland pitched forward on his face and his arms slid over the back of the chair to which he was handcuffed. He leaped to his feet and rushed out the front door of the ranch house, down the two steps and around the corner, headed for the brush out back. He paused long enough to kneel and bring his handcuffed hands to the front, then vaulted the fence and dug all out toward the stock tank. Behind him he heard the Polaris Ranger start up, and soon the unmistakable sound of it gaining, fast. He ducked around a large mesquite bush and the Ranger was on him. Blue Jack jumped from the passenger seat while it was still going full speed and the inertia of his 220 pound body knocked Boyd ten feet into a prickly pear cactus.

"You son of a bitch, I'll break your neck!" Blue Jack said as they rolled in the cactus. A round house right connected with the side of Boyd's head and he saw stars. He rolled quickly to his right and freed himself from Blue Jack's grip.

The Ranger hit him square in the back, knocking him back into the cactus. Blue Jack pounded a fist into Boyd's face rolling to sit on his torso.

Boyd rolled the other way and escaped again on the other side. With his hands cuffed in front of him he was limited in offense, so he delivered a well placed boot to Blue Jack's face. He fell back into the cactus and Boyd streaked into the mesquite.

Now a pickup truck raced around him cutting him off, and the Polaris was coming again. Boyd cut toward some brush just as the Polaris came along side and Blue Jack hit Boyd in the head with a yellow pine two by four. Boyd went down like a sack of boiled cabbage.

Boyd lay under a lake of warm gravy. Warmth and comfort pressed in on him from all directions, holding his limbs with a soft, comfortable weight. There were sounds but they made no sense and Boyd preferred to lie and feel the gravy.

A face came into view. Arthur Chailland, his father, rocked in his chair and stared at Boyd. His face was lined from years of sun and cigarettes and his gaze was unwavering. The rocker creaked the floorboards of the old house with its cadence. No word was spoken as the face continued to bore in on Boyd; stern, worried.

The first year after Arthur Chailland broke his pelvis he spent in a cast and bed. Fancy rehabilitation centers to rebuild broken bodies like his were for people with insurance or money. Broken sharecroppers got a wheelchair and Social Security Disability. Arthur Chailland had tried to fight back, but his wasted legs and crooked back wouldn't hold him up. He rolled the chair out to the barn and stood by the tractor, holding on to the tire, staring up at the seat. From the seat of that tractor he could clothe and feed his son. From that seat he could plow the field, now filled with the dried stalks of last year's cotton; but he had to get there, and stay there.

Six year old Boyd watched from the yard as Bill Hemphill, the landowner, and Odell Harrell, the hired hand who farmed the 160 acres across the road, lifted Arthur Chailland onto the tractor seat. Triumphant, he sat there, unassisted. Within a minute his flimsy muscles cried for relief and he slumped, almost falling. Six weeks later Arthur sat by the tractor again, still staring at the seat. He'd been doing sit ups in the bed, and lifting his legs to gain strength. His friends had their fields to plow and no longer came by to hoist him up. His field had been plowed by Odell's cousin. It was time to plant cotton.

The sweat made rings on the blue work shirt as Arthur leaned against the tire and lifted his withered leg to the step on the side of the tractor. Stretching upward he grasped the steering wheel and stood poised for that familiar motion that would extend his bent knee and take him effortlessly up to the seat. He made the effort and the knee buckled and he fell sideways to the ground.

Boyd hid, feeling like he'd witnessed something he shouldn't have.

Sitting up immediately, Arthur busied himself with the maneuver he'd learned; to drag the wheelchair closer, set the brake and pull up on it. Not stopping to rest, he pulled himself upright and again lifted his foot to the step. This time he pulled forward so that most of his weight was on the foot and gave another heave. Precariously he balanced on that foot, unable to rise any further, before toppling again to the ground.

This was Boyd's vision. Arthur Chailland, drenched now with sweat, trying again and again to mount the tractor. Sweat mixed with tears dripped patiently from that face that was Boyd's only family, as he drug himself upright for the tenth time, the twentieth; the next week, the next month. The face turned and looked out of the barn into the yard where the young Boyd had hidden. The distance was thirty feet, yet Boyd could see every wrinkle, every drop of sweat.

With Arthur's pain, Boyd came up through the warm gravy, awake, focused, enraged. Immobile, he opened one eye. His left arm was handcuffed to a stainless steel sewer pipe beneath the kitchen sink in Luther Dupree's ranch house. His head lay in the cabinet beneath the sink amongst the bottles of dish soap and tile cleaner, legs splayed out to the middle of the kitchen floor. There was hurried activity in the next room.

Blue Jack stood there in his desert camo cargo pants tucked into desert boots, tight brown Under Armor sleeveless T-shirt and boonie hat. He had an M-9 holstered on his belt and he stood with his hands on his hips talking to several similarly dressed militia men.

"The colonel just called. It's today, and there's been trouble already. He shot some guy who tried to slip in and take out the command center. Jerry's been wounded. He needs us there now. I've got a box of hand grenades in the truck. You, come with me. Major Hrothgar, take the men on the bus into town, the driver knows the back way. I'll secure the command center, you spread out around it. Make a perimeter a hundred yards out. Dig in. I'll bring the grenades out."

"Yes, sir."

Blue Jack dug into his pocket and took out a ring of keys. "Smith, and uh,"

"Page, sir."

"Right, Page. You and Smith close up the armory, then take care of cowboy over there."

"Yes, sir."

Blue Jack and one militiaman rushed out the door and drove away in Blue Jack's red truck. Hrothgar went across the parade ground barking orders to a few militiamen who had gotten off the bus, boarded up and the bus pulled out. It was silent for a minute or two.

"What'd he mean, take care of that cowboy?" Smith asked Page, standing on the steps watching the bus bounce down a dirt road.

"Shoot him, I guess."

"You shoot him, I'll lock up the armory."

"Don't have a gun."

"Guess we could get one over there."

They left.

Boyd sat up and pulled his hand. The handcuff was tightly closed on his wrist. He bent forward and spit on his wrist. Even before he tried to slip the hand out he could see the sheer size of it precluded any escape that way. He grabbed the pipe with the other hand and pulled, hard. The muscles of his shoulders and legs strained against the steel to no avail. Feet crunching on the gravel outside told him Smith and Page were coming back.

"How you gonna do it?" Smith asked.

"Just do it, I guess. Certainly got the gun for it." So, it was to be Page.

"You ever shoot one of those?"

"A MAC 10? All the time. Do some damage with that dude."

"Best be doin' it then. We could close up after that and take the four wheeler and get out of here."

Boyd sat up again and pulled and yanked on the pipe. Heart pounding he looked around the room for some tool to try to pick the lock on the cuffs. He had no idea how he might go about that if he found something. There was a large pool of blood where his head had lain in the cabinet and it had run out onto the floor. With his other hand he felt a baseball sized knot on the side of his temple. There was a pause, then Boyd heard the metallic click of a bullet being chambered into the MAC 10. Feet crunched on the gravel as Page walked across the drive and started up the cement steps leading into the living room.

This was it. In twenty seconds that ugly black metal gun with the ridiculously short barrel would cycle ten or twenty bullets from the spring loaded clip up into the chamber and fire them out into Boyd. It wouldn't take five seconds. Even if Page were the worst shot of the bunch, and missed with half of them, the other five or ten would be more than enough. The bullets would go through Boyd, the floor of the house, and well into the dirt under the house. If he were unsure of whether he had done the job, Page could loose another ten shots with just a squeeze of the trigger. No problem.

Boyd sat there looking around, nothing. He turned and looked at the pipe. He grasped it with both hands. Fifteen years of weight lifting had come down to the final exam. Talk of "feeling the iron", and philosophizing about strength flowing from the spirit had become part of Boyd's weekly routine. In the desert of Qatar he had lifted to the point of exhaustion many times to pass the time between his missions into Afghanistan. With his friends he had worked on each muscle group as if, on its day, it was all that mattered. Now they all mattered.

Feet wedged against the counter Boyd saw the pipe break in his mind before he applied all his force. You don't break a board with your fist by thinking about your fist stopping at the board. You see it through. He applied all the strength he had.

"Now!" he shouted with a guttural roar.

The pipe didn't break, but it did pull out from the hole in the bottom of the sink. The metal of the kitchen sink bent and the threads holding the steel pipe broke and with a metallic clunk Boyd fell backwards, free. He turned to see Page's shadow on the screen door. Page would have the machine pistol in his right hand.

Boyd rolled quickly to put his legs under him and released all his force toward the screen door. Just as Page reached to pull it open Boyd hit the door with three steps of momentum. The door came off the hinges and fell outward onto Page who fell backward down the steps with Boyd on top of him.

Boyd was unable to grab Page or the gun because the door was between them. They hit hard with Page's head in the dirt and the rest of him on the steps, on his back. The air went out of him and Boyd felt the resilience of a surprising amount of muscle. Page was not inert. He contracted at the waist and his legs came forward to continue Boyd's momentum. Boyd was pushed forward in a somersault and ended up on his back ten feet out into the yard. Boyd sat up to see Page, dazed but still in control of the gun and rolling over to sit up. Boyd would never get to him before he recovered enough to use it. He heard Smith coming around from the side of the house where he'd gone to start the Polaris. Rolling again to regain his footing Boyd leaped toward the other corner of the house, just in time to avoid a volley of gunfire in his direction by a rapidly recovering Page.

"Go around back. Don't let him get into the brush. He may have a gun out there," Page yelled to Smith.

Although two stories tall at the front and on the east side where the upstairs bedrooms were, the house was only a single story on the west side, with a low overhanging roof. Boyd could imagine Smith running around the back of the house, his gun ready to fire as soon as Boyd came running out toward the chicken coop. Boyd could run straight west, but Page would cut him down before he got to the fence. He leaped up to grab the overhang of the roof and swung his feet into the building. With a push from his feet up the wall he was up onto the roof. Three steps put him to the windows of the second floor bedrooms, locked. He repeated the leap for height and ascended to the top of the roof. He heard Smith's steps swing wide enough to see him from the rear. Anticipating the bullet that must come at any moment he raced toward the front of the house. Hesitation meant death. With a man on each side of the house there was no place to hide. Still, it looked more optimistic than it had thirty seconds earlier. Forward was the only option. Without hesitation Boyd leaped out into space over the crest of the roof, two stories up.

Page had regained his footing and was in the front yard facing the side of the house where Boyd had disappeared only a moment before. The silence was a scream. Time was frozen. As Boyd's trajectory carried him out over the front yard and Page, Boyd realized how high he really was. He also remembered how he'd always had an uneasiness about climbing things. It's one thing to fly an airplane fifty thousand feet into the air, and quite another thing to climb a ladder or a tree ten feet. Some people don't see the difference in those two situations. Boyd did. He hated that feeling more than the realization that Page still had time to look up and follow that look with the gun. Free falling was pure torture.

Boyd's trajectory accelerated downward with the lateral movement becoming less noticeable. The moment of opportunity to use the gun was past. The best Page could do now was perhaps side step just a bit and catch only a glancing blow.

Now that was past and Boyd's feet passed on either side of Page's head. An instant later Boyd's full weight hit Page's neck and shoulders. The feet passing by his face gave Page just enough warning to tense his muscles. The noise was a loud crunch but was actually made up of a series of individual cracks as Page's spine buckled. His feet remained planted, facing westward, while his upper body was carried south by Boyd's momentum. Downward went his neck and shoulders to collapse into his chest. The air went out of him with a high pitched wheeze as they both hit the ground for the second time in less than a minute.

Boyd did a parachute landing roll and ended the fall unscathed, sitting a few feet from Page's inert form.

Glassy eyed, Page lay in a rumpled heap and never drew another breath. Already a dark stain soiled his desert camo cargo pants as his bladder relaxed and emptied its contents. The gun lay by his outstretched hand.

"Where'd he go?" Smith said before he even got to the corner of the house. He was at full run, gun dangling in his right hand.

Boyd dove for Page's gun and came up with it just as Smith realized that he alone was going to have to take out Boyd, or be taken out. His legs stiffened and his toes dug into dirt as he tried to stop as he was raising his weapon.

Boyd had never fired a MAC 10 and hoped the safety was off. He pointed it in the general direction of Smith and pulled the trigger. The noise was a harsh clatter with a piercing metallic component and the empty shells flying into the air in front of his face momentarily distracted Boyd from seeing where the fusillade went. He refocused to see Smith's feet leave the ground as he was slammed backward, a surprised look on his face. Boyd released the trigger, and, in the silence, heard a high pitched yelp as Smith hit the ground on his back. His hands quickly went to his chest as he emitted another high pitched squeal, this one had a gurgle to it. He rolled to his knees and clutched his throat, gun forgotten on the ground beside him. He was facing away and Boyd could see five enlarging red blotches on the back of his brown shirt. Now he fell to the side, clawing at his shirt front as if getting it open would stop the pain.

Boyd stood and approached cautiously, holding the MAC 10 pointed in Smith's general direction. Smith had clawed up the front of his shirt to reveal the loose pattern of holes in the front of his chest. His hands were relaxing as he seemed to adjust to his situation. He looked at Boyd. Did he see? His eyes glazed. He was still.

"I'm sorry," Boyd said quickly, hoping Smith could hear. He hadn't intended to kill anyone; they'd forced it on him.

He looked back at Page, grotesquely distorted with his head and neck pushed down into his chest and his torso bent laterally.

A fly buzzed nearby to break the silence.

Boyd dropped the gun and sat down in the dirt, covering his face. In a moment he looked up to find the two men still there, dead. He retreated from their bodies, sliding backwards into the shade of the house with his back to the foundation looking back and forth at Smith and Page. His hands began to shake as he brushed the dirt off his face. He'd seen death only at funerals. When his bombs hit during the war, he'd been thousands of feet above, and usually already headed back to base. Here, death stared back.

Suddenly he realized that the job was not done yet, not even begun. He looked at his watch, it was 1500 hours, three o'clock. He rose and walked to where Page lay, his sightless eyes staring into the sun. With a grimace on his face Boyd patted Page's pants pockets and found the keys. Without looking into his face Boyd fished out the keys to the cuffs and the armory. He unlocked the cuffs, dangling from his right arm. He dropped them with the key onto the motionless Page and walked around the side of the house.

The key was in the Polaris Ranger and it started right up. He drove over to the armory where he found dozens of AR-15s. Pushing through them he found a Stoner Light Machine Gun and a box of 5.56 mm ammunition in a belt. Lying on the table next to the armory was the megaphone Blue Jack had used during the training. He threw it into the back of the Polaris with the Stoner LMG and took out after the bus filled with militia gunmen.

It was slow going for the bus as the road was little more than a rutted ranch road. Boyd could see the bus struggling in the distance to get over the uneven ground. He gunned the Polaris off into the mesquite. If he was going to take on fifty armed militiamen alone he needed at least some surprise. He looked back to see a plume of dust stirred up by his passing. He hoped the guys in the back of the bus were not looking to the south.

Flanking the bus he pulled out ahead of it and found a clearing beside the road. He careened to a halt and stood up, setting the LMG on the top of the windshield. The bus drew abreast and he fired a brief volley into the top of the windows in the middle of the bus. He grabbed the megaphone.

"Stop! You're surrounded by federal agents. Put down your weapons, raise your hands."

Boyd saw through the bus and heads began to show, having hit the floor with the fusillade. It is one thing to be a big bad boy when you're on the shooting end, but take some incoming and sobriety returns fast. The megaphone added a convincing sound of authority. They'd been hearing it for two weeks. Hands went up.

"Open the bus." The driver opened the door. "Leave your weapons on the bus. Come out one at a time."

They started coming out. Major Hrothgar was first, fire in his eyes.

"Hrothgar! On the ground."

Hrothgar hesitated. Boyd fired a volley over the bus. The man fell face down on the ground.

"The rest of you, line up, hands on the bus. Now!"

And they did.

"Driver, anyone left inside?"

The driver stood and looked back before responding, "No."

"Drive to town. Don't stop."

"Yes sir."

Boyd could tell the driver was a contractor. He seemed eager to get going, and the bus pulled out leaving fifty disarmed revolutionaries in a line, their officer face down in the dirt.

"Follow the bus."

Boyd jumped back into the seat and gunned the Polaris onto the road behind the bus, spraying dirt onto Blue Jack's men. It was just dawning on them that they'd been disarmed by one man. Well, it was one man with a machine gun.

CHAPTER FORTY SEVEN

Blue Jack bounced onto the airport property from a ranch road to the west and roared down the active runway toward Dupree Aviation, a cloud of dust following him onto the concrete. The hanger doors were open, the Gulfstream, Lear and Messerschmitt were safe, and there was no sign of the sheriff. The parking lot was nearly empty and there were no transient aircraft, except that pesky Cessna 170 that had been there all week. It looked serene.

"Go around back and secure the doors," he barked to the militiaman who had accompanied him as the truck careened to a screeching stop in front of the operations building.

"Go home," he barked at the lone receptionist in flight operations. He rushed through the lobby, M-9 holstered, AR-15 in his hand. His nose was swollen and crooked from the fight with Boyd, and he had prickly pear barbs, some having drawn blood, still studding the back of his brown Under Armor tight fitting T-shirt. He didn't notice.

The klaxon went off again as Blue Jack rounded the corner with his weapons and set off the metal detector. He was halted by the sight of blood and bullet holes more than the jarring noise of the alarm. No one responded and he hurried down the hall to the open door at the end and Luther Dupree's office. Empty.

He checked his own office, Jerry's office, and the bathroom. Empty. Skipping by the door to Luther Dupree's apartment he approached the steel door to the command center; open.

Webb Collins sat at the command module tapping something into the computer. Already he'd broken into something as the screen showed a spreadsheet of something. The Command Center; compromised!

Rage welled up in Jack Anders. This intruder had no right to be here. He'd told the colonel to get rid of this sneaky creep and here he was, still here. He took the steps two at a time.

"Get out of here!" He screamed, momentum carrying him into Webb, who was rolling backwards in the control module chair. He grabbed Webb by the shirt and yanked him to his feet, then threw him bodily to the base of the steps. He'd planned to chase him up the steps and catch him in the hall and there to give him the beating he so richly deserved.

But, Webb held his ground. The 5 ft. 7 in. 140 pound flight surgeon threw a punch at Blue Jack and caught him right in his recently broken nose. Blood splattered across the room and Blue Jack wailed in pain. Then, that demon Blue Jack kept so carefully contained got loose.

"Arrgghh!" Blue Jack grabbed Webb and threw him up the stairs, following with a round house right that caught

Webb on the side of the head and dashed him against the metal stair railing. He grabbed Webb and, shifting his weight backwards down the stairs picked him up above his head and dashed him to the ground.

"Secret Service!" Webb yelled as he hit the ground with a thud.

Blue Jack picked Webb up again and dashed him against the stairs again, this time his head hit the railing fully and he went limp.

"Stop!" Colleen Chamorro stood at the top of the stairs in the open steel door.

"Eeyyaah!" Blue Jack howled as he picked Webb's limp body up a third time and flung him all the way up the stairs striking the top step and rolling into Colleen's feet. Blue Jack was right behind Webb's lifeless body.

Colleen Chamorro raised the Beretta 9 mm Sheriff Parker had given her and fired a tight pattern of three shots into Blue Jack's chest. The bullets straightened him up and he looked at her then fell backward down the steps to lie at the bottom with his head and torso on the floor and his legs and feet on the last two steps.

Blue Jack struggled to rise, but Colleen's bullets had severed his spine and he was paralyzed. Then the pain stopped and he felt calm. There was a light and he shifted his focus to that, forgetting about Colleen, Webb, the Patriot Party, Dupree Aviation. He heard singing. A men's chorus was singing the "Horst Wessel Lied" in German; the anthem of the Nazi Party. They were young men and dressed in brown shirts similar to his. The tune, an ancient Nordic folk tune touched something in his soul and he began to sing along. That tune, with slightly different musical phrasing, is widely known as "How Great Thou Art," and was the tune Boyd had heard the militiamen singing at the end of their duty day. Blue Jack joined in and the scene changed from modern day brown-shirted militiamen to an older time and jack-booted *Sturmabteilung,* Hitler's SS troopers, then it changed again and long-haired Viking warriors with helmets and shields motioned for him to join them, and he did, and the chorus grew louder as all the young men joined Blue Jack Anders the warrior as his soul entered Valhalla, the hall of the slain.

CHAPTER FORTY EIGHT

Lt. Col. Clay Reid pulled up at the Darren County Sheriff's office with his advanced contingent of the Texas State Guard. He was soon augmented by a guardsman from Dalhart who'd gotten the recall, but his uniform was at the laundry, and he brought his brother who wasn't in the guard but was available. Sheriff Lane Parker deputized both of them and handed them badges. That made 26 plus the sheriff, the jailor and one other deputy.

"We've got two buses of Nazi militiamen coming in from Luther Dupree's ranch west of town, and we've got an undercover sheriff's deputy, my son Cody Parker, on the bus with 'em," Parker said, addressing the assembled group. "We need to do this without a lot of shooting. We don't even know if they're armed."

"Sheriff, we're here to back you up. We won't shoot unless you do," Reid said.

The two buses of unarmed militiamen Dupree had sent back to rest up for another shift had taken the paved road back to town from the ranch; 35 miles. They stopped at a stop sign by a rural grocery store and turned onto the main road to the airport and town. The first bus turned into the state highway and immediately encountered the sheriff's car blocking the road with lights flashing and flanked by Lt Col Reid's command vehicle, also with flashers, and two pickup trucks. Standing by the sheriff was Reid and a dozen of his guardsmen in uniform, weapons at the ready. The other sheriff's car came from behind the store and blocked the second bus from backing up. Two more pickups and another dozen guardsmen stepped out, guns pointed at the door.

No shots were fired; the insurrection in Darren County was over.

CHAPTER FORTY NINE

The black Messerschmitt with the white swastikas on the wings and fuselage roared over Boyd's head as he followed Blue Jack's tracks through the fence at the west end of the airport. He watched it ascend to the west and then turn north out of sight as he drove the Polaris Ranger across the active runway to the front of Dupree Aviation. Colleen stood at the doorway, a pistol in her hand dangling at her side.

"Webb's dead and Dupree's gone," she said, tears streaming down her face, but composed otherwise.

"What happened?"

"Come see," she turned and he followed her through the deserted lobby, down the hall with the klaxon still blaring, the bullet holes in the ladies room door, and the pools of blood now drying, to the open door to Dupree's office, and down that hall to the open steel door of the command center. Webb lay on his side on the steps down to the command module. His head was a bloody smashed mess and his brains were evident sliding down the side of the stair. He was most decidedly dead. Blue Jack lay dead also, at the bottom of the stairs. Three bullet holes in his chest, much like Smith out at the ranch.

"We thought you were dead too, especially after Blue Jack got here," she said, still looking at Webb.

"I almost was." He was tired, very tired as he looked at his friend, and the man who had killed him.

"It was horrible. He smashed Webb like a doll. I..I."

"You shot him."

"I never thought I'd ever use a firearm on another person. I feel terrible."

They were both silent for a minute.

"A lot's happened since you dropped out of sight," she said, turning back and walking down the hall. "Governor Rick Perry called up the Texas State Guard and they've intercepted two buses of militiamen just down the road."

"Good. Those are the guys without guns. I stopped the guys with the guns ten miles west of here and they're walking in. We need to get someone out there to pick them up before they burst in on some rancher and rearm, or die of thirst."

"How'd you do that?"

"Long story; luck really. Also, there are a couple dead guys out at the ranch. Blue Jack pulled out and told two of his men to finish me off. We had quite the fight."

"You shot two men?"

"I shot one, the other I, uh, well, I jumped on."

"Oh, and Marv Crowder is here, with your plane."

"My plane?"

"That Mustang you asked him to get. He got it."

"It's here? They told me he was fired and the Denver Secret Service office was closed down."

"He's here, and it's here, and a lot of other people are here. They're all over at the Moore County Airport in Dumas. It's about 15 miles. Here, call him." Boyd took her cell phone.

"Marv! Colleen tells me you got the Mustang."

"Yes I did. Your buddy Ben Culpepper is a great American patriot, and a tough negotiator. You wouldn't believe what I had to guarantee to get that plane down here; and he insisted on flying it here himself."

"He's a good man. I heard you were fired."

"Fired indeed, but then the Director got fired and I got rehired with a promotion, all in an afternoon. But, hey enough of that. Are you OK? We still don't know what we're doing down here."

"Well one thing we know, a fully armed Messerschmitt is air-borne with Luther Dupree at the controls. That can't be good. My friend Webb is dead, as is Blue Jack, the Neo-Nazi that was training the militia. On the other hand, Colleen tells me the sheriff and the Texas State Guard got two busloads of unarmed militia on the north side of town and I stopped the third bus ten miles to the west and got them disarmed. They're walking back so we need to get someone out there to pick 'em up."

"You work fast."

"Got lucky. Webb cracked into their database but we don't know what he found. Colleen and I are going to look around here."

"Well, your plane is ready if you can figure out what you're going to do with it."

"Maybe fly it back to Colorado."

"That would make me happy."

Re-entering Dupree Aviation they traversed the hall with the bullet holes and blood, now drawing swarms of flies as the doors had been open. Dupree's office was open and in disarray. Boyd opened a drape and beheld an internal window into the hanger where the Messerschmitt had been.

"Sits and looks at his baby," Boyd said, looking at the now empty hanger. "Let's start there." They opened a back door and entered the hanger.

"Smells like gas," Colleen said.

"And oil, and brake fluid, and lubricating fluids; the smell of active piston era aviation. Ahh, the scent of heroes."

"To you, maybe, the scent of death and destruction to the rest of us," Colleen retorted without a smile.

"Look at the tracks across the grass toward the runway," Boyd said, pointing out the open hanger door. "He cranked it up and just gunned it out the door and up. The Messerschmitt was made to take off from a grass strip."

"Nifty."

"Handy in a war that moves about."

"Like I said, nifty." There was no humor in Colleens' voice.

"Look here," Boyd said, drawing Colleen's attention to an open crate of 20-millimeter ammunition. "Each one of those would blow the roof off your car, and he can fire four a second."

"You love this stuff too much."

"Hmm, doing some modifications," he said, pointing out a pile of electronic equipment on a work bench. "Looks like he took out the ILS, HF radio, GPS navigation, LORAN, and some black boxes I don't recognize. Some of it looks old, some is new."

"Why?"

"Don't know. Maybe upgrade, maybe cutting weight." He looked around and added, "Don't see any indications of building a fuel tank. He must be cutting weight."

"Let's see what Webb found. He gave his life for something," Colleen said.

They traversed Dupree's office and stopped at the top of the stairs, Webb's lifeless body and that of Blue Jack stretched out below them.

"I can't go down there, I'm getting sick again," she said. Boyd stepped gingerly over Webb and Blue Jack and approached the command console. Sitting down he moved the mouse and the screen came on. It showed a list of the membership of Delano, when the members were initiated and who nominated them. Scrolling down was another list, all the donors to the Patriot Party in the past decade; names, addresses, Social Security Numbers.

Boyd retraced his steps back up the steps and encountered the sound of Colleen vomiting in Dupree's bathroom.

"I've got to get out of here, the smell…. Yurrph!" She retched again, then struggled to make herself heard. "Couldn't we cover them up or something?"

"Yeah, I'll look in Dupree's apartment and get a blanket or something, at least for Webb." He made a quick search of the simple apartment Dupree had used when not staying at the ranch and found a blanket and covered Webb.

"Nothing much there," he said returning to the office. He went to the desk and rifled through it. "Or here."

"Boyd, the wall."

He looked up, "Wow. That's it!"

Pinned to the wall and so large that it had at first looked like wallpaper was a schematic drawing of a an airplane.

"Is that his dream sheet?"

"No, that's his target. Let me have that cell phone again."

It was a engineer's drawing of a Boeing 747 with electrical and hydraulic lines highlighted. In one corner was a schematic of a GE jet engine.

"Marv, where's the President today?"

"Get right back to you."

"The President? How can you tell?"

"Incredible. This has all been a kabuki play; a real life drama staged by Dupree to get us to this exact point. Don't you see, he's been leaking all the news stories, he deliberately implicated the Boston mob in mortgage fraud with John Rigdon's ranch to get Congressman Kelly, and probably took me out there that night so I'd be part of catching on to it.

He brought Blue Jack here and helped him to have the Nazi training camp he'd dreamed of, knowing that at some point they'd hit authority and there'd be headlines; Webb didn't crack the computer downstairs, it was on and open to lists of Delano and the Patriot Party. He wants all this found!" Boyd paused, then said, "Say, why hasn't Marv called back?" He dialed Marv's number.

The cell phone gave a busy signal.

That's when the GPS system went down. Cell phones ceased to function. A million worried travelers began calling the airlines, the FAA, Dallas Fort Worth International Airport, the White House, the FBI, the Secret Service; all the land lines clogged up and shut down.

The GPS based Instrument Landing System at DFW ceased to function and they reverted to their older radar based ILS, slowing down departures and arrivals. With airliners reporting their GPS navigation out the system slowed down to one approach and one departure at a time, stacking inbound aircraft in giant circling patterns east and west of the Dallas metropolitan area.

"How far is that other airport?"

"Takes about half an hour to get over there," Colleen replied.

"Let's take the Cessna," Boyd said, rushing out the door, through the lobby and out the front. The Cessna was parked on the refueling ramp. It started right away and they taxied out toward the main runway.

Hyde Fleetwood was still in the Dupree Aviation parking lot, hunched down in the front seat of his car talking with Luther Dupree on the cell phone. When it quit he smiled, started his car and leisurely drove out the drive.

CHAPTER FIFTY

Boyd tried the Unicom "open air" frequency on the Cessna's radio but the chatter over the impending shutdown at DFW drowned out communication. He tried the emergency guard frequency attempting to get through to Dallas Center but that was tied up as well.

"Good thing we're not on fire and about to crash, nobody would hear us," He said, announcing again on the open frequency that he was turning onto a downwind leg at Moore County Airport in Dumas.

The windshield shattered.

"Boyd!" Colleen screamed.

The Cessna was rocked by a dozen hammer blows on the wings and fuselage.

"Hail?" She screamed.

"Bullets," he replied, pulling the yoke fully back against his chest and slamming his right foot down on the right rudder pedal. The black Messerschmitt roared by not a hundred feet above them. The nose of the little plane pulled up and it briefly gained altitude before losing power and stalling. It fell off toward the right wing. "That was Dupree, he's using his machine gun and not the cannon, or we'd be toast. Hold on."

The Cessna spun wildly out of control, dropping straight down.

"Uh, hand me that clip board there," he said, debris was flying about the cockpit. When she didn't respond he reached over her and retrieved a clipboard. He still clutched the yoke to his chest as he looked at the numbers he'd written on it before takeoff. "3984. Remember that number." He craned his neck around, searching the ground which was fast approaching.

"What?"

He pointed to the altimeter without looking, "That's the number that will be there when we hit the ground."

"Hit the ground?"

A few hundred feet off the ground Boyd pulled his foot off the rudder pedal and pushed the yoke back forward, the little plane corrected its stall and was now in controlled flight, diving straight toward the ground. The airspeed indicator rose to over seventy knots and Boyd pulled the nose up to only a thirty degree dive. The ground continued to rush up and at the last moment he flared and they touched the ground at seventy knots in a field of wheat stubble, not a mile from the Moore County Airport. The wheat stubble made a loud roar as the wheels hit it first and before they started bouncing on the plowed furrows. Boyd cut the engine and pulled the yoke back again. The plane came to a stop and Boyd was already out of his seatbelt and opening the door.

"Get out!" He jumped to the ground and Colleen opened the other door. "Grab the tail, help me with this!" He called as she was slow to respond. "Pull it up." He scanned the sky for the Messerschmitt.

Numbly Colleen complied. Together they lifted the tail of the small aircraft and its heavier nose fell to the ground, tail pushed up into the air. Boyd pulled out his survival knife, still strapped to his ankle and rushed to the wing plunging the knife into the thin sheet metal. Gasoline poured out over his hand.

"Got a light?" he asked gaily, scanning around the debris of the cockpit looking for and finding a butane lighter. Colleen stood by staring blankly. Boyd lit a piece of paper with the lighter and tossed it toward the plane. Instantly a loud "Whoomp" pushed them back and the plane was engulfed in flame.

"Lie in the stubble, hide under the smoke. Here he comes," Boyd said, diving under the tail to be under the cloud of smoke billowing up from the front of the Cessna. Colleen followed just as the Messerschmitt passed overhead with a roar. The wheat stubble caught fire and drove them further and further from the hotly burning Cessna. They stayed in the smoke just in front of the leading edge of the fire, fanned by a steady prairie breeze. Once more the throaty roar of Dupree's machine passed overhead and then was gone.

"He thinks he got us," Boyd said triumphantly as he stepped over the burning edge of the stubble.

"I think he did," Colleen said, then kneeled and vomited again, mixing what little was left in her stomach with the black ash on the ground. "How'd he know?"

"Somebody must have called him. He couldn't have remembered the call sign of the Cessna and come back from wherever he was. It also tells us that we're not in his plans from now on."

"It's already Dupree one, Chailland zero. You sure you want to continue?" Colleen asked, wiping her face off with a disposable tissue. A pickup truck was lumbering over the wheat stubble from the nearby airfield to pick them up.

CHAPTER FIFTY ONE

The P-51 looked regal sitting in the shade of the hanger that had held two crop dusters. As the pickup with Boyd and Colleen approached, Ben Culpepper and Marv Crowder and a gaggle of mechanics in civilian clothes rushed over. They'd witnessed the shoot down and seen the Messerschmitt swoop by, headed south.

"Boyd! Are you OK? It looks like the war with Dupree has started," Ben Culpepper asked.

"Trying out his new toy," Boyd replied, jumping out of the truck with Colleen. "Do you think he saw what you've got here?" He nodded toward the Mustang.

"I doubt it; we'd pushed it all the way under the roof just in case."

Turning to Marv Crowder, Boyd asked, "Marv, what did you find out about the President?"

Marv hesitated for a moment, eying the little crowd around them. Deciding they were part of the same team, he proceeded.

"We've got a problem. The entire GPS system must be down, nobody's cell phones are working, so I used my satellite phone, which is just for such an eventuality, but the Secret Service Command Center won't take my call. I called the White House situation room, but I lack the credentials to get in there. The internet is up, so I sent emails to those places, but I haven't heard anything. I did get the Chief Field Agent, the guy who rehired me. There's a battle going on in Washington right now. He said that I had the full authority of the United States government behind me and to proceed as I see fit, but not to expect any help."

"What? How can that be?"

"The big problem is the Department of Defense. Some units began refusing orders from the Pentagon, saying they were taking orders only from the President. To reassert his control, the SecDef executed a dispersal contingency plan that had been in place for years. Then the President called the Chairman of the Joint Chiefs on the phone and summoned him to the White House. He went. In person the President told the chairman to expel the SecDef from the Pentagon and take orders only from the President. While the chairman was out, the SecDef closed down the Pentagon, put tanks around the perimeter. The chairman can't get back in."

"So we don't know where the President is?"

"No. I alerted the Chief Field Agent that Dupree may be targeting Air Force One, and he's going to find out where it is today and get back to me on my satellite phone. In the meantime, I've been in touch with Lt Col Reid of the Texas State Guard. He's on his way over here from Dalhart. He now has nearly a hundred guardsmen with more on the way from Midland and Ft. Worth. He tells me there's a strange development at Ft. Hood. Much of the garrison went to Qatar, but what's left is supposed to be confined to quarters, and to make sure they are, the Texas State Guard is positioned at all the entrances to the post. It's a standoff. He tells me he's hearing the same thing from other states; a federal/state stalemate. It hasn't gotten to shooting yet, but somebody somewhere might lose his head and pop off some rounds and the fight would be on."

"So, it's about control and who is to be in charge?" Colleen asked, standing there in the khaki slacks she'd worn to work that morning, a dirty blouse and a holstered Berretta 9 mm pistol on her hip. Marv had brought Secret Service badges for everyone and hers was pinned to her belt.

"Right," Marv said. "The President is the president, whether he was ever in Delano or not. So, he's the ultimate authority, at least over the executive branch, but some of his own appointees are resisting, still holding on to control of their agencies. Over at the Capital we've got committee hearings going around the clock, and bills mandating this and that being brought forth every hour. Each side is trying to expose something about the other and confirm their own authority."

"Who's in charge here?" Boyd asked, just as Lt Col Clay Reid appeared in his command vehicle with the deuce and a half behind and two dozen pickup trucks following, all filled with uniformed Texas State Guard men and women.

"I guess we'll see," Crowder said, breaking away to greet the convoy. The two men shook hands and engaged in earnest conversation for several minutes. Soon Crowder was on his satellite phone while Reid talked on a radio as the Texas Guard established a perimeter and posted guards at the entrance to the Moore County Airport.

"Boyd, you need to meet someone," Ben said, directing Boyd's attention to a dapper man in his late forties standing with the crowd that had been working on the Mustang. "This is Milt Fry, the chief pilot of the Commemorative Air Force in Midland, Texas. I called him right away when Marv told me what was up. He's the only guy we know of who has flown both the Mustang and the Messerschmitt. He came in on that Cessna 210 over there this morning and brought along some mechanics that know this old warbird better than I do."

"Happy to meet you," Boyd said.

"We did the major overhaul of Ben's plane a few years ago, and we helped Dupree get his Messerschmitt airworthy after an overhaul in Germany three years ago. We know both the planes. We had no idea Dupree was up to anything. We thought he was just another pilot who made enough money to buy his dream plane."

"If it does come down to me and him; who has the advantage," Boyd asked.

"The better pilot is usually the answer to that question." Fry held up a picture of a Messerschmitt bf-109 "Dupree's plane is the bf-109 G, built in 1943. He's got one of the only operational Daimler-Benz DB 605A engines in the world, and he's had German mechanics working on it from day one. It's an inverted V-12 and gives him 1455 horsepower. His max speed is going to be around 400 knots at 20,000 feet." Fry walked back to the Mustang as he talked about his passion, the Messerschmitt. Four greasy mechanics went back to work loading the last of six 50 cal machine guns into the wing of the Mustang as he talked. Boyd, the lanky jock pilot leaned against the wing with Colleen at his side, adjusting the Beretta holstered on her hip. Ben, the chubby crop duster in dirty coveralls leaned against the fuselage of his treasure. Soon they were joined by Marv Crowder and Clay Reid.

"The Bf-109 is not versatile, and it's not easy to fly. To achieve what they wanted, they had to give up some important features that you may be able to exploit if you go up against it. The wing is very thin. At the time of its design, they felt they needed that for speed. And, indeed, it did produce a very fast aircraft. But, it has the main spar, or structural member running lengthwise down the center of the wing. There is no room for fuel or armament. The landing gear are too close together and, for some unknown reason angle out from the body. It's a bitch to land. Now look at the tail. It's too small with limited rudder and not enough horizontal stabilizer, and as a result it's a relatively unstable aircraft. It does fine when zipping along at 375 knots, and it turns well, but in tight maneuver down near the stall speed it departs controlled flight at the most inopportune moments. You never know. The really good pilots seemed to plan through the loss of control to some recovery maneuver at just the point an inexperienced pilot would find himself spinning toward the ground," Fry wobbled his hand in demonstration and dropped it toward the pavement.

"Contrast that with this beauty," Fry said, relaxing and becoming more aware of his audience. He pointed out the thicker wing of the P-51 and looked at Culpepper. "Within this wing are six machine guns and how much fuel?"

"About ninety gallons, each side," Ben said, enjoying the show.

"And look at those wide, forgiving landing gear," Fry said as the group looked down at the Mustang's wheels. "Now look at the tail on the Mustang. It's tall and thick, and it has plenty of rudder. This particular aircraft here has the Packard V-1650 supercharged V-12 that delivers 1490 horsepower at 25,000 feet. It has a maximum speed of 437 knots and stalls at 100 knots. So, you have more power, more speed, and more fuel in a more stable aircraft."

"I feel better," Boyd said laughing.

"This plane has some drawbacks too," Fry said, patting the Mustang. "It doesn't stall easy, but when it does, it does it in spades. It's hard to recover. Even with all those machine guns, it doesn't quite have the punch the 109 has with its 20 mm cannon. I don't know for sure, but I think the 109 could turn inside a P-51." Fry was thoughtful, painfully so for Boyd.

"How do I shoot him down?" Ben asked.

"The Messerschmitt is really compact. The front is all engine, from skin on top to skin on bottom, no non-essential parts to absorb fire. The middle is all pilot. Put a round through the cockpit and you got him. The radios are behind the pilot, and the fuel tank is about here," he said, pointing on the Mustang to an area a couple feet behind the canopy. "There is no armor. I wouldn't waste time trying to shoot the tail off or putting holes in the wings. Go for the big stuff."

"No armor? I thought all these planes had armor to protect the pilot," Boyd said.

"This one does. Behind the pilot, unless Ben took it out, and in back of the engine," Fry said, looking at Ben.

"No armor behind. The plate in the back of the engine is the firewall and doesn't come out. There's also a kidney shaped plate in front of the engine that protects the headers and the tank of the cooling system. Hell, the radios are where the armor behind the pilot used to be. You gotta have radios," Ben said defensively.

Boyd stood up and felt his back arch a bit as he looked at the fuselage where the armor wasn't.

"What strategy do you recommend?" One of the mechanics asked.

"First, the 109 won't have enough fuel to do much more than get up to altitude, fight for fifteen minutes and glide back down for gas. So, you can stall him and he'll have to break off. Second, both of the aircraft take muscle to fly; there is no hydraulic assist like you guys are used to in your modern fighters. Being the younger man, you can wear him down. Your plane is bigger and has more control surface so you'll have more to pull, but he's how old?"

"Pushing sixty," Boyd said.

"On the other hand, he's been flying the 109 for three years and you have, what, one flight in the Mustang?"

"This is probably just academic. Dupree will likely fly his plane to Mexico and disappear and in a day or two we'll be having some laughs while we work to get these machine guns out without the ATF coming down on us," Culpepper said.

CHAPTER FIFTY TWO

Acting Secretary of Defense Dan Ames strode into the command center in the basement of the Pentagon. Everyone in the room came to attention.

"As you were, gentlemen. What's the situation?" He sat at the head of the table, surrounded by admirals and generals – all the Service Chiefs except the Air Force. The aides and executive officers stood around the walls of the room, and the control room behind the glass was filled to standing room only.

"Mr. Secretary, the President is in grave danger." The Chairman of the Joint Chiefs began the meeting. "We caught an Air Force Colonel at Base Operations at Andrews Air Force Base calling someone named Dupree on a satellite telephone just as Air Force One was taking off today. We interrogated him and he wouldn't tell us much, but we located the telephone he called. It's in Wizard Wells, Texas. That's just north of Dallas. Then the GPS went down. We think that was sabotage, probably by the Chinese. They infiltrated the control center at Schriever Air Force Base and contaminated the data controlling our satellites. Fortunately, none of the Army or

Navy satellites were involved, and the National Reconnaissance Agency satellites are sound. Then Air Force One lost all radio communications."

"How did that happen?"

"We think it was a small fire, sir. We know they're proceeding on course because the FAA is following them, but we can't raise them on the radio."

"Surely there's redundancy in the system."

"Yes, sir. But there was a clear air lightening strike, or something, which hit our antenna here today and knocked out our VHF and UHF bands that we use for direct link to the President."

"I thought the President was going to be in Washington tonight," Ames said.

"A diversion, sir, to mask his trip to the National Education Association for a major address. He was planning to make a speech and get right back to DC."

"Where's the meeting?"

"Dallas. He's due in at 18:45 local."

"Just at dusk."

"Yes, sir."

"And no GPS, so DFW will be backed up. Chaos in the skies."

"Right, sir. We're developing a contingency plan now."

"Can't you get some fighters up; a CAP over Dallas?"

"When the previous SecDef executed the dispersal plan it put a lot of our resources out of reach. Then the Commander of the Southwest Air Defense sector scrambled his fighters from the Texas Air National Guard for a nuclear scenario and sent them to Holloman Air Force Base in New Mexico. They're two hours away from Dallas, sir."

"Incredible. So, tonight was to be the big night. The President flies into a trap and my predecessor and his buddies in the Senate were all set to take over in the confusion after a fiery crash; a coup d'etat in the United States of America."

"Sir, I wouldn't know about that."

"We have one thin line of defense left," Ames said, turning to the control room and holding up a piece of paper. "Get me Special Agent Boyd Chailland of the Secret Service at this number in Dumas, Texas."

CHAPTER FIFTY THREE

An old Phillips 66 gasoline truck with Oklahoma plates bounced down the dusty road and into the drive of the Moore County Airport just as the telephone in the office rang. One of the men standing around the P-51 was the airport manager and he sprinted into the office to answer it.

"Special Agent Boyd Chailland! Phone call. Says it's urgent."

The crowd went silent. Boyd rushed to the office.

"Boyd, this is Dan Ames at the Pentagon Command Center. I'm the Acting SecDef. Marv Crowder has kept me up to date on all that's happened down there. Now we know why, how, and when. The President is due in Dallas in less than an hour; 18:45. Air Force One is flying without radio communication, and DFW is in crisis mode without GPS. It's clear to me that some in our own organization have been behind a plan to assassinate the President, and Luther Dupree has been their tool. He must be stopped."

"Yes sir."

"Get that Mustang up."

"This flight suit has always been big in the shoulders, it should fit you fine," Ben said, stepping out of the oil stained flight suit he'd worn every time Boyd had ever seen him and standing in his boxer shorts. "The parachute is in the jump seat in the back of the cockpit, better get it cinched up tight now."

There was urgency and a certain sadness in all of this. Boyd had worn the latest in flight gear his whole career, usually on missions where having fireproof clothing was not really that important. Now that it very well could be, gasoline is far more flammable than jet fuel, he was wearing a suit that was soaked in lubricating oil. When had the parachute last been repacked? He climbed the wing and leaned into the cockpit to retrieve the parachute and saw the inspection tag was fairly recent. He felt better as he jumped back to the ground.

"Got that gas all the way from the refinery in Oklahoma City. 115/145 av gas, hotter than even the high lead fuel they used in the Mustang when it was new. Marv Crowder asked me what was the best and I told him. That's going to add a lot of power," Ben said excitedly as the gasoline truck pulled up to the Mustang and pulled a hose toward it.

Boyd stripped down to his shorts and climbed into Ben's flight suit. As he bent over to pull up the legs Colleen and the mechanics standing behind him could see the large purple bruise spreading out from his torso from the fall onto Page out at the ranch, and the lump on the back of his head with blood matting his hair from Blue Jack's blow with the yellow pine two by four.

"Boyd, are you OK?" She asked, smelling the blood and two days of sweat.

He turned toward her, a quizzical look on his face. "Babe, this is what I do, remember?" He zipped up the flight suit, zipped the flight boots, and climbed back onto the wing. One of the mechanics, a former crew chief, joined him and helped strap him into the Mustang.

"We took the gate off the carburetor and adjusted the prop governor. When you flew it before, take-off power was at 3000 RPM, now it will be 3400. You had about 61 inches of manifold pressure before, now you'll have 80 or 90. Be careful and try not to stay in full military power too long, it will run hot." Fry said, standing on the wing on the other side.

"This is the cocking mechanism for the guns," Ben said, having climbed up behind the mechanic strapping Boyd in. "It's run by a compressed air cylinder. Arm it as soon as you're up to altitude. The plane shakes when you fire the guns, but not enough to throw off your aim. They're aimed to converge at a hundred yards. You have maybe thirty seconds worth of ammunition. If you have to get out, jettison the canopy and trim the nose down, then turn inverted, unstrap the seat belt, and let go of the stick. The plane will flip nose up and throw you out."

Comforting, Boyd thought as Ben handed him his helmet from Buckley. The crew chief reviewed the instruments and some of the basics of starting and flying the plane that Ben had taught him the month before. Ben jumped down and sprinted to the office to adjust the radio.

"Mustang One, do you read me?" Boyd acknowledged the transmission.

The crew chief jumped down from the wing and attached the external power source to start the engine. The crowd backed away. The diesel engine on the power source sprang to life and then Boyd hit the starter switch, and the big four-blade prop began to slowly turn. The Mustang coughed a couple times and then caught. Black smoke shot out of the six exhaust ports on either side of the fuselage. Instantly the wind from the prop washed over the hanger area, blowing debris and knocking over a stepladder carelessly left leaning against a counter.

Feeling the powerful engine throbbing just in front of him, with the knowledge that this was not a joy ride but real combat gave Boyd a rush of adrenalin that masked his fatigue and the pain in his head and back. He checked the gauges again and gave a thumbs up to the crew chief and the crowd, pointed once at Colleen and saluted them all smartly before turning his attention to the ramp and adding power. The noise increased and the P-51 rolled toward the end of the runway.

CHAPTER FIFTY TWO

The sun was just a bright rim on the horizon as Luther Dupree climbed for altitude coming off the grass strip at Wizard Wells, Texas with a full tank of gas. He armed the guns in his Messerschmitt as he turned east and flipped through the frequencies of a simple VHF radio, chuckling at the chaos in the air traffic control system.

"But I've got..." was repeated over and over as pilots argued with Dallas Center that was diverting and delaying their flight plans.

He circled unseen upward, no transponder, no flight plan; a speck in the evening sky. At twenty thousand feet he leveled off and looked down at the blue twinkle of the swimming pools in the northern suburbs as they caught the fading sunlight.

The sun was down now, and darkness spread like a shadow across the west. Dupree turned east and scanned the horizon for a blinking red light at about heading 060 from his location. To the south of that direction he could see dozens, no hundreds of blinking lights in a holding pattern of delayed airliners Dallas Center was stacking from 15,000 to 35,000 feet over east Texas. He looked back over his shoulder at a similar pattern on the Ft. Worth side of town. He felt better than he'd ever felt in his whole life.

In a few minutes the entire world was going to change and most of the people who had helped him change it were going to find out that it was his plans being realized and not theirs. It was a patriotic move, really. Hubris and greed in high places was going to be laid bare and violence was inevitable as the long knives of revenge took their toll. America would writhe as its government collapsed, and Luther Dupree would be rich and gone. America was going to be a better place, thanks to Luther Dupree.

There was the light. Slowly descending from altitude a white 747 was coming from the northeast directly into DFW. Dupree turned north and, as the plane crossed under him, dropped his left wing and pointed the nose straight down. He allowed the wings to slowly rotate as he plummeted towards the earth, and looked up to watch the 360 degree panorama of Dallas at dusk. The airspeed increased to 400 knots and he throttled back to save fuel, adjusting the prop to slow the dive.

Dupree began to pull the nose of the Messerschmitt up as he crossed behind Air Force One and it proceeded to the Outer Marker of DFW at an approach speed of 250 knots. The Messerschmitt swooped below Air Force One then pulled up and traded speed for altitude as it approached from behind at 350 knots and veered slightly right, gaining on the starboard wing and its two engines.

CHAPTER FIFTY THREE

The big white 747 lumbered along unsuspecting at just the location Carswell radar had said the bandit would be. Now focused like a laser, the Department of Defense was using all available resources in the Dallas-Ft. Worth area to find Dupree and inform Boyd on an obscure frequency. Boyd throttled back and went into a shallow dive from 12,000 feet, expecting to just follow it in and watch its tail. Something black and without navigation lights plummeted down behind Air Force One. It was not so much visible as it was detectable by the ground lights it blocked out as it passed. Boyd pushed the nose of the Mustang down with mounting alarm as he scanned the twinkling lights beneath the President's plane. The Messerschmitt swooped up out of the shadows rapidly approaching Air Force One from behind. Boyd opened the prop control for maximum rpm and pushed the throttle through the gate to maximum and felt an instantaneous power surge. He was vertical, three thousand feet above the 747 and approaching from the west.

Fire shot out of the nose of the Messerschmitt and impacted the starboard outboard engine of Air Force One with bright explosions and pieces of metal flying off. Now in a screaming dive, speed approaching 425 knots, Boyd was only a few hundred feet above and approaching from the port side. He rolled to the left and as the 747 passed he opened fire. The night was illuminated by the tracers of six fifty caliber machine guns, but the fire was well ahead the 109 and served mainly to alert Dupree to Boyd's presence and force him to let up on the President's plane.

Instantly Dupree turned into Boyd's dive to get out of the fire and quickly flew under as Boyd's plane screamed down behind Air Force One. Boyd pulled up headed east and turned back to the south to find Dupree already turned and crossing Air Force One's path in front coming after Boyd. As Boyd pulled the stick with all his strength to bring the nose around and complete the turn his aircraft crossed the Messerschmitt's nose and fire shot out of it sending a stream of tracers in front of Boyd. He flew through it.

There was a flash and explosion and the whole plane shuddered for a moment. The impact was clearly visible from the cockpit. One twenty millimeter shell hit the front of the Mustang just below the propeller. The engine began making a clanking sound, but didn't quit. Boyd watched Dupree pass beneath him as he climbed out of the stream of cannon shells and continued a clockwise climbing spiral to put him above and behind Air Force One.

"Damn!" Boyd said out loud. He'd only been in the dogfight for 30 seconds and had had the element of surprise, speed, altitude, and power in his favor and he was losing. Still, if Air Force One landed safely, he'd have done his job. He continued a clockwise spiral upward.

Either the climb or the damage to the engine was causing a major drop in rpm and power and Dupree was gaining on him, coming in a counter clockwise spiral from below. Boyd looked up but couldn't see the stars; the windshield was covered with oil. Oil pressure began to drop so he adjusted the prop control to let up on the engine a bit. Some engine is better than no engine. The clanking got louder and the airspeed dropped to 220. A line of tracers from the 109 chased up at him and he slipped rudder to the right to avoid it. Dupree followed the same maneuver and fired to his right so he slipped left as their scissoring spiral continued upward. Seeing that he was going to stall and be a sitting duck, Boyd elected to exit for another maneuver. He dropped his nose and right wing and pulled a hard right turn to the north.

Dupree turned to the north also and got off a quick snap shot that missed behind Boyd. With less speed, the Mustang turned quickly and the two adversaries were closing head on. Simultaneously they fired again. The small caliber guns on either side of the Messerschmitt's nose gave thin continuous parallel lines of fire toward Boyd, and in the center was a discontinuous line that seemed faster and straighter and through which Boyd hoped he would not have to fly again. Boyd's brighter and more numerous tracers converged in front of Dupree and Boyd saw pieces fly off the Messerschmitt as it passed through them. For an instant there were tracers like fireflies on either side of Boyd's canopy and then the Messerschmitt broke to Boyd's left and they passed.

The burning 747 continued making slow progress toward the brightly lit DFW, now surrounded by the twinkling diamonds of ten thousand street lights stretching like a blanket toward the brighter concentrations of the two centers of the Dallas-Ft. Worth metroplex. It was almost completely dark.

Heart pounding, Boyd realized he was out of breath from the exertion of handling the plane with such quick and drastic maneuvers. He began to plan more of the same. Dupree was twenty years older and had a bad leg. He couldn't keep up the pace much longer. Could he?

Boyd flicked his aircraft straight up and scanned the lights below hoping to see Dupree circling around for another head on encounter. Oil pressure was at zero and the engine was missing frequently suggesting that he'd been hit in the crankcase and one or more rods were gone. That would explain the loss of oil. His altitude was 9,000 feet and his airspeed was 110; near stall. He dropped his nose and scanned where Dupree should be now if he'd turned for another head on encounter.

Fat and unsuspecting, the Messerschmitt was in level flight headed east. Boyd was diving straight down on him. Just as Boyd pulled the trigger and blinded himself with tracers in the night sky, Dupree turned sharply left and the fusillade missed. Unlike poor dead Page out at the ranch, Dupree had looked up.

With altitude and speed again Boyd was able to pursue Dupree, but then a streak of flame darted down the side of the Mustang. It was not continuous, more a flicker every second or so. His speed declined just as he was closing on Dupree. Dupree yanked left again and just eluded Boyd's gun sight. Even without power Boyd could finish this if he could just get his nose inside a few more degrees. He pulled the stick with all he had, the Messerschmitt was tantalizingly close, yet the gun sight was just at its tail. Slowly the sight lost ground as the 109 turned inside the P-51. Now the sight pointed to a spot well behind Dupree's accelerating plane and Boyd broke right to avoid the hunter becoming the hunted. He yanked upward but the engine was gone, sputtering, flames now constant, canopy again coated with oil, Boyd had to point the nose down to prevent stalling.

Dupree popped up, pulled his nose through vertical and dropped down on Boyd's sitting duck Mustang.

Flanked by tracers Boyd heard the thunderous hits of numerous 20 millimeter cannon shells as well as the more frequent higher pitched machine gun bullets rock his plane. The engine exploded and sent a sheet of fire backward over the canopy. The Messerschmitt banked left when he banked right and they were apart.

Silence was broken only by the rush of air by the canopy. Boyd quickly closed off fuel flow to the dead engine and was gratified to see the flames dampen. He craned back to see if he should dodge again, but the night sky was empty. Again, Dupree had left him for dead.

In the distance, the crippled Air Force One was lighting the night sky with its fire. The 747 entered the perimeter of the airport; dark because of the lack of houses and street lights. It had less than five miles to touch down; 2 minutes 30 seconds at 160 knots. From the west Boyd saw the shadow approach again.

With a dead engine and on fire to boot, Boyd knew he should jettison the canopy and jump. He wagged the wings and found the controls still worked. Air speed was near stall. The cockpit was dark. He had one last chance to complete his mission. He dropped the nose and turned east.

CHAPTER FIFTY FOUR

"Daddy! Is that Grandma's plane?" The little girl said to her impatient father standing on the observation deck at DFW. He was looking off to the east, smoking a cigarette.

"Grandma's plane is stacked up over there, honey. She won't be here for hours."

"It's burning!"

"What's burning?"

"See," she pointed.

"Holy shit!"

Bright yellow flames punctuated by the flashes of 20-millimeter shells impacting the starboard side inboard engine lit the night sky as Air Force One came into view on final approach to DFW. Five seconds later the staccato reports of the explosions rocked the onlookers, like the delay in a big fireworks display between the flash and the bang. Then, in full view of thousands of stranded travelers and airport workers a dark gray airplane with white swastikas on the wings and tail swooped past the burning plane and came straight down the runway, pulled straight up in front of the shocked onlookers, performed a perfect Immelmann loop to come screaming straight down at the runway before turning back for a head on pass at the plane carrying the President of the United States.

Just as the Messerschmitt opened fire on the port engines, another aircraft dropped down from the night sky; a battered, smoking, dead stick Mustang came over the starboard side of Air Force One and its six 50s flashed, blowing pieces off the smaller German plane and kicking up dust and dirt from the ground below. The Mustang dropped in front of Air Force One just before it touched down on the end of the runway.

The Messerschmitt dodged the Mustang's fire by yanking up and right and was gone.

Air Force One landed on the main runway of DFW and was immediately surrounded by fire trucks. The Mustang hit the grass beside the runway and bounced along wheels up until it encountered a crossing taxiway where it screeched across, did a 360 degree turn and came to a smoking, shuddering stop. It was 6:45 PM. The President's plane was right on time.

At 8:55 PM the Messerschmitt hit Rich Mountain north of Mena International Municipal Airport in Mena, Arkansas, 218 miles to the north. It burned completely to ash, twisted metal, and a few charred bones of the pilot.

CHAPTER FIFTY FIVE

August 11th was the greatest news day in the history of the world. The media had all night to gather the story; and what a story it was. A neo-Nazi assassination attempt on the President of the United States using a restored Nazi plane in front of thousands of witnesses was just the beginning. There was something for everyone in the newsroom; reporters, analysts, and specialists from all the news outlets outdid themselves in hyperbole and headline-grabbing new developments.

Forty passengers on Air Force One relived what Air Force bomber crews in World War II had experienced; the terrifying power of the Messerschmitt 20-millimeter cannon shells as they pierced the cabin and exploded on the wings and engines. Each news organization scored its own exclusive interview.

With only a handful of flying Messerschmitts in the world, it was less than an hour before everyone knew it was Luther Dupree who'd tried to kill the president, and that led attention to the "Insurrection in Dalhart," as it would forever be known. Sheriff Lane Parker was the new instant celebrity, standing there in his cowboy hat and sheriff's uniform with that cannon he carried for a sidearm. He related over and over again how his men, with the help of the Texas State Guard had stopped a hundred armed insurgents.

The bus driver sold his story to Fox News, and was a one day celebrity as he related how a fusillade of bullets shattered the windows in his bus and a single unknown Secret Service agent with a machine gun casually resting on the roll bars of a Polaris Ranger had stared down 40 armed Nazis. Polaris made their biggest ad buy of the year to follow every showing of the story with a fifteen second spot of the Polaris Ranger.

Initially the Nazi militiamen were held in a fenced compound in Dalhart under the supervision of Sheriff Parker and the Texas State Guard, and a scary bunch they were with their shaved heads, facial tattoos, and brown shirt uniforms. Media swarmed the fence, filming, and trying to interview these sullen sociopaths. It was a circus for a few hours, then swarms of defense lawyers showed up eager to do pro bono defense work and make a name for themselves. They filed writs of habeas corpus demanding to see a judge that very day, and most of the Nazis were released.

Amazon paid Cody Parker, the sheriff's son, a million dollars for his exclusive story about infiltrating the neo-Nazis and helping to disarm them. Amazon's ghost writer was in Dalhart by breakfast on August 12th and worked with Cody night and day. Their book *Blue Jack and the Nazis* was released a week later in exclusive Kindle format for $9.99. Amazon made back its million dollars in less than 24 hours.

Then it got ugly. As the feel-good stories of small town heroes saving the day began to wear thin, emails between Trusten Polk and the SecDef and Congressman Kelly were leaked, and that tied all the Delano members to a presidential assassination attempt. Analysts began to go from how to why, and it wasn't long before a clear picture of an attempted coup d'etat in the United States emerged; Trusten Polk was the liaison, Luther Dupree the tool, someone still in government had to be the mastermind. Accusations led to hearings, to indictments, to trials, resignations, dismissals, a groundswell of new politicians appeared in the next election cycle; but all that took two years – two good years to be in the news business.

CHAPTER FIFTY SIX

Slowly, painfully, Boyd made his way up the hill through the trees, noticing that a crash site burned with gasoline smells different than one with jet fuel. He had a fractured lumbar vertebra from jumping off the roof onto Page, and a fractured skull from when Blue Jack hit him with the yellow pine two by four. They'd rushed him to Parkland Hospital from DFW after the crash because he could barely stand, and the doctors had insisted he be admitted. He called Colleen on his cell phone and showered and put on some scrubs for pajamas, and then snuck out a back door just ahead of a phalanx of reporters that had figured out who he was and where. She met him at a service entrance and they roared away into the Texas night together. Now he was up in Mena on August 11th with the first of the FAA accident team.

"Can you get DNA from that," Boyd asked the examiner.

"Probably not, but we've got teeth. See, there?" A charred skull peeked out from the ashes, teeth intact. "Pretty clear what happened," the man said, exuding the confidence of one who's been to "hundreds of these." "Missed the runway, was going around. Hit the mountain."

Boyd turned to look back to the south at Mena International Airport. How did Dupree miss a straight in approach and have to go around?

"We shouldn't allow these old planes to fly; they aren't airworthy," the man said, sifting through the wreckage.

It had sure as hell been airworthy the day before, when it had turned inside, out climbed, out gunned and shot down an experienced Air Force fighter pilot in a faster more stable aircraft. No, there was nothing deficient about this plane, or the pilot who had flown it. Boyd said nothing, his head pounding from his concussion the day before.

"He's dead, Boyd. Give it up," Marv Crowder said, back in the Secret Service office in Denver in late September.

"He's not dead."

"He's dead! Dental records match perfectly, the plane matched perfectly, right down to the serial number on the engine," Marv responded, laughing at Boyd's intransigence. "On top of that, they found a hanger at Mena he'd rented that had a gassed up getaway car, $100,000 in cash and fake identification papers. Boyd, he's dead."

Boyd rose and walked to the window and looked out; then he turned abruptly and said, "Marv, Luther Dupree found a new way to do a Ponzi scheme, a way nobody had done before, and he stole how much money?"

"A hundred million we've found so far."

"The plane crash that killed Trusten Polk, or Howard Swilley, was just an accident. The lab found a tiny defect in a third stage turbine blade, and it broke on its own. All the plane crash did was to speed up the plan Dupree had all along, to use Polk to expose Delano. To make it more dramatic he finds the one man in America who personifies the Nazi mentality and sets him up with the dream training camp stocked with the cream of the sociopathic misfit world, and unleashes Blue Jack to wreck whatever havoc he can, just for publicity!"

"Yeah, looks that way."

"Then he shuts down the GPS system; just for two hours!"

"Yeah. They figured out it was corrupted data and got it back up."

"No. He let it come back up, because he planned to be finished with killing the president by then."

"OK."

"Then he comes within a hair of killing the president in front of half of Dallas in a way that will be remembered for a thousand years."

"You stopped him."

"I got lucky. Luther Dupree is the best pilot I've ever seen. He is smart and strong, and focused, and he absolutely knows his aircraft inside and out."

"He's had three years to practice."

"Exactly!" Boyd turned from the window to face Crowder. "This man leaves nothing to chance, and he doesn't care who he ruins or kills to have his way. And you tell me he misses an approach to Mena airport on a clear night and hits a mountain four miles away? No, Marv. No."

"It was dark."

"A good pilot can land an airplane in the dark. They have lights on the runway; it's like driving down a superhighway."

"He was wounded. You shot him."

"He was not wounded; not bad enough he couldn't fly. He didn't have enough gas after our fight to get anywhere but back to Wizard Wells. The Messerschmitt only carries enough gas for half an hour. He crashed two hours later. He went to Wizard Wells, gassed up and flew to Mena. He couldn't have done that if he were wounded."

"So you think it was all a stunt?"

"A stunt?" Boyd was angry now. He took a step toward the center of the room, putting him right in front of Marv's desk. "A stunt? Marv, Luther Dupree took down the government of the United States with this 'stunt.' When the voters get through with Congress there won't be an incumbent left. He exposed Delano and used that as a club to destroy the whole political culture, and all because the system RIFd him twenty years ago."

"Revenge?"

"Yes." Boyd responded quietly, the argument over. Then he turned back toward the window and looked out for several seconds. "He turned Blue Jack loose on my best friend; bashed his brains out like he was killing a rodent. I'll get him for that."

Boyd stood there for a minute during which nothing was said, then he turned and went down the hall to a temporary office they'd given him and closed the door, still angry. He kicked the desk as he rounded it and sat in the chair for a moment, then turned to face the window, then restlessly swiveled back to the front. Sitting on the desk was a book that Ben Culpepper had given him for his birthday the week before, *The Blond Knight of Germany,* the biography of Erich Hartmann, the German ace who shot down 352 Allied planes during World War II. He picked it up and found his place and began reading. Half an hour passed, during which Boyd read mechanically, just going through the story. Hartmann was relating his 7th Squadron's retreat from the Crimea in Russia in 1944. He tells of removing the cockpit armor and radio from his Messerschmitt bf-109, leaving a compartment large enough to fit a man; two if they slide back into the rear fuselage. He was able to save his crew chief from the Russians by flying him out of Russia this way.

Stunned, Boyd sat bolt upright. This book is the complete story of an extraordinary fighter pilot and absolute master of the bf-109 Messerschmitt and it is widely known and read. The book seemed to tingle in his hands; Luther Dupree would have read this book years ago. Boyd thought back to the avionics left on the workbench in the Messerschmitt hanger at Dupree Aviation, the funny plane crash, the skull smiling sardonically out of the ashes.

The dentist in Amarillo had been interviewed by the FAA, over the telephone. He had pulled Dupree's dental file and looked through the demographics, and looked briefly at the dental x-rays and hadn't remembered the patient. He'd sent along the x-rays and gotten the originals back, case closed.

"Take another look at your notes," Boyd had asked, calling that afternoon.

The dentist was busy, he didn't want to.

"Please, just look at your notes again. You might see something."

Silence, rustling papers, then, "Oh, that's the German guy."

"German guy?"

"Yeah, I remember him now. He'd had some dental work done in Germany, good work, but over the years it worked out. I replaced a couple fillings."

"German guy?"

"Yeah, thick accent."

"Little guy?"

"Yeah, about five seven."

"They usually hit the mountain coming in from the north, usually at night. Get a little off course and, well, it happens every year," the airport manager at Mena International said the next day in answer to Boyd's question about Rich Mountain. He and Marv had flown in from Denver in a rental.

"Every year someone hits that mountain?"

"At least one a year. Not from the south very often, though."

"Humm." Boyd stood looking north at the mountain. "Not that impressive from here. We've just come from Denver. Big mountains there."

"It's impressive on a dark night, or in weather."

"You have surveillance cameras?" Boyd asked.

"Yeah, we've had some vandalism and that's the VOR beacon over there, so we set it up to watch that as well as the building here."

"Got video from August 10th?"

"Sure. We keep it for a year."

At 8:57 PM on August 10th a parachute landed right at the confluence of the north/south and east/west runways at Mena International. A man gathered the parachute and limped across the grass to the parking lot, threw the parachute into the trunk of an older model Toyota Camry and drove away.

CHAPTER FIFTY SEVEN

Luther Dupree took a sip of old bourbon poured over a single ice cube made from Mountain Valley Spring Water in his living room in a quiet comfortable home in the Garden District of New Orleans. Gold, he mused smugly, is the fugitive's best friend. Forget all those wire transfers and fake front companies. You want to hide money, turn it into gold and carry it someplace. It's heavy, but a million dollar's worth is only 36 pounds. You can cash bullion coins anyplace; hell they even advertise on television for the privilege. He had carried enough gold to this safe house to last well into old age, and there was more stashed in safe boxes around the country.

He picked up the TV remote and turned it on. It was late October and the debacle of governance in the United States had been providing him with considerable pride and satisfaction as each news cycle still brought shocking revelation and speculation, sweeping away careers and reputations in a tsunami of backlash. He was out of it now, in his carefully constructed new identity, and didn't dare insert any additional news leaks. He'd done enough.

He heard a noise. He switched off the television; it was still there, in the house somewhere. Wary, he picked up his Beretta automatic and walked to the front window and looked out; empty street, no neighbors working in the yard. He stood silently, listening. It was coming from the back of the house. He checked windows on the sides, the back yard, stood at the bottom of the stairs. It was a machinery noise coming from the spare first floor bedroom he'd used mainly for storage. He'd probably left something on, he thought. He strode through the back hall and stopped again at the door, the noise was coming from inside. He opened the door.

Bees! A thousand bees swarmed out through the open door, surrounding Luther Dupree in a swirling mass of anger and pain. He was stung twenty times in the first ten seconds, and bees were crawling into his ears and up his nose, and his mouth. He ran panicked to the front of the house, managing to elude half the swarm, but still covered with insects.

"Argghh!" He stumbled down the front steps, looking frantically for something to get the bees off him.

A blast of cold hit Dupree from behind and he was engulfed in a cloud, which did immobilize some of the bees.

"Secret Service! Luther Dupree, you're under arrest!" Two SWAT Team members with CO_2 fire extinguishers continued to spray Luther and the bees, and two Secret Service agents with guns drawn rushed to cover him while a fifth SWAT Team member tackled him and wrestled his arms behind him to be cuffed.

Boyd Chailland strode around the corner of the house, dressed in suit and tie with his M9 holstered. He casually walked over to the cuffed Dupree, struggling to scrape bees off his back.

"That's him," Chailland said, not fooled by the new Hemingway beard or the longer hair.

"How'd you find me?" Dupree asked later, both arms and legs cuffed to the gurney in the emergency room of the new LSU Charity Hospital.

"You're too smart to have left the fake identity until after you'd stolen the money; we figured you started with the identity, and made yourself a loan just to see if it would hold up. It did, until now. We went back to the bank in Baton Rouge where you worked and looked for loans made to a single man your age; found you in an afternoon. We've been watching you for two weeks."

CHAPTER FIFTY EIGHT

Hyde Fleetwood had never trusted Luther Dupree. He'd helped Dupree fake mortgages, insert them into the MERS database, watched Dupree maneuver them through the system and sell them to big commercial banks. He'd built the elaborate partnership with the Boston mob, which was made with a double cross in mind from the beginning. He'd marveled at how Dupree found a way to get a virus into the GPS command center from Thule, Greenland; a master criminal. No, that new identity Dupree had given him wouldn't be safe. He was pretty sure they'd find Dupree, and when they did he'd trade whatever he had for whatever he could get; and even more than what was left of the money, they were going to want to find the man who knew how to take down the GPS system.

Fleetwood knew another ruined university professor who had been kicked off the faculty a few years before he was. This man was susceptible to every kind of substance he could lay his hands on, from scotch to cocaine. When Fleetwood found him he was on the verge of being evicted from the cheap apartment where he lived. He was sick, alone, forgotten. Two weeks later he was dead, buried by a backhoe naked in a field a hundred miles from Boston with his hands and feet cut off and his teeth sawed out. Fleetwood checked out of rehab in December, a new man.

www.ingramcontent.com/pod-product-compliance
Lightning Source LLC
Chambersburg PA
CBHW060147260626
47160CB00001B/158